Caged Eagle

ALSO BY RICHARD ROHMER

FICTION

Ultimatum (1973)
Exxoneration (1974)
Exodus, UK (1975)
Separation (1976)
Balls! (1976)
Periscope Red (1980)
Separation II (1981)
Triad (1981)
Retaliation (1982)
Starmegeddon (1985)
Rommel & Patton (1986)
Red Arctic (1989)
John A.S. Crusade (1995)
Death by Deficit (1995)

NON-FICTION

The Green North: Mid-Atlantic (1970)
The Arctic Imperative (1973)
E.P. Taylor (1978)
Patton's Gap (1981)
How to Write a Best Seller (1984)
Massacre 747 (1984)
The Golden Phoenix: The Biography of Peter Munk (1997)
Mustangs Over Normandy (1998)

OTHERS

Poems by A.H. Ward
Practice & Procedure Before the Ontario Highway Transport Board
Report: Royal Commission on Book Publishing
Raleigh on the Rocks: The Shipwreck of the H.M.S. *Raleigh* (2002)

Caged Eagle

A NOVEL

Richard Rohmer

St. John's, Newfoundland
2002

©2002, Richard Rohmer

Le Conseil des Arts | The Canada Council
du Canada | for the Arts

We acknowledge the support of The Canada Council for the Arts for our publishing program.

We acknowledge the financial support of the Government of Canada through the Book Publishing Industry Development Program (BPIDP) for our publishing program.

All rights reserved. No part of this work covered by the copyrights hereon may be reproduced or used in any form or by any means—graphic, electronic or mechanical—without the prior written permission of the publisher. Any requests for photocopying, recording, taping or information storage and retrieval systems of any part of this book shall be directed in writing to the Canadian Reprography Collective, One Yonge Street, Suite 1900, Toronto, Ontario M5E 1E5.

Front Cover Art: Robin Ledrew
Cover Design: John Andrews

∞ Printed on acid-free paper

Published by
KILLICK PRESS
an imprint of CREATIVE BOOK PUBLISHING
a division of 10366 Newfoundland Limited
a Robinson-Blackmore Printing & Publishing associated company
P.O. Box 8660, St. John's, Newfoundland A1B 3T7

First Edition
Typeset in 12 point Bernhard Modern BT

Printed in Canada by:
ROBINSON-BLACKMORE PRINTING & PUBLISHING

National Library of Canada Cataloguing in Publication

Rohmer, Richard, 1924-
    Caged eagle: a novel / Richard Rohmer.

ISBN 1-894294-48-3

    1. World War, 1939-1945--Aerial operations, Canadian--Fiction.
2. Canada. Royal Canadian Air Force--History--World War, 1939-1945--Fiction. I. Title.

PS8585.O3954C34 2002   C813'.54   C2002-903077-3
PR9199.3.R58C34 2002

Author Garth Peters' Notes to Reader

I want you to know where, as the author, I am and where I'm coming from as I write this book. First of all, you should know that I'm a senior citizen, really senior with God only knows how many months or years left to me. So if I'm going to tell you my tale of sex, violence, warfare, corporate intrigue and personal history, I really have to get on with it.

Second, you should know I'm serving time in a penitentiary. The main reason I'm putting pen to paper (no fingers to keyboard from me) is to pass the time of day. Mind you, they've put me into one of those soft, open prisons where inmates live in comfortable cottages with one or two other inmates. There's TV, a grocery store, a golf course. It's like a country club with strict rules. No escaping, please. You can have private visits from your wife or friend of whatever sex. And, yes, this place isn't in America. It's in the place they call lotus land, British Columbia, in the Canadian Rockies.

What got me started this writing goes this way. Some of my fellow inmates (they're mostly of an age to be my grandsons) asked me to tell them about my escapades during the Second World War. As a fighter pilot in the U.K. and Europe I had a few, believe me. I told them about how, after the war, I became one of Canada's most famous and successful businessmen, an entrepreneur is the catch word today. The story of how a young teenager out of Pompano Beach, Florida, did that Canadian success thing intrigued my listeners (and myself) as I've dragged my stories out of my big memory box. With a few exaggerations, of course.

My fight with my bitch of a daughter who seduced the Prime Minister into putting her into the Canadian Senate was a difficult story to tell. Got me emotional. You'll find out when you get to it.

The sessions with my little gang usually lasted about an hour, usually over coffee in the mornings or drinks before dinner. Yes, we were in a penitentiary.

After the first session, I decided to tape what I was saying. It occurred to me that I should have a record. I wasn't sure why, but it seemed like a good idea. And thank goodness I did because those transcribed tapes are the foundation for this book.

As you'll see, I've been an active aviator since I was eighteen, and a fairly competent pilot at that. So now I'm an old bird but still an eagle even though I'm caged in this penitentiary.

And why am I in this goddamn prison? I'll tell you that later.

Garth Peters
Author and former senator
10 September 2001

1

It was September 20, 1943. The slight, thin-faced squadron commander was sitting at his desk, a collapsible table with its legs on green grass under a spacious canvas tent. He looked up from the papers that Flying Officer Garth Peters had handed him.

Squadron Leader Frank Chesters was the commanding officer of 430 Squadron of the Royal Canadian Air Force. The squadron flew the Mustang I aircraft, with its Allison engine. This US-made fighter aircraft had been ordered from a set of drawings presented by North American Aircraft of California about a year before Pearl Harbor by a desperate Washington based British Purchasing Commission. 430 Squadron RCAF was a fighter reconnaissance unit tasked for low-level recce operations—never higher than 7,000 feet—vertical and oblique photography, artillery fire direction, attacks against targets of opportunity such as enemy trains and barges, and, of course, visual reconnaissance—which meant finding enemy tanks, guns, headquarters and being able to pinpoint them on the map with exquisite accuracy. The eyes of the army. That would be the job of 430's pilots when D-Day arrived and the assault against the German coastal fortifications got under way, whenever that was to be. Before D-Day the task was train busting, and photographing No-Ball sites (V1 Buzz bomb launching ramps) that had just been bombed and other important targets.

Chesters smiled affably, well aware that the very young pilot—'God, he looks about sixteen'—was ill at ease and nervous as he reported to his unit and its commander for the first time. Peters was fresh from his conversion course onto the Mustang and into the skills of the reconnaissance pilot at 41 Operational Training Unit, the OTU, at the Royal Air Force Base Hawarden in Wales.

"Sit down, please. Cigarette?"

Peters took the cigarette then reached for his Zippo lighter and sat down.

Chesters sized up the boy, young man. Perhaps five eight, slim, broad shouldered, wavy, thick brown hair close cropped, high forehead, tucked-in ears, the taut smooth skin of a well-conditioned nineteen-year-old, a thin upper lip over straight white teeth indicated possibly a tendency to aggressiveness—but how was Chesters to really know—high ruddy cheekbones below, near-black eyebrows above two of the bluest eyes Chesters had ever seen.

A good-looking, all-American boy, a real Jack Armstrong type, Chesters thought as he wondered what Peters' personality was like, what was between those tucked-in ears, the stuff you couldn't see in the brain that made the young pilot function.

"You're American, I see. Florida. You joined the RCAF on your nineteenth birthday, one month to the day before Pearl Harbor, right?"

"Yes, sir. I've thought about transferring to the American Air Force but I don't know where I'd wind up, what they'd do with me. You know."

"Sure. So you've stuck with the RCAF and we're glad to have you on 430 Squadron. You're nineteen?"

"Going on twenty. I'll be twenty next month on October 11."

"So you have seventy-eight hours in the Mustang. What d'you think of our big, beautiful fighter?"

Peters momentarily rolled his eyes toward the roof of the tent, a smile on his face. "You said it, sir. Beautiful. Handles like a solid, brand-new Cadillac. I haven't driven a Cadillac. I'll own one, at least one, someday. But that's what I think about the Mustang, even though she's a little heavy, you know, heavy for dogfighting."

Chesters agreed. "Too heavy is right. The Me 109 and the Focke Wulf 190, they can turn inside us easily. So if you're bounced, what d'you do?"

"Don't try to stay and fight because the 109 and the 190s 'll kill you for sure. Roll over and head for the deck with the throttle through the gate. The Mustang's so heavy and so perfectly streamlined it can outrun a Jerry aircraft easily."

The squadron commander nodded. "Good answer. But what if you're on the deck when you're attacked? You can't dive to pick up speed. What d'you do then?"

"Break to port or starboard when the attacker's within firing range."

"You mean just outside firing range."

"Yes, sir, just outside firing range. Then get your butt out of there as fast as possible. Throttle through the gate. But if you're trapped and you have to dogfight, then that's what you do, dogfight. With six .5 machine guns and two .303's firing through the propeller you've got plenty of firepower - if you can get one of those bastards in your gunsight."

"Sounds as though you've picked up a few clues at the OTU. I'll fly with you in the next few days so I can get some idea of how you handle situations. You'll be assigned to A Flight. Dick Manser, Flight Lieutenant Manser, is the Flight Commander. You'll like him. Big, happy guy. But tough, demands a lot. And he's got a great singing voice. Excellent pilot. It's late in the day, almost six. Did they assign you to a tent, get you moved in, okay?"

"Yes, sir. They've put me in a tent with a guy, Mark . . ."

"Mark Tyler. Mark's been with the squadron for about

six months. You'll get along with him okay. He's a bit older than you are. He's from a place called North York, a farming area north of Toronto. Don't know much about him except he says his father is a farmer and into horses."

As Chesters stood to end the discussion, Peters got out of his chair and said, "Well, I haven't met him yet. The officer who met me at the train station . . ."

"At Ashford."

"Yeah, Ashford. A very small man. Very."

"That's Hart Massey, Flight Lieutenant Hart Massey, our senior administration officer who doubles as our intelligence type. His parents had a choice, either an operation that would stop his height growth at the age of twelve, or he would go blind."

"Not much of a choice. Anyway Massey told me that when you and I were finished he'd take me to the pub where most of the squadron's having supper tonight. He said Mark would be there and it'd be a chance for me to meet everyone."

"Good idea." Chesters placed his wedge cap firmly on his head, then tugged down on his Air Force blue battle dress jacket with his pilot's wings on the left chest and under them the white with diagonal purple-striped medal ribbon of the Distinguished Flying Cross.

Chesters stepped outside the tent and Peters followed.

"Isn't that a beautiful sight?" Chesters asked.

The two men stood looking down the long dirt airstrip toward the muted orange ball of the sun lowering toward a thin copse of trees well beyond the field. Silhouetted against the clear September evening sky sat the squadron's fourteen Mustangs, wing tip to near wing tip, in a line safely near the southern edge of the strip, their sleek glistening noses canted slightly upwards, tails solidly down, their camouflage painted, low-bellied fuselages sitting on strong wide legs. The superb new fighting machines resembled a flock of

Canadian geese preparing to leap into the still air. Behind the squatting aircraft, large, light brown servicing tents stood in a long line continuing westward to the far reaches of the tactical airstrip that army engineers had carved with their huge-bladed tractors out of the pristine country estate of the absent Lord Strobolgi. The airfield was at a short distance to the west of the ancient town of Ashford, some thirty miles south east of Luftwaffe-beleaguered London.

"Quite a sight, sir. This is the first experimental airstrip, isn't it, where the army engineers come in and take a farm field and turn it into an airstrip?"

"That's right. When we invade France—God knows when that's going to be—this squadron and all the other recce units and all the Spitfire and Typhoon squadrons—hundreds of aircraft will have to move to the beachhead as soon as it's established. That means the army engineers working with Second Tactical Air Force, 2nd TAF people have to develop standards and procedures so the army can go into pre-picked locations with their great goddamn caterpillar tractors, level the ground and, presto, you've got an airstrip."

"The squadron ground crews with their vans and tents will have to be totally mobile, sort of a self-contained movable village, won't they?"

"Yeah. And they're going to have to cross the English Channel on landing craft. The Channel's usually choppy. You'll see that when you do the low-level crossing on your first operational trip."

"When will that be, sir? Next week?" Peters' voice had a note of hope.

"Christ, no! Maybe a month from now. You've got a helluva lot of training to get under your belt."

Disappointment was written on Peters' face. "I thought that's what we got at 41 OTU."

"41 OTU is one thing. 430 Squadron, an operational

fighting unit, is quite another. First of all you've got to get to know the people you'll be flying with. Got to know how they fly and what they're like as people. You've got to practice battle formation in pairs and fours. You have to practice low flying while you're navigating and map reading at 260 miles an hour. Dogfighting and air firing. Vertical and oblique photography techniques have to be honed. The list of things you have to do before I'm prepared to let you go on ops is as long as your arm!"

Chesters' tone softened. "Look, it's time for you to meet the gang. As you said they're all at the pub. Hart Massey'll take you there. Believe me, you'll need a guide. You have to cross several of Lord Strobolgi's fields and climb over about ten fences. It'll be dark by the time you get there. I'll join you later."

Peters found Massey in the administration tent and they set off. The small officer led the way, his wavering flashlight—'torch' as the Brits called it—cutting the lowering darkness as they crossed Lord Strobolgi's rolling pastures and climbed steps over centuries-old stone fences.

"It's a bloody route march," Massey muttered, then giggled. "Wait till you try getting back to the airfield in this bloody darkness with half a dozen pints of mild and bitters under your belt."

"I could do it with my eyes shut." Peters laughed.

"Bullshit," Massey responded. He stopped and pointed ahead, "There it is, the Shepherd's Cross. We call it the Shepherd's Crotch—the finest farm pub anywhere."

Squinting his eyes to see in the dark, Peters could make out the black silhouette of an angular, narrow, pitched roof looming against the background of the night sky. Not a light to be seen. It was as if the building was dead. But the blackout, of course. Then he heard it—the noise of voices lifted in raucous song wafted across the cooling, damp night air of the remaining quarter mile between them and the Shepherd's Crotch.

"Sounds as though they're well into the sauce," Massey observed as he moved on at a quickened pace, "and I'm in desperate need of a scotch!"

Massey knew exactly where the entrance door was located in the black, nearly invisible wall of the Shepherd's Cross. Peters couldn't see it in the darkness but tiny Massey went without hesitation to the center of the ancient building, grabbed the unseen door handle, turned it and pushed.

Stepping inside the long entrance hall, the pair were immediately enveloped in the dim light of a bare electric bulb, a mix of human-heated and cigarette-smoke-thickened warm air and the lusty roar of a dozen male voices singing to the tune of "Deutchland Uber Alles," a ribald song with words that included what Peters and Massey were hearing at that moment "Auntie Martha's gone and farted, blown her arsehole inside out!"

The raucous singing was coming from a room at the far end of the hall. Massey shut the door quickly. "Blackout, y'know. That figure you see through the doorway down there is the squadron's jovial choirmaster, Dick Manser, big Dick as he's affectionately called—sometimes."

Manser's tall, slightly portly body moved to the rhythm of the raucous song, his round face glistening with happy perspiration as he led the unseen squadron through the last bars of the obscene activities of Auntie Martha. Peters stopped at the doorway while Massey scuttled through it anxious to get to the bar for his scotch.

The song finished but the noise and hooting went on. Manser turned and held out his hand. "You must be Peters. I'm your flight commander. A Flight. Welcome to 430 Squadron, the best goddamn reconnaissance squadron in the world—at least when it comes to singing." He smiled a crooked, slightly buck-toothed smile, shook Peters' hand,

and shouted to the bar man: "A pint of mild and bitters for—what's your first name? For Garth here." Manser ran a hand through his thick crop of black hair and turned to face the boisterous crowed of young pilots in their blue battle dress uniforms, pilot's wings on their left chests, some wearing their flat hats, some smoking furiously, all talking and laughing as they sat around the rough-hewn tables of the Shepherd's Crotch, swilling pints of mild and bitters and devouring thin, butterless tomato sandwiches.

Manser shouted over the din, "Pay attention, you guys!" The noise subsided and all eyes were on the new boy. "This is Garth Peters. He's just joined the squadron. Give him a big welcome!"

Cheers rang out and glasses were lifted. A gravelly voice floated from the back of the room. "Garth Peters, that's a helluva name. A lot better than Hangin' Dick!" which was another of the names given to Manser affectionately by rude squadron members.

"Up yours, Tyler!" Manser shouted. He turned to Peters who now had his own pint of brew in one hand and a freshly lit cigarette in the other. "C'mon, I'll introduce you to these idiots. That dork in the corner is Mark Tyler. Been with the squadron about six months. He's my deputy flight commander. Good pilot. Comes from a farm somewhere north of Toronto."

"So the C.O. said."

Manser took him around the room and actually remembered everyone's name. Red Moore, Jack Watts, Freddie Bryans, Butch Lowndes, Jack Taylor, Ed Winiarz, Ed Geddes, Butch Butchart, Clem St. Paul, and in the corner, Mark Tyler.

Tyler was the only one of the crowd to stand up to shake Garth's hand. He was a good head taller than Peters, broad shouldered, lean, with close-cropped black hair and a matching thick mustache. A handsome bastard, Peters thought, looks something like Clark Gable.

As Tyler stood towering over him slightly unsteady on his feet, Peters was already resentful of this man. Maybe it was the good looks or the fact that as the deputy flight commander of A flight Tyler would have authority over him. Whatever the mix was, Peters decided he didn't like the big farmer. Peters' instant hate was born out of simple visceral jealousy. But he wouldn't show his dislike. One thing he had learned from his lawyer father, or maybe it was in his genes, was to hide any outward show of what he was feeling, particularly any emotion that was a reaction to another person. He wasn't always successful when it came to some young female who turned him on. But at his age there hadn't been too many of those, not enough to suit him by any means. Cool. He prided himself in being cool, playing things cool, just the way his daddy did, that cool Florida legal alligator he hated yet tried to emulate, tried to please.

If nothing else, the young American was ambitious as well as confident of his own ability. He wanted to be the best, to be at the top, and he'd use very trick, every device, every weapon to get there, even if it meant doing a distasteful kiss-ass routine. If he was going to get ahead in 430 Squadron, be a flight commander or maybe even take over command of the squadron somewhere down the road, he'd never do it if he alienated Tyler or Manser or anyone else in authority. No way. Peters' motto, unspoken, would be kiss ass or rub ass, whatever was required to keep him on the path to the top.

So while Peters' mind told him that he was intensely, instantly jealous of the handsome, tall, arrogant son of a bitch, Peters' face showed nothing but a smile of pleasure at what he was hearing.

"Glad to have you here. Have a seat, and how about another mild and bitters? Gotta keep your kidney's flushed out, eh, Jack?" Tyler poked his table and drinking mate, Jack

Watts, a chunky, round-faced happy sort, whose infectious laugh was a sort of giggle.

"Dandy eyes, Mark!" which was Watts' way of saying "Damn right!"

"Jack's the flight commander of B flight," Tyler announced, "so you better pay attention to what he says, eh, Jack?"

"Dandy eyes, boy!" Watts agreed. "You've got a funny accent, Pete. Where are you from?"

"Florida. Pompano Beach. Grew up there. But you're the ones with the accent, you and Mark, not me."

Watts giggled, "Guess you're right. You sure look young, Pete. Maybe sixteen. A lot younger than us old boys, us twenty-two year olds. The C.O. will be scared to death letting a child fly one of his precious Mustangs on operations against the wily Hun." Watts giggled again.

"Wait a minute!" Peters reacted. "I'm twenty and I'll be twenty-one soon and I can fly the Mustang as well as anybody on this goddamn squadron. I'm ready to go on ops tomorrow!"

Tyler snorted, "Nothing wrong with your ego, is there? We'll find out what you can do with a Mustang. Hey, Dick!" he shouted across the room to Manser, "little Peters here thinks he can fly the Mustang better than anyone. I'd like to give him a little workout in the morning, OK?"

Manser came over to the table, his toothy smile belying the hardness in his voice. "Peters, have you been telling these two turkeys you're a real hotshot in the air?"

Watts giggled, "Now, Dick. He just told us he could fly the Mustang as well as anyone on the squadron, that's all."

"And I want to find out if he can," Tyler added.

"I'll give you two aircraft at nine. You'll do close formation, battle formation, then a dogfight session. After that you can do some aerobatics for us, Peters. Put on a show for us older guys. And, Mark, I'd like all of this inside a two-mile radius of the airstrip. Don't want to miss one minute of Pete's performance. What d'you think about that, Peters?"

"Shit hot, sir."

Manser laughed. "I'm not sir. The C.O. is. Now it's time for a song." He went back to his singing position by the door, ducking on the way to get under one of the low wooden ceiling beams that had been there since the Shepherd's Crotch was built in 1613. "All right, lads, how about 'Sixpence, I've got sixpence, jolly, jolly sixpence?'"

* * * * * * * *

Peters checked the clock on the instrument panel. Time to start the engine. He motioned for the crewman to start cranking the engine's energizer. When the mechanism reached a constant high whining pitch, he pushed the 'start' switch which engaged the starter. The Mustang's huge three-bladed propeller began to turn slowly, then picked up speed as the engine came to life firing on all cylinders, belching thick gray smoke out the line of exhaust ports down the sides of the aircraft's long nose.

Satisfied that the engine was idling properly, Peters did the required run-up to near takeoff power, checked the propeller pitch-change function and all his engine instruments. Then back to idle. The Mustang was okay and ready to go.

He looked to his left down the line to Tyler's aircraft parked four spaces away, its propeller turning. Peters pressed his radio transmit button as he signaled the ground crewman to take the chocks away.

"Red Two to Red Leader. Ready. Over."

"Red Leader. Taxing now."

Peters was tense, his whole young being taut, working at

maximum intensity as his brain focused totally on his gun and camera platform, his Mustang.

He had only one goal—to show these bastards, Tyler, Manser, the whole goddamn squadron. He hadn't stood at the top of his class on the Tiger Moths at Windsor, then the Harvards at Aylmer and on the Mustangs at 41 OTU, for nothing. He'd show them! Make fun of him, would they, because he looked so young.

Tyler taxied past in his green and brown camouflage-painted Mustang, his leather-helmeted head, goggles up, nearly touching the top of the aircraft's "bird cage" plexiglass hood. Releasing his toe brakes on the rudder pedals, Peters moved the throttle forward with his gloved left hand. The powerful Allison engine roared in response and the propeller began to pull the huge fighter aircraft in the first movement of what was to be one of the most challenging hours in the life of Garth Peters.

He followed Tyler out to the northern button of the north-south strip the army engineers had bulldozed and levelled. Tyler stopped his aircraft on the left side of the holed metal grillwork that had been laid out at each end of the airstrip to provide a solid starting point for the fighters when the strip was rain-wet.

As instructed by Tyler during the pre-flight briefing on what he intended during the one-hour flight and on what Peters was to do, Peters swung into position on Tyler's right, his port wingtip about two feet behind Tyler's starboard wingtip and out and away from it by a foot.

Both pilots completed their brief run-up checks—pitch full fire, mixture full rich, ten degrees of flap, fuel on a full tank, the radiator cooling vent set. Tyler looked at Peters who gave him the thumbs-up sign. Tyler's right hand, palm vertical, moved from next to his head forward toward the windscreen. He did that three times. It was the hand signal to 'go.'

As Tyler 'poured the coal' to his engine Peters did the same thing, moving the throttle gradually, but smoothly and quickly to near full takeoff power, knowing that Tyler would use enough but not full power for takeoff so as to give the man flying tight formation on him some throttle/power leeway to stay in position.

This was hand-eye coordination in the extreme. Not for one second could Peters take his eyes off Tyler's aircraft. His focus was on the wingtip of the leader's aircraft because in flight Peters would put his wingtip about a foot inside Tyler's wingtip and about a foot behind it. That was *tight* formation. Anyone who could fly that kind of formation on a good, smooth leader was a first-class pilot.

As soon as both aircraft were off the ground, their pilots' left hands switched to the control column, reached down to the right near the floor to haul up on the undercarriage lever. Immediately the wheels began their slow lift up into their waiting wing-root wells where they disappeared behind covers that clamped shut.

Now in the air Peters could concentrate on really getting into his tight formation. As he moved his wingtip in yet closer, he could see the anxiety in Tyler's head movements. Then the twitch call came: "Red Leader to Red Two. Hey, take it easy. Not so close!" Behind his oxygen mask cum radio microphone, Peters smiled as he thought, "You chicken bastard. Thought I couldn't fly tight formation, did you?"

"Red Leader. OK. I'll back off six inches."

The tight formation lasted ten minutes with Tyler putting his number-two man in line astern, then on his port side, then back to the most comfortable position, on the starboard.

Through it all Peters had his aircraft exactly in position. In the smooth air of that cloudless, high-pressure area blue sky, there was no air turbulence to knock the Mustangs around, which would have made Peters' formation challenge even more difficult. As it was, the newcomer was well pleased with his performance. His concentration and hand-eye coordination were complete. He congratulated himself on how well he was doing and mentally rubbed Tyler's nose in the dung heap along with the noses of all the pilots and groundcrew standing down there waiting for Peters to make a fool out of himself because he couldn't dogfight or couldn't do aerobatics. Peters knew they wanted the squadron hotshot, Tyler, to make mincemeat out of him, to humiliate him, to give the cocky young whippersnapper a lesson he'd never forget, to put him in his place. Well, they could all get stuffed. If any of them had seen a better display of tight formation, he'd eat Tyler's shirt.

Then the battle formation session got under way, with the two Mustangs crisscrossing the airfield, their droning Allison engines cutting the pastoral morning quiet of the farms surrounding Lord Strobolgi's estate and filling the ears of the upturned heads of the watching 430 Squadron.

The instant Tyler gave the order: "Red Section. Battle formation. Go!" Peters broke to his right from his tight starboard formation moving out to a position 200 yards from Tyler while flying at the same level—about 2000 feet above ground—but slightly behind, perhaps an aircraft's length, behind the leader.

Battle formation was always used when over enemy territory or in airspace where enemy aircraft might be operating. Instead of the pilot of the number-two aircraft (or three and four if it was a section of four Mustangs) having to keep his eyes on the lead machine, in battle formation he could keep checking the sky for any "bogeys" (uncertain identification) or "bandits" (the enemy for sure) approaching from above or the sides or from behind, the most vulnerable area of all. While constantly swivelling the head to look for bogeys or bandits, the number-two pilot would have to maintain his position in relation to the leader and not get ahead of him or too far behind.

Holding position straight and level was one thing. Negotiating turns was the big challenge. Ideally the leader would call a turn ninety degrees to the left or right. Anything more or less made the turn more difficult for number two.

When the leader called a turn to port, the left, Peters, sitting way out on Tyler's right, had to move smartly to put his machine into a tight turn to the left, always checking where Tyler's slower-turning aircraft was. When Tyler finished his ninety degrees turn to the left, Peters would have to be in his exact battle station position two hundred yards out but on the *left* side of the leader. No small feat. It was most difficult to achieve even after many hours of practice.

In the ten or so minutes of battle formation over the area of Lord Strobolgi's estate, Tyler called five ninety-degree turns. At the end of each one of them Peters was in perfect position, two hundred yards out, slightly behind, at the same altitude and smiling, knowing that Tyler would be cursing!

The next session was the dogfight. As briefed, the pilots broke off formation and climbed to 5000 feet, with Tyler positioned two miles west of the airstrip and Peters two miles to the east.

At Tyler's order both headed for the airstrip and each other, with Peters heading down the north side of the east-west runway and Tyler just to the south of it. When they passed each other the dogfight was on, each pilot hauling back hard on his control column to throw his Mustang into a steep turn to the left. The objective was to get onto the tail of the other guy and therefore into a position to shoot him down. The man who maneuvered onto the tail of the victim was the winner and clearly the pilot with the superior flying skills.

Years later when Peters became a business tycoon and wanted to describe the wheeling and dealings necessary to make a hostile bid for a company, his mind would go back to that day over Lord Strobolgi's estate and Ashford, Kent, and he'd say, "It was like a goddamned dogfight and I won"—just as he did on that September morning in 1943.

As soon as Tyler had flashed by in the opening pass, Peters not only hauled into a steep turn to the left he also pulled the Mustang's nose up, almost vertically into the sun, and rammed the throttle forward breaking the protecting wire that normally prevented absolute full power. Then as the heavy machine slowed to almost stalling speed, he put down ten degrees of flap to give the wings more lift and the Mustang a much smaller turning radius. Peters immediately had a height, turning radius and speed range advantage over Tyler who was still steep turning three thousand feet below wondering where Peters (sitting in the blinding orbit of the sun) had gone. It was all over in three minutes with Peters dropping down behind and right up Tyler's turning tail.

"Red Two to Red Leader. I'm right up your jaxxy at one hundred yards and with my six point fives and two 303s I am about to shoot you out of the sky. Want to try again?"

Tyler did want to try again. "Red Two, that was a fluke. We'll go back to our original start positions. Let me know when you're ready."

"Red Two. Wilco."

Once again Peters reported ready when he was in position to the east of the airstrip. Then the two sleek aircraft were thundering toward each other, the pilots ready to begin the deadly dogfight dance.

Again as they passed the circling began, each man trying to turn his aircraft inside the turning radius of his "enemy" so he could bring his gunsight to bear on the other aircraft and then lay off sufficient deflection—aiming ahead of the target—that the hail of bullets from the Mustang's eight machine guns would strike the fast-moving target. This time the two opened the maneuvering by continuing the steep turn to the left, circling, each trying to turn inside the other.

Garth's machine shuddered on the point of stalling as the heavy force of gravity drained the blood from his head, bringing him to the point of near blackout. Easing the turn slightly, he could see Tyler's machine turning at the opposite side of the invisible circle the two aircraft were carving in the smooth morning air. They were at a turn stalemate with neither gaining on the other.

Peters thought "Enough of this!" Still in a steep turn at shuddering stall point, he pulled back sharply on the control column while ramming as hard as he could on the right rudder pedal. The huge machine instantly flicked upside down and rolled out to the right as Peters neutralized the controls and shoved the throttle full forward past the already broken wire into the emergency slot. The controlled high-speed stall and flick had done two things. It had put Peters' aircraft into a steep right turn and at the same time had slowed the Mustang's forward speed momentarily. Tyler, suddenly overtaking the other aircraft, couldn't duplicate Peters' manoeuver so he desperately tried to turn his machine from its steep left turn into an equally steep right turn to follow the turning direction Peters was now in. But Tyler overshot, arcing by Peters without a chance of getting on his tail. As Tyler went past slightly above, Peters stopped his turn, rolling his machine upwards, his emergency power bringing his speed up rapidly. There in front of him at two hundred yards twisting into the middle of his gunsight was Tyler's Mustang. "Red Two to Red Leader. I'm on your tail and my camera gun is rolling. You're dead!"

The exultant Peters, bursting with the euphoria of a triumphant boy winning the game against all odds, let out a whoop of victory, and shouted into the dead microphone in his face mask: "Screw you, Tyler, you asshole. I can take you or any other sonofabitch on this fucking squadron. You can kiss my ass, you big prick!" Pressing the transmit button he said, "Red Two to Red Leader. Breaking off now. As briefed I will commence my aerobatics."

There was no response from Tyler. The bastard's probably sulking, Peters thought with a pleased smile on his face. He turned his Mustang toward the airstrip about one mile to the southeast. He headed toward the west end of the east-west runway, gathering speed as he descended to his altitude of choice, 1000 feet. He would use the runway as his guide line.

I wonder what the people on the ground are saying now about that inexperienced sprog pilot, Peters thought. Screw them all!

To hell with it. He'd start his aerobatics at 200 feet. His Mustang roared down the runway, speed 325 mph. Lifting the nose slightly he executed a perfect four point roll to the right. Straightening out he pulled the Mustang straight up. At the top of the arc and upside down he rolled out with the nose pointed down toward the center of the strip. It was the first half of a Cuban eight. Thundering down to 50 feet above the center of the runway, he completed the second half of the Cuban eight, again cresting back to the center point of the runway. Then it was a haul back on the stick to take the Mustang straight up. Climbing vertically Peters was about to show his spectators something they'd never seen before. He'd show those idiots!

With the engine pounding at emergency power, propeller pitch full fine, Peters kept an eye on the horizon to ensure his machine was vertical and on the airspeed indicator. The airspeed on the heavy aircraft was dropping off rapidly, 100 mph to 75 mph, well below stalling speed. Then in a space of two seconds the vertical Mustang stopped all forward upward speed and started to slide backward. A tail slide. Peters pulled the throttle back sharply to cut the engine while he kicked hard on the right rudder to throw the nose of the Mustang to the left as it picked up its tail sliding downward speed.

Slowly the nose started to swing to the left, then the Mustang accelerated as it passed the horizon, moving quickly again to the vertical but this time with the nose pointed straight down and the airspeed indicator shooting up like an uncoiling spring.

Down the runway again at 350 mph and 50 feet. As the Mustang heading west passed over the east button of the airstrip, Peters smoothly rolled the machine onto its back. Inverted, he flew it down to 10 feet above the centerline. Past the west button he went another 400 yards, then with full emergency power on he began the first half of an outside loop, pushing with all his might against the control column to force the aircraft through as short a bunt arc as possible. At the top of the outside loop—which no one on the ground had ever seen a Mustang do—with his aircraft level and only 10 m.p.h. above the stall, Peters let the nose fall slightly to pick up speed to 125 m.p.h., the normal approach speed for landing. At the same time he moved the undercarriage lever to 'down' and selected 20 degrees of flap.

He was going to land the beautiful Mustang straight off the top of an outside loop! Unheard of.

Peters could see the green light of the Aldis lamp winking at him from the airfield traffic controller's shack positioned just off the runway and midway down its length. He was cleared to land. He looked around for Tyler's Mustang but it was nowhere to be seen.

Engine power at just above idle, Peters gently lowered his Mustang to a perfect, smooth three-point landing on the runway's grassless, sandy loam surface, a low scud of raised dust following in the lessening turbulence of the slowing aircraft. Peters reached down to unlock the steerable tailwheel. Then as the Mustang came to an almost full stop he turned it sharply right to clear the runway and get onto the rough grass taxiway to taxi back to 430s dispersal area.

He was surprised and annoyed when he looked to his right during his turn off from the runway and saw Tyler's aircraft also turning off the runway not more than twenty yards behind him. Christ, what a stupid thing to do, landing so close behind. When the tail of the Mustang was on the ground, there was no way you could see over that looming nose. You were blind straight ahead. Bad, dangerous airmanship, Peters thought. I'll let Manser know about this in no uncertain words! On second thought, I'd better leave it alone. I've rubbed Tyler's nose far enough into the deep shit as it is. And Manser and the C.O. and everyone else would have seen him land up my ass. Somebody'll chew him out, or maybe they'll be feeling sorry for him.

Since Tyler had turned off the runway first, Peters had no choice but to follow, which he did, at a safe distance. The two Mustangs, weaving slowly from side to side so their pilots could check straight ahead, made their way to the dispersal area spots they had left a little more than an hour earlier.

Peters taxied into and through his machine's parking slot, then stood on the left brake to pivot the aircraft in a complete 180-degree reverse. Using the throttle to move the smooth running Mustang forward, he watched for the groundcrewman's signal to stop. When it came he brought the aircraft to a halt, locked the brakes, pulled the mixture back from full rich to shut-off lean. As the engine sputtered to a coughing halt, he turned off all the switches and reached to throw open the bird cage hood up from the left side of the cockpit.

In an instant the bug-eyed engine mechanic, a corporal whose name he didn't yet know, was on the wing root beside the cockpit ready to help him out, saying, with an awed-filled voice, "Jesus Christ, sir, where in hell did you learn to fly like that? Fantastic, sir. Absolutely fucking fantastic!"

Peters peeled off his brown, sweat-soaked leather helmet and grinned as he unhooked the safety harness that had held him snugly in place during the violent maneuvers he had put the Mustang through.

He laughed, "My daddy was a hundred pound sonofabitchin' Florida alligator with wings. Born with wings, boy. A tough, mean flyin' gator. I've got his genes."

"And his balls, too."

"I reckon so." Peters stood up in the cockpit and punched the six-inch round parachute-harness release plate in front of his flat stomach. He then lifted the right shoulder strap over his head to grasp it and the left strap with his left hand, leaving the right hand free to grab the windscreen for balance as he stepped out of the cockpit.

Turning on the wing root to jump off the trailing edge he saw Tyler walking toward him carrying his own parachute and followed by all the squadron's pilots including C.O. Chesters and a beaming Manser.

If Tyler was upset, he didn't show it. There was a broad smile on his face as he came up to the shorter man and stuck out his hand. "That was some exhibition. Congratulations, kid. Where in god's name did you learn to fly like that?"

The corporal—Mitchell, as Peters later found out—couldn't resist the temptation—before Peters could reply he shouted, "Says his daddy was a hundred-pound Florida gator with wings!"

Tyler laughed. "That's your new name. Gator with wings. Gator for short. Great flying, Gator. You can fly with me anytime."

"I'd be happy to—but on one condition." There was no smile on Peters' sixteen-year-old-looking face.

"Yeah. What's that?"

"That you don't land your fucking Mustang right up my

ass," Peters snarled. "That's downright piss poor airmanship."

"Listen, kid, get one thing straight. I'll land my airplane wherever I choose, even on top of yours. This is an *operational* squadron not some prissy cream-puff training command station back in comfy Canada. And I don't have to take that kind of shit from some cocky, pain-in-the-ass Yankee teenager!" Tyler shouted down at the mask and helmet marked face of an unrepentant Peters. Tyler turned and stalked off through the approaching crowd of pilots, his face beet red with anger.

When the chatter of congratulations subsided, the squadron leader asked Peters, "What's with Mark? He looked as though you just kneed him in the crotch."

Peters snorted derisively. "Well, he deserved a knee in the crotch. Didn't you see him land right behind me, right up my jaxxy? I gave him a piece of my fucking mind about it. I mean, that's poor, dangerous, stupid airmanship of the worst kind."

"Is it?" the C.O. asked, his face turning grim. "Did he tell you his fuel pressure started to act up when he was watching you do your aerobatics? He should have landed immediately but he wanted to wait until you'd finished your thing. His engine quit as he was taxiing into his parking slot."

Peters was unconvinced. "I didn't hear him report any emergency."

"That's because he was on the emergency frequency."

Manser, his jovial side turned off, added, "Sounds to me as though you owe Mark an apology, kid. You may fly like a frigging angel but you'd better loosen up more than somewhat if you want to fit into my flight."

"And into 430 Squadron," Chesters agreed. "Look, you've just put on a superb flying exhibition. You make us all look like flying fledglings. Congratulations again. But I think you should tell Tyler you're sorry and that you'll buy him all the mild and bitters he can drink tonight at the Shepherd's Crotch." He smiled at Peters, looking for a conciliatory reply.

Inwardly Peters was thinking, 'Screw you and the whole fucking lot of you. I'm right and Tyler's absolutely wrong. Unforgivable what he did, fuel pressure or no fuel pressure.' Outwardly his words came, "You're right, sir. I'll do it, I sure will."

It was not the first time and by no means the last that Garth Peters would be thinking one thing and saying exactly the reverse—if the situation dictated that, for his personal advantage, he should avoid the truth.

2

At 430 Squadron's base at RAF station Gatwick, Gator Peters carefully wrote an entry into his flying log book. His late afternoon entry recorded that on that day April 12, 1944, he had flown Mustang I serial number AG346 on an unusual sortie from the Canadian Spitfire wing's base at Tangmere on the south coast of England, a short hop down from Odiham. He had flown with 411 squadron of the Royal Canadian Air Force under the command of Squadron Leader George Keefer. In terse terms the entry (his nineteenth operational sortie against the Hun) stated that he had been airborne out of Tangmere at 10:30 a.m. and landed back there at 11:35; that the squadron's target had been two freighters in Dieppe Harbour; and that he had taken photographs of the Spitfire squadron, one of the best in the business, on its way across the English Channel. What it did not record was that he had pulled a stupid, dim-witted stunt at Dieppe that almost cost him his life. Imagine being shot down, killed at Dieppe of all places. Gator Peters knew that Dieppe was where, on August 19, 1942, the attacking Canadian army led by the Essex Scottish and the Royal Hamilton Light Infantry was sacrificed, massacred by the waiting and ready, deadly accurate, German 88mm guns embedded like coveys of lethal snakes on the high cliffs that had a commanding view of the entire pebbly Dieppe beach, the killing ground below.

It was those same German 88s and tracer-laden 40mm guns that had almost blown Peters out of the sky that morning. As he wrote he shook his head momentarily in disbelief that he had committed a dumb error, that he hadn't thought through the consequences of what he had been doing.

By eight o'clock that evening of April 12, Gator Peters was in his favourite London pub, the Vine. It was conveniently located on a narrow lane running north off Piccadilly a few steps away from Piccadilly Circus and the Regent Palace Hotel, where he'd been lucky enough to get a room for the night.

He'd also been lucky enough to be introduced to the gorgeous blond daughter of the Vine's buxom, motherly bartender, Mary Roberts, by now an old acquaintance of six months' standing. Back in November he, Dick Manser and Jack Watts had stumbled upon the Vine one late afternoon during a sortie into London from Gatwick where the squadron was based for the dreary winter of 1943/44. From then on they had been back at least twenty times to the comfortable, wood-paneled, smoke-and-chatter-filled welcome of the Vine and Mary Roberts.

Peters, by now known only as Gator, was sitting at the bar of the Vine, chatting up Mary as she served the pub's thirsty customers. That night, not too many people were there after the supper hour. Maybe it was the light April rain that kept the usual crowd away. Mary was about his mother's age, Gator guessed. She was a chunky, bright-eyed woman with a delightful Cockney accent. Peters loved to listen to her chirp away, with her opinions about this, that and the other thing, as she puffed at her usual cigarette. That evening she was enjoying a Canadian Sweet Caporal from a carton that he had managed to grab from the huge wooden box in the squadron's dispersal office. Gator himself smoked the Sweet Caps but he much preferred the cigarettes he couldn't get—the straight and powerful, no-nonsense Camels from the US of A.

As he was talking with Mary, she looked past his shoulder toward the blackout drapes of the front entrance. Her face broke into an even broader smile than usual, as if someone had just presented her with an unexpected gift of great value.

"Julie!" she exclaimed.

Peters turned, his blue eyes wide, staring at the dark-haired vision of beauty, slim, tall—about his height—with beautiful teeth, full lips, and carrying a small suitcase. Who in hell was this? Likely one of the thousands of prostitutes that prowled Piccadilly Circus in the blackout. Didn't matter. The girl-judging part of Gator's mind immediately gave Julie an A plus—and would he ever like to get his hands on her even if the price was higher than was right.

Mary downed her cigarette, swept around from behind the bar and clutched Julie, kissing her on both cheeks saying, "Julie, luv, how wonderful t'see you! What're you doing here? What a lovely surprise. Is it a holiday or somethin? Is school all right? You haven't been turfed out or anyfing like that, have you?"

"Aw, Mum," Julie laughed, "you ask so many questions."

So that was a daughter of marvelous Mary. But so different even in her accent. What little he'd heard Julie say told him she had what an American would call an 'ordinary English accent,' not a Cockney one.

"It's Thursday. The school's closed tomorrow. Some sort of special convention for the profs. I wrote and told you I was coming. Didn't you get my letter?"

Mary's hand flew to her mouth. "Cor luv a duck! Of course I got it, my sweet. Sort of slipped my mind. Blimey. Here. Come and sit down at the bar. I'll get you somefing t'eat. You must be starved. And a glass of milk?"

"No, Mum. Not a glass of milk. A gin and tonic, please. Remember, I'm eighteen now . . ."

"Sure'n you can do anyfing you want, I know. And this here's my young American friend Gator, Peters all dressed up in his Air Force officer's uniform so he looks like one of them bleedin' Canadians. You talk to Gator and I'll get you some food, some steak and kidney pie. Never mind the rationing. Tell her what you were doin' today, Gator, that Dieppe thing and all."

As Mary poured a gin and tonic for each of them—as it happened Peters was finishing off his second when the beauty appeared in the doorway drapes—Julie, perched on the bar stool close to Peters, said to him "Dieppe? Tell me about Dieppe. Mum said you were there today. How could that be?"

Gator Peters straightened his back, smoothed down the front of his Air Force blue uniform jacket, which was resplendent with polished brass buttons and near-white, crown-in-the-center pilots' wings above the left chest pocket.

"Before I take you to Dieppe, or anywhere else for that matter, I must say that you're so different from your mother. It's quite remarkable."

"Yes, well, you see, I have my father's looks. He's tall and, well, lean and mean. Dark haired, brown eyes, with a regimental sergeant major's waxed mustache because he is an RSM."

"Really. What about him? Where is he?"

She shook her head. "I really don't know. He's with his regiment somewhere in North Africa with the Eighth Army, that sort of thing."

"But your accent. It isn't like your mother's at all. And what about your school?"

She gave a low, throaty laugh. She took his proffered Sweet Caporal and waited until he had lit it for her. "Actually my father's from Farnham Common out to the west of London near Slough. He doesn't have the famous Cockney accent like my mum and he didn't want me to have it. Mind you, there's nothing wrong with the way my mum speaks. It's just that he and my mum too, wanted me in schools where I would learn to speak English with a 'propah' accent."

"Which you sure do."

Julie nodded, dragging deeply on her cigarette. "It's because I've been to the right schools and I've spent a lot of time with my grandmother, my father's mum, out at Maidenhead. That's where my school is. You know. Maidenhead's on the Thames not far from Farnham Common actually."

"I love the way you say 'ectually' instead of actually."

She giggled as she drew on her cigarette, looking directly into his eyes through the twisting, wispy smoke. "You have the bluest eyes, really. And what's this name of yours—Gator is it? Strange name."

"For a strange person, I guess. It's short for alligator. There are lots of them where I come from in the States. Florida that is."

"Florida? Are you from Florida? Crickey, would I ever love to go there some day."

Her mother, busy behind the bar, overheard that remark. "Here now, Julie. You're not supposed to use 'Crickey!'" She said to Peters, "That's Cockney, y'know, and we've spent a bleedin' fortune getting her to schools an'all to get her to speak proper."

Her mother went back to her chores as Peters said to Julie, "Maybe someday you'll get to Florida. Who knows, you might even get there with me."

She looked at him coyly over her glass while she sipped her drink. "Yes, that might be great fun, it really might." She lowered her eyes, and took another puff on the cigarette. "You're a very attractive man, don't you know. I'll bet you have a way with all the girls."

Peters didn't know quite how to respond to that unexpected opening. Momentarily flustered he blurted out what he was thinking, "I'd sure like to have my way with you."

"No one's ever done that." Julie blushed. "Now, tell me about Dieppe. It's just across the Channel isn't it?"

Peters nodded. "Yeah. It's a port. Not big. But important to the Germans. It lies in a sort of bowl with big cliffs on each side of the entrance from the Channel. I mean tall cliffs. And the Jerries have loaded the cliffs with anti-aircraft guns, all kinds of them. Jesus, have they ever." He shook his head and looked at his near-empty glass as his mind went back to what he had done that morning. Really stupid.

Speaking slowly he explained to Julie the background: his squadron's role, the Mustang fighter and its camera equipment and the task he had been assigned that day to fly with the squadron and take pictures of it in close formation as it left Tangmere and pictures of the Spits bombing a special target in France near the coast.

"But just as we were being briefed by the squadron commander—there was a change of plan. Somebody had spotted two freighters in the harbour at Dieppe and some big wheel at higher headquarters decided the squadron should go after those instead of the original target.

"So off we go to get into our aircraft. But my leader, Jack Prince, I was flying number two to him, his aircraft wouldn't start. So after some quick discussion with the C.O., I was to do the trip by myself with an extra Spit flying cover for me. The oblique camera in my Mustang—it points off to the left side slightly down and slightly behind and it sits right behind the pilot—the camera was loaded and set to go.

"There was only one glitch, one problem. I didn't have the same radio frequency that the squadron used for its normal operations. So I would have to communicate with the squadron leader through my Spit number two on the emergency frequency. Then he'd switch channels and talk with the leader. It also meant that I couldn't hear the squadron's chatter or the orders the leader was giving.

"So off we went. Beautiful weather all the way across the Channel. I took shots, pictures of the squadron in beautiful formation. But as we approached the coast—we were flying at about 5000 feet—there was a layer of thin cloud that stretched out from the land like a film of thin gossamer. You couldn't see through and it wasn't very high, maybe at two thousand feet, well below us.

"So my number two, the Spit lad, tells me the squadron leader's having trouble finding Dieppe. There's the odd break in the cloud but he can't find Dieppe. I'm way off to the side and about half a mile behind the squadron and I can't hear them. But I'm the ace recce map reader. If he can't find Dieppe, I sure as hell can. So I start to look down through the holes in the clouds to find the place. Nothing. Then suddenly I look up to check the location of the squadron and it's gone! Disappeared! What in hell am I going to do? I've lost the whole goddamn squadron. When I get back to base and tell them what happened, they'll laugh me right out of my squadron. Panic, I was right on the verge.

"Then I saw it—one Spitfire, the last one of the twelve and he was going straight down through a hole in the cloud following the rest of the Spits. He was about to drop his bomb. So at least I knew where they were and where Dieppe was." He paused and asked Mary for another gin and tonic for both of them and they lit up fresh cigarettes. "So what did you do?" Julie asked.

"I decided I had to get a shot of Dieppe Harbour, a shot of those two freighters so we could see if the Spits had hit them. I mean, that's what I was there for, right? The coast runs north and south and I was heading north when I saw that last Spit. I couldn't just follow him down because I didn't have a bomb. I had my camera sticking out the side and if I just went thundering straight down I'd never get a picture. But if I did a low run from north to south just a bit of a way out over the channel, I could get a perfect picture—or so I thought.

"I told my number two to follow me down but to stay well out and away from the coast while I did my photo run. Down I went and leveled off over the water about the same height as those cliffs I was telling you about and maybe a hundred yards out from them. I was heading south at over 400 miles an hour. My high speed was the only thing that saved me. As I approached the break in the cliffs where the harbour is located, all hell broke loose. The flak, the anti-aircraft fire, was unbelievable. I had made the worst mistake of my life. It hadn't occurred to me, hadn't crossed my mind, that every gun in Dieppe would've been firing at those Spits, would be red hot and loaded for bear. And were they ever! All this stuff coming at me was so bad, the flashing of the flak shells bursting around me was so bright and I was so scared—I actually ducked, stuck my head down into the cockpit. All I could see even looking at the floor were these goddamn flashes. I was sure I'd bought it. Stupid, that's what it was. Stupid. So that's my story of Dieppe this morning."

"Your Mustang wasn't hit?"

Peters smiled and shook his head. "Not a scratch."

"What about pictures? Did you get any?"

"Yeah. Strangely enough in the middle of all the flak crap, I remembered why I was there and I got the camera going. There are the two freighters in the distance but I really wasn't close enough. You can't tell if there's any damage to them. But I got the pictures, that's what's important. I saved my squadron from humiliation."

"More important, you saved face for yourself even though it almost cost you your life."

"Saved face," Peters mused. "That's an interesting expression. You save face by doing whatever's necessary to avoid being humiliated or lessened in the eyes, the regard of others. Think that's about right?"

"Yes, that's good enough, I suppose."

"Yeah, never back down, never give in. Always look for a way to back down, or give in without appearing to. Always find a way to, as you put it, save face. That's a good rule to live by."

She put her hand on his knee for a moment. "You certainly lived and survived by that rule today. That's quite a story, Gator, your Dieppe thing." Julie was emotionally caught up by the tale of his vivid brush with death. She had a strong urge to put her arms around him and comfort him. He was so young and looked so vulnerable.

As Julie would discover later, Garth Peters was not a vulnerable soul. Vulnerable appearing, yes, when it suited him—as it did that evening in the Vine as he sat close to an innocent person who was in transition from child to woman, and vulnerable. He hoped she was vulnerable.

"Will you have dinner with me tonight, Julie? I'd love to spend the evening with you, get to know you."

She looked toward her mother busily drawing pints of ale and mild and bitters, pulling down on the huge enamel handles that are the trademark of every British pub. "Mum is getting steak and kidney pie. At least she said she was. Why don't we just stay here? We can sit over in the corner there or we go upstairs to the restaurant. How would that be?"

Peters quickly decided to go up to the restaurant. Anything to get away from the eyes of Mum, who would be watching over her little chick like a mother hen keeping an eye on the newest randy rooster in the barnyard. He calculated he wouldn't be able to get Julie away from Mary tonight. The mother and daughter would be on their way home (wherever that was) on the tube as soon as the Vine closed at eleven, after Mary had sung out the ritual call, "Time, gentlemen, please!"

But there was always tomorrow and many tomorrows after that. What he'd settle for tonight was a little close formation. He'd get his wingtip as close to her as possible, maybe even touch her fleetingly like a hummingbird touching the nectar of a full flower. His wingtip, as he called it, began to harden.

He picked up his battered, blue officer's flat hat from the next barstool, put it on his head at a jaunty angle, made sure the top brass button of his uniform jacket was undone as only fighter pilots could wear them, stood up and took her soft hand, saying, "OK, Julie. Tell your Mum we're going upstairs to do a little close formation." He smiled down at her, "I'm going to the W.C.. Then it's upward and onward for the two of us. Upward to the restaurant and onward to the stars!"

Julie smiled. Through her cloud of cigarette smoke came her soft words, "Silly goose!"

* * * * * * * *

That first evening at the Vine ended with Peters stealing a long, searching, tongue-touching kiss to which Julie, readily responded as they came down the hidden-from-Mum's-view stairwell from the restaurant.

There was just enough time left for Gator to grab a taxi and get to Victoria station to catch the last train back to Gatwick. Julie agreed to meet him for dinner the next night. They'd meet where? Not at the Vine. Mum didn't have to know what they were up to. Not at the Piccadilly tube station. Too crowded. Green Park station just west down Piccadilly near the Ritz. He'd meet her at the ticket taker's booth. Six o'clock.

Gator didn't tell her then but he decided he'd take her to dinner at the Stafford, a small Victorian hotel in St. James

Place just behind the Ritz, a few steps away from Green Park station. He had stumbled across the Stafford and its comfortable lounge bar which had become a favourite gathering place for Canadian fighter pilots. No Brits please and certainly no low-life bomber pilots allowed. If you couldn't wear your top button undone, if you weren't on Spits or Hurricanes or on the Mustangs, then in the Stafford bar you weren't comfortable, let alone welcomed by the crowd in their Air Force blue officers' uniforms.

A delightful, small hotel away from the beaten track, the Stafford was. And the food wasn't all that expensive. For a man with no money except his meager military pay to live on, watching the pennies was important. With no big wealth, no millions of quids or bucks in his family back in Florida, Garth Peters had always had to earn his own spending money, make his own way in the world from the time he had left his Pompano Beach high school two years before. Was it only two years? The spring of '41 and here he was a full-fledged operational fighter pilot, a goddamn good one at that, flying one of the best aircraft in anybody's world—the Mustang I.

No money to live on except his frugal military pay—this was true—up to a point. Gator Peters was extraordinarily skillful at the card games of blackjack and red dog and at other gambling pursuits. Between training and operational sorties during their on-duty shifts, he and most of his 430 Squadron mates spent many of their waiting hours in card combat.

As it happened, he had been unusually lucky in the past few days, so lucky that he'd been able to accumulate winnings totaling £98, a goddamn small fortune. He'd taken most of it, £62, ten shillings to be exact, from the man he loved to hate, Mark Tyler, who seemed unconcerned about losing. Gator couldn't figure out why a farm boy from some place called North York wouldn't be moaning and groaning and upset about losing that kind of money. It would have given Peters much pleasure to see the pain of losing on Tyler's movie-star good-looking face. But Mark just shrugged off his loss, saying, "I'll get you later, you bastard. I'll get even." A typical loser's statement.

Peters took an early train out of Gatwick and by five in the afternoon he was in Victoria Station flush with his wad of winnings and revved up by the anticipation of being with Julie. Gator decided he'd increase his chances of getting her into the sack. Instead of taking a room at the usual hotel—the Regent Palace on the north edge of the hub of London's nightly blackout action, Piccadilly Circus—he had booked into the Stafford. A small single room on the rabbit warren third floor which was reached after a shaky ride in a lift that looked like an open brass-wire fence coffin stood on end.

All that Gator Peters had to do was invent some credible excuse for getting Julie up to his room after dinner. But he had to get her up there early in the evening so there'd be plenty of time before he had to deliver her back to her Mum at the Vine before closing time. He wasn't sure how he'd entice her up there but he'd think of something.

He had time for a quick bath in the common tub down the hall. Had to be sure all appropriate working parts—especially his wing tip and the two big bombs that hung from it—were clean and fresh if the evening's operational sortie was to be successful.

Julie was half an hour late when she walked unhurriedly through the ticket taker's booth at the Green Park tube station. She smiled at a happy Garth Peters, who but thirty seconds before had been the most disconsolate American in London because he was certain he had been stood up, his pride growing more deeply wounded by the moment.

And didn't Julie look smashing, he thought, his mind using one of the many words he was beginning to pick up from the British. Smashing indeed. A coat was draped over her left arm, hiding her purse. She wore a tight-fitting black dress, low cut in the front to show a cleft of white eye-catching cleavage above not too large, high breasts accentuated by her slim waist and flat stomach between narrow yet attractively rounded hips. They undulated ever so carefully as her long shapely legs mounted on high black heels carried Julie toward Peters.

She reached up her face to kiss Peters on the lips saying, "Mind the lipstick, luv." Her tongue found his for only a tantalizing moment as she pushed her hips and pelvis up against his. As she quickly backed off from Peters, who was startled by her appearance and aggressiveness, Julie apologized, "Sorry to be late, Gator."

"It's okay. The main thing is you're here. And d'you ever look smashing!"

She giggled, taking his arm and turning him toward the entrance steps. "Where are we going?"

"The Stafford," he replied, moving up the steps arm in arm with her.

"The Stafford? What's that, a restaurant? I really don't know much about the center of London. I really don't. I know where the Vine is and Piccadilly Circus is and all that lot. But apart . . ."

He helped her on with her coat. "The Stafford's a hotel. A small one." He pointed as they stepped out of the tube station entrance on the south side of Piccadilly and looked across the grass and lofty trees of Green Park standing between them and Buckingham Palace in the distance. "The Stafford's over there, just to the east of the park where those bomb-damaged buildings are. The Luftwaffe hit those but missed the Stafford right across the street. You'll see. We walk down the path over there toward the palace, then we cut through on a little narrow path between those gutted buildings, and there we are on St. James' Place and the front door of the Stafford. Come on. It'll only take us two minutes."

They walked, still arm in arm, down the Green Park path striped by the motley shadows of the trees blocking the rays of the rapidly descending evening sun.

"What time d'you have to . . . ?"

"I have to meet Mum at the Vine at closing time. And what about you? Are you catching the last train back to Odiham?"

"No. I'm staying in London tonight." He decided to spit it all out. "As a matter of fact I have a room at the Stafford."

Julie stopped walking and spun him around to face her. Looking him in the eye her face appeared shocked. "Garth Peters, are you telling me you're up to something? she demanded.

Peters didn't know where to look, at his feet, off into the trees, or up at the sky. Finally he looked into her eyes where he could see a hint of amusement, just a hint, but enough to suggest she was putting him on. Was she?

"I have to be honest with you. Something like that's crossed my mind. After all, you're . . . well, you're a very attractive girl."

"And you're a very attractive young man who's going to tell me over dinner that he has to make every moment count because he has to go out in his flying machine, in his fighter Mousething . . ."

"Mustang."

"Yes, Mustang, every day to do battle, every day and he doesn't know how long he's going to survive and all that sort of thing. So you need sympathy and love and caressing while you can get it. Right?"

When the English-lilted words stopped, Julie's smile told him she knew she had the situation taped. Garth bent down to kiss her but she laughingly gave him her cheek, saying, "Come along now. I'm sure they're waiting for us at the Stafford. You did make a reservation, didn't you?"

"Of course?"

"Dreadful. Bloody awful," were her words when they entered the cul-de-sac known as St. James Place, where the Stafford stood whole and undamaged on the east side of the street, while on the other loomed the angled hulks of the five or six-storeyed residential buildings, gaping brick walls, roofs gone, staircases going nowhere, a bathtub high up in the open. "And just think," Julie said, "the Nazis were able to hit those buildings, knock them for six, and here right across the street no more than fifty feet away stands the Stafford with not a mark on it! A bit of grime and dirt or else it wouldn't be respectable. But not a bloody mark!" Garth led her through the narrow front doors of the Stafford, past the concierge's cubbyhole on the right, then the reception desk, and on the left the waiting, rickety room-for-two lift. They walked on worn dark carpet into the tea and sitting room and off to the left into the hotel's dining room through a wide drapery-protected entrance. Solid oak doors had once hung there when the house that was now the hotel was built as the London residence of one of young Queen Victoria's more influential and certainly wealthy ministers.

"Rather quiet in here, isn't it?" Julie remarked after they were seated by the maitre d'hotel suitably dressed in white tie and tails.

"Yeah," Peters agreed. "Well maybe it's a little early. There'll be other people in for dinner for sure." He looked around the compact dining room with its ten or twelve tables all gleaming with polished silverware, water and wine glasses, and lit candles on immaculate linen tablecloths.

Julie fished in her purse for cigarettes. Peters used her matches to light one for her, asking "What would you like to drink?"

"I'll have one of those things Mum tells me you Americans like. Haven't had one before. A martini please. A gin martini, with an olive."

"Ice?" a pleased Peters asked. Pleased because a martini on her empty little stomach would certainly help in reducing Julie's resistance against getting into that rickety elevator, let alone flying a little close formation with his wingtip which was already showing signs of getting airborne. Sitting close to her, almost touching, on the comfortable brocaded wall seat, Peters was stimulated and aroused by her femininity and the possibility that he might be able to put his hands on her before the evening was finished.

Three martinis, and two glasses of red wine each, steak dinners, coffee—and many cigarettes later—then it was time to leave the Stafford's dining room.

Peters strengthened by his martini and wine-hazy euphoria, was about to make his move. There had been much hand holding, leg rubbing against leg and even a touch of fingers on legs under the protection of the folds of the tablecloth that reached almost to the floor. He guessed that she was ready and he certainly was.

But it was Julie who spoke first. "What about that room of yours. Don't you think I should see it? It's still early. And besides I can use your loo."

"My what?"

"Your WC, your water closet, your toilet, darling."

"Oh, yea, sure. I'll get the bill." For some reason Garth Peters would always remember that bill when he went back to stay in the Stafford, even more than fifty years later. It was four shillings and sixpence for dinner and drinks—which would cost him £120 at the turn of the century.

And he always remembered that long evening with the inebriated Julie. In a way those few hours were in the end probably the most costly of his life yet paradoxically the most rewarding.

The ride up to the third floor in the swaying, clacking brass cage of the Stafford's lift gave Peters a chance to put his strong left arm around the already tipsy Julie to steady her. It was also an excuse to do what he had been lusting to do all evening, hold her to him. She giggled when his arm went around her waist. "Ooo, I like that," she whispered when his hand moved up to cup her breast with a finger finding the erect nipple under a thin brassiere.

When with a loud clatter the lift cage arrived at the third floor, the two were in a full body-to-body, mouth-to-mouth, writhing embrace with no ending—until they heard the words coming from outside the lift.

"I say, old boy, are you and the lady about done? Sorry to interrupt but I really must get down to dinner."

Peters, face flushed, cap still on his head, broke away from Julie. Peering out through the lift's mesh he could see the blue uniform of an Air Force officer with the four stripes of a Group Captain, pilots' wings and two medal ribbons on the chest—a DSO and a DFC, a round, mustached face with a balding head.

"Yes, sir. I just have to help the lady out, if you'll open the door please."

Julie, her lipstick smeared, was half carried out of the lift and down the hall by an embarrassed, eager Garth whose wingtip was in full extension after being flown straight onto and flattened against the moving target of Julie's hard responsive belly during their brief moments in the lift.

Peters did not fumble with the room key. He thrust it directly into the lock, penetrating fully and turning it immediately.

She was against him in the darkness as soon as he shut the door and slipped the lock home, her fingers working feverishly on the buttons of his jacket, then his shirt as he ripped off his tie. He took her head in his hands to kiss her, without stopping the frantic fingers massaging his penis beneath the fabric, then undoing the belt and below it the buttons of his fly.

Suddenly his bare wingtip—long, large and pulsing with

his young blood—was in her caressing hands. Her lips left his to trace a slow path down his light haired chest, a nibble at the side of his navel followed by an excruciating forever pause before her soft wet mouth and gentle teeth's edge found the rounded tip of his already moist penis which she took into her mouth while her hands gently kneaded his testicles.

The sensation was overpowering. Garth knew he had to delay her or it would all be over for him in an orgasmic flash. He reached down under her still covered arms to lift her to her feet so he could begin to undress her. Her mouth was again on his, as his hands pulled up the skirt of her dress and stroked the backs of her taut bare legs. Hands rising up to her buttocks he stopped, exclaiming, "Gawd a mercy! You don't have any panties on!"

"Of course not. They're rationed!" Julie replied. "And besides neither have you. Not now anyway. Where's the bloody bed? Just a minute, let me get me frock off and the rest. There we are. And you've got everything off now, 'aven't you? Right. There we are all bare and don't you feel lovely and hard. And you've got your protection with you, haven't you, luv?"

"Protection?" he muttered.

"A french safe. You don't think you can make love with me without a french safe, do you? C'mon, Garth. I haven't been had by a man before, haven't gone all the way. Fooled around a bit."

"Yes, I can tell," Peters thought. "I have half a dozen. Will that be enough?"

He moved a hand from her buttocks slowly around to the moist open pouch between her thighs, massaged there while kissing Julie with increasing passion. The kissing moved down to her hard nippled breasts, to the flat stomach and then to that wet pouch Peters had been fantasizing about.

"Find the bed, luv. God, please find the bed." Protection had been driven from her mind by passion.

Peters did not do what he promised. In the next hour they devoured each other with their hands and mouths, reaching several individual climaxes of such soul-rocketing, mind-lifting magnitude that neither had experienced before.

They lay exhausted trying to gather the will and strength to get up, dress and walk the half mile or so to the Vine where Julie had to be delivered up to her Mum.

"That was wonderful, bloody marvelous," Julie whispered into his ear, nibbling on it, her hand holding his 'bombs' under his temporarily withered four-times-in-two-hours record-making 'wingtip.'

"Time to get up, luv. Not your wingtip, but us. It's ten of eleven. Off we go. I'll use the biffie while you get dressed. Turn on the light, there's a dear."

Peters sat up, fumbled for the bed lamp and switched it on. For the first time he could see the gorgeous body that had been his and had had him in its hands for the all too short, exquisite moments, moments the like of which the two of them had never experienced before and might never live through again. As his appreciative eyes consumed the contours of Julie's near-perfect body with its mouth-watering love lines and precious places, he pleaded, "God, Julie, do we have to go?" He could feel another stirring in his groin.

She laughed and sat up, saying, "We do. We do," as she bent over, breasts swaying, to give a quick good-night kiss to the unwithering wingtip.

He watched her stand and, facing him, stretch—arms high like a cat about to jump to a higher place.

"I think I could fall in love with you, Julie."

"And what will your wife think about that?" She dropped her arms and crossed them in front of her breasts.

"Wife? Not me. I'm not married. No way. I swear on a stack of bibles!"

She was amused, "With no pages in them. It doesn't matter, Gator. I like you just the way you are. But this love thing, I'm not really ready for that. After all, I don't really know you. I . . . I don't know nothing about you."

"Anything."

"What?"

"I don't know anything about you—not 'nothing.'"

"Are you correcting my bloody English? Well, you can get stuffed, you can." With that she picked up her clothes from the floor and marched into the bathroom, slamming the door behind her.

When she emerged from the biffie, he apologized for correcting her, saying it was the way his lawyer-father had raised him. "I may have an extra-funny Florida American accent, but I can tell you my Daddy used to climb all over me if I used the wrong English—like a double negative or got my hers and shes mixed up."

"Not to worry, Gator. As a matter of fact it would help me if you'd let me know if I did something, said something wrong like that. You're forgiven." A light brush of the lips kiss so as not to smear the fresh lipstick. "We really do have to go."

As they stepped out of the lift, Peters turned to go out the front door, but Julie asked, "Isn't there a back way out? We have to hurry."

He was reluctant to leave through the bar because some other fighter pilots might be there, people he knew. Peters wasn't worried about being seen with a smasher like Julie— no, he'd be proud of that and the assholes at the bar, whoever they were, could eat their hearts out. But if there was a gang he knew in the bar, he and Julie might have to stop and have a pint with them. It would be bad form not to. And Julie would be in trouble with her Mum if she wasn't at the Vine shortly after closing time—at least by the time Mary had cleared the last customers out, cleaned up and was ready to go home, which was usually about twenty past eleven or maybe eleven thirty. It was five minutes to eleven. They really had plenty of time to get to the Vine. Might even take a taxi.

"OK. We'll go out the back way through the bar and Blue Ball yard. We'll go this way."

Holding her hand he led her through the lounge, past the dining room where a few people who were still at a table could be heard through the drapes now covering the entrance, into a short corridor with the men's loo off it, then a short jog to the left and into the bar.

Gator Peters knew there were fighter pilots in the bar. He could hear the loud chatter and hubbub as soon as he and Julie had stepped into the lounge. There must have been eight or ten pilots along with half a dozen women they'd brought with them—found on the street. The air was dense with cigarette smoke and filled with the noise of flying stories and rude jokes being told, propositions being made and the smell of mild and bitters, lager, gins and tonic and whatever else was going down the hatches.

The barkeep, Louis, was singing out his "Last call , gentlemen, please" to the groans of the men in their uniforms, top buttons undone, their young faces flushed pink by their happy all-evening carousing. Just as Julie and Peters were at the heavy blackout curtains covering the door to the Blue Ball Yard and he was about to pull the first layer back so they could get out, a voice that he recognized called out.

"Hey, Gator. Where're you going? Hey, come and have a drink, and how about that beautiful chick you've got with you. God, Gator you've really scored tonight."

Apparently slightly drunk, but still fairly sharp, Mark Tyler—all six foot two of him with that Clark Gable looking face, straight black hair, black mustache, crooked smile with perfect white teeth, cigarette hanging from his lips—left his cluster of drinking friends at the bar to walk a few unsteady steps to the caught couple.

"Hey, Gator, how about introducing me to your chick here."

Peters could see that Julie was quickly sizing up the movie-star good looks of Tyler, a man who could turn any woman on—and knew it.

She didn't wait. She stuck out her hand. "I'm Julie Roberts. Pleased to meet you."

Tyler pulled the cigarette out of his mouth and took her outstretched hand and did not let it go.

"I'm Mark Tyler. Gator here and I are on the same squadron."

"Canadian, aren't you? I can tell by the accent—and the Canada patches on those wide shoulders of yours."

Tyler snorted, "Wide shoulders? They're broad. Have to be to carry the load of your friend Gator here. I'm his deputy flight commander. Taught him everything he knows about flying. Right, Gator?"

The sullen and sober Peters was getting angrier by the moment, as well as jealous, as he saw the way Julie was looking at Tyler. It was as if suddenly Gator didn't exist.

"Tell me Julie, how did a good-looking girl like you ever get hooked up with the likes of Gator here?"

He was staring down at her, his eyes dropping to the cleavage. She thought, if only she'd been able to fix the bodice an inch lower before she left Gator's biffie. Julie took the opportunity to let this gorgeous man know where to find her.

"We met at the Vine. It's over by the Piccadilly police station. In the lane going to it from Piccadilly Street. My mum tends bar there."

"And that's where you're off to now? Surely you're not off to the sack somewhere when you've got the likes of me available!" He threw his head back and roared with laughter just as Gator's right hand clenched into a fist and hit his uplifted chin from underneath. The blow threw Tyler staggering backwards, his shoulders hitting full on the back of one of the pilots standing at the bar. The two of them crashed to the floor. Tyler's pint of mild and bitters was thrown against the small bar's picture-laden wall, the glass shattering loudly like a gun going off. As he lay on the floor, Tyler shook his head groggily while full consciousness returned. His eyes focused on that 'little Gator prick.'

He could see the woman clawing her way through the blackout curtains. She was gone. But there was Gator, sneaky little bastard. "Hit Mark Tyler when he wasn't looking, would he? I'll fix his clock."

Tyler lay on the floor long enough to make sure that all his senses were in full operation. Having all that booze in his system was a handicap but that no-warning cheap shot to the chin had gone a long way toward sobering him up. At least the rotten little son of a bitch hadn't hit him in the mouth, hadn't knocked out any of his precious teeth.

He got to his feet slowly, glaring across the barroom at Peters. Realizing that Tyler was rapidly pulling himself together, Peters quickly assessed his choices. There weren't any. He could only stand and fight. Tyler moved toward him, fists up in boxer style. Just as he pulled back his right arm to punch, two of Tyler's drinking mates rushed to grab his arms and hold him back.

Dick Manser and Jack Watts were on him, Manser saying, "Don't do it, Mark. We can't have a fight in here. They'll never let us into this place again" Watts added, "For Christ's sake, you'll get poor Louis fired. If you want to clean his clock, go out in the yard. We'll referee."

Peters was shocked to see Manser and Watts. He hadn't noticed them at the bar earlier. Now he was more than somewhat embarrassed that he'd taken his shot at Tyler in the presence of the two people in the squadron whom he liked best.

Tyler stopped struggling. "OK. Let me go, you guys.

This yellow prick'll probably try to hit me while you're holding me back. I won't hit him unless he comes at me again."

His two squadron mates warily released him, expecting him to lunge at Peters. But he didn't. Tyler tugged at the bottom of his uniform jacket, eyes riveted on Peters.

His spat out words were for Manser. "Dick, tell this snivelling, sneaky alligator asshole who hits a man when he's not looking, tell him to get out of here before I drag him outside and beat the absolute shit out of him."

Manser's words for Peters were, "You heard him. And as far as I'm concerned if you don't get your ass out of here, I'll help him drag you out the door."

"Me too," Jack Watts joined in. "A fair fight when a guy's looking's one thing. But dear Jesus, to hit a man when he's not. You better get out of here while the getting's good."

Peters looked around the room, then looked at Manser. "Where I come from, the men are gentlemen. They're a lot more civilized than you apes from Canada. In my country when a man insults your woman in your presence, you do something about it. Mister gorgeous here insulted Julie. Talked to her as if she was a slut. He didn't give me any choice." He smiled cockily, still not looking at Tyler. "Tell your overgrown farm boy I'd be happy to take him on out there in Blue Ball Yard or anywhere else, because when I'm finished with him that pretty face will be so badly cut up he'd look more like Frankenstein's monster than he does now."

Tyler couldn't contain himself. Peters' words filled him with a blind, uncontrollable rage. He leaped at him, swinging hard at Gator's head with a right uppercut intended to take his head off. Peters ducked. As the huge fist went by he launched a skilled boxer's flurry of left jabs and right crosses to Tyler's wide-open face and gut, his dancing footwork carrying him out of range of Tyler's next and last wild swing. Tyler, still raging, had his head snapped back four times in rapid succession as Gator's left fist hit him squarely in the face with powerful short jabs that flattened his nose and cut him open above both eyes. Tyler was finished off by a vicious right to the stomach, which brought him crumpling on his knees to the floor.

It was all over in less than a minute. Peters looked around the room. Awe and astonishment were on all the faces.

Peters straightened his officer's flat hat still on his head, shook his hurting left hand to get the pain out like a dog shaking a limp toy, and walked to the door leading back into the hotel. He turned to Watts and Manser and said, "This Florida high-school boxing champ will see you back at Gatwick, gentlemen. And tell my fearless deputy flight commander there on the floor that I expect him to be on duty and fit when A flight begins its shift tomorrow at noon, so he can bravely and with valor lead us all in glorious battle against the wily Hun." He was enjoying his own sarcasm.

"A final word before you leave," Dick Manser said. "If you want to stay in 430 Squadron, Gator, then after what's happened here tonight, you're going to have to be wilier even than the Hun. You hear what I'm saying?"

"Yeah. Even wilier—and I will be."

3

The telephone line was weak and laced with static scratches. Peters had had a difficult time even trying to get through to Julie's number. Over the ten days since their session at the Stafford he had tried several times to reach her at the number she'd given him in Slough, her mum's house. But always no answer.

He would have gone into London to the Vine to find out from Mary where Julie was, but his commanding officer, Squadron Leader Frank Chesters, had ordered him to stay away from London for ten days, or else. Chesters couldn't formally impose such an order on Peters and certify it in writing. He had no authority under the RCAFs King's Rules and Orders, KR&Os. But the C.O. laid it on him anyway as punishment for his striking Tyler and fighting in a public place.

The morning after the scene at the Stafford, Manser and Watts had gone to Chesters to report what had happened. It was a serious matter, not only the assault of one officer against another, but more important it was a dangerous situation morale-wise to have bad blood between two pilots who were supposed to work and fly together.

Chesters heard their story and asked some questions, including, "What d'you two think I should do about it?"

Manser's response was, "Wait till you see Tyler's face when he checks in at noon." That was when the A Flight pilots were to go on duty until the following day at noon when they'd be relieved by Watts' B Flight people. "Gator cut him up pretty good. Nothing really serious—no teeth lost, no broken nose. But two black eyes and cuts on the cheeks and over the left eye. That'll tell you there really was a fight in the Stafford bar."

Watts added, "I think you should transfer Gator to B Flight. Get him away from Tyler. Keep the two of them apart as much as possible."

"You mean, if I decide not to turf him out of the squadron. It might be better if we got rid of him. Right?" Chester's question was a nice one.

"He's too good a pilot," Dick Manser replied. "Sure, he's a cocky, know-it-all Yankee kid. But he can sure fly and he can sure take care of himself."

"I agree," Watts said. "We sure don't want to lose him. Not right now, anyway. We're about to move to Odiham and back into tents to get ready for D-Day. Our reconnaissance and photo-recce sorties, particularly in the Normandy and Pas de Calais areas, are increasing in number every week. We've got a lot of time and effort invested in this kid. Don't turf him. Give him another chance—and let me have him in B Flight."

"I'll think about it," was the only commitment Chesters would make.

That afternoon, after taking a good look at Tyler's puffed and cut face and having a few words with him, Chesters asked Peters to join him in his office. "Want to have a little chat."

An apprehensive Peters followed the C.O. into his office. Chesters shut the door and sat behind his table-desk, the same one he'd had at Ashford when he'd welcomed Peters to 430 Squadron last September, seven long months earlier.

"Is the old man going to have me court-martialled? Is he going to throw me off the squadron? What the hell's he going to do to me?" Peters mind was filled with questions. He was nervous and afraid, but there were no outward signs. All that Chesters saw was the aggressive, confident, unrepentant face of a twenty-year-old man who looked like a sixteen-year-old boy.

Chesters calmly went through all of the facts and factors, the Stafford incident, Peters' abilities and handicaps—mostly personality problems. His responsibilities as an officer and as an operational fighter pilot; his duties to his squadron mates and to the squadron itself. And the question whether he really fitted in, whether he belonged on 430 or any other squadron.

The C.O., a fair man, gave Peters every opportunity to tell his side of the story, particularly Tyler's provocative words to Julie. "Tyler and I got along okay up until last night, he said "and we can probably sort things out in the next few days."

"Probably," Chester agreed. "And I'm going to help make that happen. What I'm going to do, Gator, is this. I've thought a lot about whether to send you to another unit, get you off the squadron."

Gator was on the edge of his chair. This was it. If the C.O. said he had to go, then he was gone. No appeal. He could apply to go to the American Air Force and maybe get on Mustangs there, or he could stick with the RCAF, perhaps go to a Spitfire squadron. What he wanted to do most in this world was fly the Mustang I and stay on 430 Squadron.

Chesters said the words, "But I've decided to keep you, Gator, at least for the time being. Which means that if you screw up again, step out of line in any way, you're gone. D'you understand that?"

"Yes, sir, I do. I sure do."

"First thing you have to do is apologize to Mark Tyler. This is the second time. He will have to apologize to you for insulting your girlfriend, and you'll have to say you're sorry for beating the shit out of him."

Peters was on the verge of balking but quickly thought better of it. "Yes, sir."

"I'm going to transfer you to Jack Watts, to B Flight, so you'll be out of Manser's and Tyler's hair."

"That'd be great, sir. I like Jack Watts a lot."

"And for some reason he likes you. In fact, it was Jack who persuaded me to keep you."

"I owe him."

"Goddamned right you do. Now, to make the cheese a little more binding I want you to stay away from London for the next ten days. You can have your girlfriend come down here, stay at one of the locals. But I want you here in Gatwick."

"A form of punishment, sir?"

"You might call it that. I call it a signal. A signal to the rest of the turkeys on this squadron that when somebody screws up, there are consequences. You do understand, don't you, Gator?"

"Yes, sir. I sure do."

Chesters picked up the portable phone on his desk, turned the crank on the side of its holder box and said into the speaker. "Has Flight Lieutenant Tyler arrived back? He went to see Dr. Metzler. He's here? Send him in please."

Peters was shocked when Tyler came into the office. His face was a puffed mess. The cut over his blue-black left eye socket had just been stitched together and bandaged by the squadron's medical officer, Squadron Leader Bill Metzler. His right eye also was black. Both cheeks were red and swollen. His nose, where Gator had deposited two left jabs, wasn't broken but was puffed up around the nostrils. The cut under that square manly jaw where Peters' first blow had landed hadn't needed a stitch but was lightly covered by a small bandage and tape.

Inwardly Peters was patting himself on the back as he viewed the damage he'd so skillfully done to this big, conceited, beauty-boy Canadian farmer. Outwardly he was putting on a contrite and "I'm really sorry" look.

"You wanted to see me, sir?" Tyler asked, ignoring Peters' presence.

"Yes. Sit down, Mark. Gator here is prepared to apologize to you for what happened last night and I'd like you to consider doing the same for the things you said to his girlfriend. Gator?"

Peters stood up. "Mark, I'm sorry. I'm really sorry about last night. I just lost control. I get very protective about the women I'm with. And, well, I shouldn't have hit you. I mean, I apologize, Mark. I'm really sorry."

Tyler stiffly struggled to his feet to face Peters. "I'm even sorrier than you are. Look at my face." He grinned. "I apologize for what I said to Julie . . ."

Peters was startled that Tyler had remembered her name. A slight caution signal was triggered in his mind.

"And to you. I was in my cups, I guess. I hope we can put this behind us and be friends." He stuck out his hand.

Peters took it saying, "I hope so too, Mark. I'll work on it." He returned the grin.

"So will I."

"Okay, you guys. Get out of here. And, Gator, since you're new in B Flight you have the rest of the day off. So go and find Jack Watts and have a chat with him."

"I sure will, sir."

From that day, Peters, grounded at Gatwick from going to London, had been trying in vain to reach Julie by telephone. Ten days later he was free to go to London if he wished to do so, the C.O. had reminded him. If he wished to do so! Christ, being away from Julie and not even being able to find her or talk to her had just about driven him up the bloody wall.

But there she was on the line. It was Sunday afternoon and he'd finally scored.

They could hear each other fairly well over the weak, scratchy telephone line, well enough for him to detect a certain reserve, a certain lack of enthusiasm in her voice.

"I'm not sure I can see you again, Gator, much and all as I'd like to."

He couldn't believe what he was hearing. "Julie, why not? God, after that wonderful evening we had together . . ."

"But that was how long, about a week and a half, and I haven't heard a word from you and you haven't been to the Vine, at least my mum hasn't seen you. What was I to think?"

"Well, I've tried to reach you. Telephoned a hundred times and no answer. And I couldn't go to London to the Vine or anywhere else."

"Why not?"

"Well, the C.O. grounded me, ordered me not to go into London for ten days because I had a punch-out with Tyler at the Stafford. He and I had a big go-round after you left. It's all behind us now. We've apologized to each other and actually we've gotten along not too badly since."

"Yes, I've heard about that."

"How could you hear about it?" His tone was accusatory.

Sounding flustered she replied, "Well, through my mum. Someone from your squadron's been into the Vine so she's heard all about it."

"So you knew I was ordered to say away from London."

"Yes, I guess I did. But, Gator, the real reason I can't see you is . . ."

"Why not?"

"It's because . . . well you know how quickly things happen in wartime. I've become engaged to get married, Gator. I mean I love him deeply. With you, well, I hadn't gotten to the point of loving you. We just had our wonderful time together. So, Gator . . ."

"Julie, how could you do this? You know I love you!"

"But I don't love you. Look, there's really nothing to talk about. We had a lovely time together and that's it. I'm going to get married in a week—next Saturday actually—and you're going to be invited to be the toastmaster at the wedding reception."

"I'm what?"

"Toastmaster or master of ceremonies, whatever. The whole squadron's being invited. The wedding will be at the Anglican church in Gatwick—all my friends and Mum's can get there by train—and the reception'll be at the King's Head, the pub with the big restaurant."

Peters was absolutely bewildered. "Why's the whole squadron being invited and why am I going to be the toastmaster? What in heaven's name is going on here?"

"What's going on is that I'm marrying your friend Mark Tyler, that's what."

He couldn't believe what he was hearing. Garth Peters was in emotional shock for the first time in his life. "Jesus Christ, you're marrying that big farmer, that hayseed Tyler. You've gotta be kidding! You're putting me on, Julie."

She laughed. "Gator, darling, I'm not putting you on. Mark Tyler and I are madly in love and we're going to be married next Saturday. He's come up to London every single night since you knocked him for six and we've just had a bloody marvelous time together."

Through clenched teeth Peters muttered, "I'll bet," then, "Strange, I've seen him every day, talked with him, sort of become friends, and he hasn't said a word to me about this, about you."

"That's because he's not only gorgeous, he's also very clever. Wouldn't you say?"

"Julie, I'm a very jealous man when it comes to women. Jealous is an understatement. Get it from my daddy and his daddy. I can't bear the thought of even thinking of you in bed making love with another man, let along doing it with Mark Tyler. This hurts Julie. It hurts real bad."

"Don't be jealous, Gator. Don't be mad at us. Be happy for Tyler and me. And please be at the wedding. Be the toastmaster, won't you?"

He didn't respond.

"Mark's going to be here any minute. I'll tell him we've talked. And I'll tell him you're happy for us and you'll be delighted to be the toastmaster. All right?"

"Who's going to be the best man?"

"Dick Manser."

4

The chore Garth Peters hated most in this world was writing a letter home to his mother or his daddy. Usually it was to his daddy. Sometimes he became overwhelmed by the guilt of receiving so many letters and care packages of Florida fruit, chocolate and whatever special goodies could be crammed into a box that had to survive weeks of travel on trains, trucks and the long U-boat-plagued voyage across the Atlantic and now the English Channel as well. When all that guilt had piled up to the point where he couldn't bear it, he would get one of those flimsy blue airmail letters-without-an-envelope the Brits had invented and scratch out a few lines. As few lines as possible which meant only as many as necessary to kill the guilt.

Today was the day to write *that* letter. Low cloud and rain lay over the entire Beachhead area from the US Omaha Beach on the west through the British and Canadian army sectors on the east of the Orne River, and up against Caen right through the whole of Normandy and across the plains leading to Paris.

There was no flying because of the cruddy weather. So Jack Watts and his on-duty B Flight pilots were holed up in the "chateau" the large farm house allocated to 430 Squadron as their waiting place, where the pilots waited for the telephone call from the Wing Commander Operations—who was known as the Wingco ops—asking for two or four pilots to go to his trailer to get briefed on the task that the Army 'brown' jobs at Montgomery's 21 Army Group headquarters wanted done. It could be a visual reconnaissance of a particular set of roads, or a photo recce—low oblique photo run at a Jerry gun emplacement—or an artillery shoot, an Arty-R, directing the fire of the big guns when the usual air o.p's (army air observation posts), army spotters in their small light aircraft Austers couldn't hack it because of lethal 88s, the anti-aircraft, anti-tank, anti-everything guns the Germans used with deadly accuracy.

The chateau was on the south side of the westerly end of the airstrip known as B8. The British engineers had carved it out of farmers' fields about eight miles to the north east of Bayeux. B8 had been completed on D-Day plus four, June 10, when 430 Squadron and its sister RCAF squadrons—414 on Mustangs and 400 on unarmed, high level photo Spitfires, Blue Birds—started to use it for refueling after sorties starting from their temporary Royal Air Force base at Odiham early in the morning. No need to fly back to England to refuel, though it was necessary to go back there for overnights.

That procedure lasted until D-Day plus ten, June 16, when 39 Recce Wing's entire compliment of personnel, vans, trucks, tents and other equipment arrived at B8. After a rough channel crossing they had landed at the Mulberry Port—Churchill's tactical portable port that had been prefabricated over several months, towed across the channel, sunk, and in operation just after D-Day at the beach at Arromanches north of Bayeux.

Jack Watts, Vince Dohaney, Pappy Dunn, Ed Geddes, Butch Butchart and Jack Taylor, the lusty members of B Flight were in 430 Squadron's pilot's waiting room, a huge second-floor chamber of the chateau at the western end of the B8 airstrip. All except Peters were sitting at the folding tables engaged in playing Red Dog, a card game that was the gambling fad of the moment. Tall windows opened to a full view of the button of the west end of the airstrip. Watching the bouncing landings of their Mustangs or 400 Squadron's

Blue Bird Spitfires returning from operational sorties normally provided critical amusement for 430 pilots who were waiting for their turn to be briefed for a mission. But today those windows were shut against the rain, and Red Dog was in full command in clouds of cigarette smoke.

Gator, fed up with the bad cards he was being dealt, had left the game, grabbed a chair, spread out the blue airmail letter form on the broad, smooth sill of a window near the corner. Using a pen he'd borrowed from Vince Dohaney of Plaster Rock, New Brunswick, he began writing to his father. It was the first since the second of June.

Normandy France

July 20, 1944

Dear Dad:

When you receive this, remember that what I'm writing is going to be censored, probably by some army liaison officer turkey (they're all nice guys). They're with us in our wing organization to brief and debrief us because our job is to work as the eyes of the army. We're supposed to see what Jerry's doing, where his tanks and guns and vehicles are and report them and even take photographs of them. Sometimes we direct artillery fire. The other day I ranged on a target and then a whole goddam division fired at the target, maybe a hundred big guns. They were all over the place when the shells landed. D-Day was spectacular. I was over the Canadian beach Juno at 500 feet—the cloud was low—when the first landing craft and troops hit the beach just before 7 in the morning. What a sight. Miles out to sea I could see the warships firing their big guns at targets right under us. Looked like Christmas tree lights winking out there behind the black smoke from their firing. I had the best seat in the house. And because I'm writing, you can tell I survived.

We're living in tents in an apple orchard next to our airstrip. I dug a slit trench and put my safari cot in it for sleeping. The tent's under an apple tree. Jerry usually comes over at night—he's afraid to come in daylight—and the whole night sky lights up with our anti-aircraft guns pooping away at him. What we have to be careful of is the shrapnel from the exploding shells. You can hear the stuff falling through our apple trees. So what I do is put my steel helmet over my you-know-what so it won't get cut off. The world would end for us Peters if we didn't have our peters, wouldn't it?

The food is great. We have one of the world's best chefs, Stradiotti, and a scrounge officer who can find eggs, chicken and beef anywhere. All the other airfields and the army live off spam, canned beef and all that cruddy stuff.

I'm flying a lot. When the weather's good, a couple of

operational sorties every day. Three on D-Day. And the C.O. thinks my work is good. I'm flying as lead pilot now almost all the time. We operate in pairs or fours and usually about 5000 feet or below. Easy pickings for the Jerry ack-acks.

Get along well with most of the guys. I had (and still do) a problem with a guy in the other flight. Stole a girlfriend—I was in love with her—right out from under my nose, the bastard. He actually married her! Tough to take. As you say, Dad, don't get mad, get even!

I got even last night. This guy, a farmer from somewhere north of Toronto, a real hayseed who looks like Gable, really gets into the sauce which is where he got last night. Hammered. He had just come back to the beachhead after a three-day special leave in England with his new wife, Julie. Special. He must have some pull somewhere. I was at the mess tent (dining room) bar by myself, minding my own business, and this idiot, smashed, but still standing and talking, comes over to me and starts boasting about what it's like making love to his wife, the girl he stole from me. He thought that was a big joke and he'd really get me upset. Well, he got me upset. I was furious. I was all set to beat the shit out of him. But I'd done that once before and besides he was smashed. So I got even. I told him I knew all about making love with Julie because I'd been there before him.

That was it. The sonofabitch threw his beer in my face, swore at me, swung at me and fell flat on his face. You'd be proud of me. I didn't hit him when he was down. I just walked out. But if he'd been sober and said and done the things he did, beer in the face etc., I would have laid him out. Have to control myself because I just see red when I think of that hayseed, let alone think of him in bed humping Julie. Can't avoid it. Like father, like son, as they say in Pompano Beach. I'm running out of space. Tell Mom if you're talking with her that her care packages are just great. Much appreciated. I am also enclosing a photo.

Love,
Garth

Garth Peters 1944

5

Peters was in the mess tent having a leisurely Stradiotti breakfast of bacon and eggs with just the right amount of ketchup on the side. B Flight wasn't on duty until noon so there was no hurry. Gator was shooting the shit with the giggly Jack Watts and buddha-like Vince Dohaney about their egg-scrounging trip the afternoon before. The journey took them all the way to the towering cathedral and town below it on a huge rock island called Mont St. Michel far to the west in US held territory. No eggs were found, but seeing and exploring Mont St. Michel was an unforgettable experience well worth the ride in the C.O.'s jeep, sweet talk borrowed by the persuasive Watts.

They paid no attention when the field telephone jangled its peculiar hand-cranked (at the other end) ring at Stradiotti's cooking end of the tent.

Then Strad himself, a one-time professional wrestler with cauliflower ears to prove it, shouted, "Flying Officer Peters. Sir, the Wingco ops wants you at his van and he said *now*, sir."

"Shit. What can the old man want? What the hell have I done now—I haven't punched out that asshole Tyler lately. I sure could have last night. And we're not on duty 'til noon," Peters muttered, unhappy about being summoned during his off period.

When he knocked at the van door and stepped in, Peters was shocked to find Mark Tyler there with Wing Commander Bunt Waddell. They were standing talking, looking at maps laid out on Waddell's plotting table.

"Come on in, Gator." Waddell smiled a welcome. "Coffee?"

"No, thank you, sir, I'm coffee'd out."

"Okay. I called you because we've been tasked by Montgomery himself, the old boy actually spoke to me directly, believe it or not. He wants us to do a special sortie, a photo recce. It's really important. So I decided I wanted the two best pilots in 430 to do the job. I asked your C.O. who should do it and he nominated you two. Okay?"

Tyler said, "Yes, sir," while Peters, still shocked and trying to sort out what he was hearing, merely nodded his head.

"Come over here, Gator, so you can see the map while I take you through the basics of this thing. Myles Eadon will brief you later on the details of the target." Captain Myles Eadon, a British army intelligence officer, was one of the better ALO's, air liaison officers, on 39 Recce Wing. He would also be responsible for the debriefing when they returned from their sortie.

Waddell said, "Look I know you two don't fly together. You're in separate flights but you're both pros. Shouldn't be any problem. Mark, you're senior. You'll lead. But it's basic that when you get to the target you'll both photograph it instead of the usual thing of the number two standing off and covering the leader's tail while the leader does the low photo run. Monty has to have photos of this place, absolutely must, so we have to cover all the bases."

Bunt Waddell, a thin-faced, long-jawed, handsome man, his brown wavy thirty-year-old full head of hair slightly ruffled, bent his lean six-foot frame over the maps and pointed, his index finger jabbing at a spot on the north side of the Seine River west of Paris. Christ, that was a long way from the beachhead! Nobody from 39 Wing had gone that deep into enemy territory.

"It's a long way, guys. I know what you're thinking. I'll

talk about routes, flak and Luftwaffe fighter bases between here and the target. But let me tell you what the target is."

Tyler said it. "It better be shit hot, sir, to risk going in that far. Holy Christ!"

"It is shit hot and you better believe it. Your target, it'll be low oblique shots of course, is the castle on the north bank of the Seine at this place, La Roche Guyon. The castle is the ancestral home of the Dukes de la Rochefoucauld. They say it's a magnificent stone structure, a medieval castle in the real sense."

"So what's so special about this castle?" Gator had to ask.

"What's special? Well, let me put it this way. Monty defeated Field Marshal Erwin Rommel in North Africa and, as you know . . . Rommel is in command of the German forces facing all the US, British and Canadian armies under Montgomery's command here on the beachhead."

"Don't forget the Poles and the French, sir," Tyler reminded him.

"Right. So Rommel, the Fox of the Desert, is the man Monty has to defeat."

"The castle, sir. What about it?" Gator put the question again.

"Monty says it's Rommel's headquarters. His intelligence people say it is. And high-level photos, from a 400 Squadron Blue Bird Spit that did a run over it a couple of days ago, show what appear to be 88s around the castle and staff cars in the yard." He took a stack of photographs from his desk. "Here. You can see the castle, the river and the town. The castle's built right up against a high cliff. The stone to build the place was quarried right out of the cliff. Monty thinks they're using the quarry tunnels for offices, storage, air-raid shelters, that sort of thing. What he wants is a bunch of closeup shots from 200 feet not 40,000. And you'll get a bottle of champagne if you catch Rommel at the door of the castle waving as you go by!" Waddell laughed and the young pilots nervously laughed with him.

"Let's talk about the route," Waddell said.

"Before we do that—when are we supposed to do this sortie?" Tyler asked.

"Now. As soon as you're briefed and ready."

"What about the weather from here to there?"

"Supposed to be 10/10ths overcast at 2000 feet over the target and 7/10ths broken with a base of 7000 feet from here to about your half-way point."

"Sounds good. What d'you think, Gator?"

"Yeah, sounds okay. We'll have to decide whether to do the run across to—what's the name of the place?—yeah, La Roche Guyon, on the deck or just under the cloud base."

"I'd vote for the deck. That way we can avoid radar and it's almost impossible to see us from above. Almost, that is," Tyler suggested.

"Yeah. But if we're at say, 2,000 feet, and we get bounced by Jerry fighters, we can roll over, head for the deck and leave them far behind."

"True. But just under the cloud base you're so easy to spot, like a black beacon against the white or grey of the clouds."

"So, okay. We'll do it on the deck," Gator allowed.

Waddell said, "You two sort that out." He pointed at the map again. "There's a Luftwaffe fighter base here near Mantes Gassicourt not far from your target. They have both Focke Wulf 190s and Me109s that we and the USAAF haven't cleaned out yet. My suggestion is you avoid that airfield like the plague. Cross into enemy territory here just north of Caen and rollercoaster through the usual heavy 88 flak there. Do that at 5,000 feet plus or minus, then head for the deck. Go east, perhaps steer 070 until you hit the Seine then turn right and do your run down to La Roche Guyon."

He was back to the vertical photographs again. "Dirk Bogarde, one of the lads at APIS—the army air photography photo interpretation section—says there are 88s and 40-millimeter guns on the west and east of the town on the flats on each side of the Seine. And also on top of the cliff about half a mile on the east and on the west of the ruins of the ancient Donjon tower here just above the castle."

"I guess the question is whether they'll open fire for fear of giving away the presence of the headquarters there. Or whether they'll just let us drive by," Tyler observed.

Gator nodded. "But if we do this right and stay on the deck, they won't even know we're coming. We'll be long gone before they can get to their guns."

"Let's hope so." Tyler frowned. "How long is this going to take us?"

"About an hour there and an hour back," the Wingco replied. "It's about 250 miles. So you shouldn't have to worry about fuel, although you may want to lean your mixture on the way out just to be on the safe side."

"So why," Gator asked, "does General Montgomery want these photos? What's he got in mind? Since I'm going to risk my ass to do this, it would help if I knew why."

Waddell shrugged. "He didn't say and I didn't ask. Anyway, if you were shot down and taken prisoner, it would be best if you didn't know."

"Maybe Monty wants to send Rommel a birthday present or something like that and he wants to know where to drop it. Who knows," Tyler added.

"That just about covers my end, gentlemen," Waddell said. "If you'll go and see Myles Eadon now, he'll finish off the briefing."

Peters' face didn't show it but he was furious about having to fly with Tyler. His hate for the pompous prick was overwhelming. And to have to fly as his number two! How humiliating. Neither Waddell nor Tyler saw the emotion etched on Peters' face at that moment. The powerful pangs of jealousy soared in his soul. His mind went straight to Julie and their fantasy-like short time together. Now this horse's ass of a farmer had taken her. Unbelievable. He guessed that Tyler had been so drunk during their skirmish in the mess tent the other night that he didn't remember Peters' taunting statement that he'd made love to Julie before Tyler had her. Just as well. Peters said nothing, his mind working furiously as he listened.

"Too bad your father's in such bad shape, Mark," Waddell said. "Sorry to hear about it."

"Thank you, sir. There's no hope of recovery. I don't know how long he's going to last."

"And you're the only child, aren't you?"

"Yeah. My mother died three years ago so there's just my dad and me."

"I've told you before. I can arrange compassionate leave for you to go and see him."

"It's too late, sir. He wouldn't know I'm there. It would be a waste of time. I'd rather remember him the way he looked the last time I saw him. Big, robust, hearty, full of life, busy in the horse barn just as if he were in his thirties. A great man. Accomplished a lot in his lifetime."

"Well, I wish you luck, Mark. I know you and Gator'll pull this Rommel thing off for Monty." He turned saying, "Isn't that right, Gator?" But Peters had left the tent without the others knowing he'd gone and was on his way to the A.L.O. van.

"Strange," Waddell mused.

Mark said, "He sure is. He hates my guts. See you later, sir."

"Ah, there you are old chap," the leonine-headed Myles Eadon greeted Peters. "Been expecting you. Looks like a wizard op coming up, eh what? Rommel no less. Absolutely wizard. Where's Tyler?"

Peters' face plainly showed his unhappiness of mind. "He'll be along in a minute—if he can find his way."

"Well, well. What's this all about? Are you unhappy about doing this sortie?"

Gator shook his head. "No. Only about having to do it with Tyler."

"Not to worry. It's only this one sortie." Eadon, who acted older than his mid-thirties, had taken a kind of fatherly interest in young Peters, a sort of cultural outsider who Eadon could easily see had trouble fitting into this peculiar Canadian squadron.

The same greeting was heard as Tyler entered the tent. "Ah, there you are old chap."

"So enjoyed meeting your Julie at the wedding. Lovely girl, you lucky sod. Now chaps, let's get down to business."

"Here are your maps with the bomb line on and all. You'll have to draw your track on it and do all the usual navigation preparation yourselves. Are you going on the deck?"

"On the deck," Tyler replied. "After we get past the Orne, we'll go down to treetop and stay there until we start the photo run on the castle."

"Right. The photo run. Oblique cameras, 14-inch for you Mark, 8-inch for Gator. Not more than 300 feet above the ground, please, and no more than 200 yards out from the target. That'll put you tracking easterly down the north bank of the Seine." Eadon had put up a detailed map of the La Roche Guyon area which showed every hedge, lane, building, woods and roadway.

Pointer in hand Myles Eadon was into his lecture. "You'll want to be ready to switch your cameras on just about here." The pointer went to the map at the river's edge just to the west of the castle.

"Let me tell you chaps a bit about this lovely place La Roche Guyon. By great good fortune I spent a couple of days there back in 1938. Holiday sort of thing. We—my wife and I . . ."

"I thought you were big on mistresses," Mark joshed.

"It's getting off on them that I'm big on," Eadon retorted. "Anyway we took a barge trip down the Seine to Le Havre. But the bloody barge broke down at La Roche Guyon. So we had two unplanned days there. I know the Wingco has briefed you. Probably told you everything you need to know, flak positions, enemy airfields, that sort of thing. Right? So I'll fill you in on the village and what we think the layout is in the castle which is Rommel's headquarters according to intelligence. That's what your cameras will or will not confirm."

Slumped in a collapsible wooden chair, his flat hat shoved to the back of his head, like Tyler, Gator looked almost Army in the khaki trousers, shirt and jacket all the RCAF pilots had been permitted to buy from a nearby US Army stores depot. The khaki was worn instead of the Air Force blue battle dress that looked like a German uniform to any American, Canadian or Brit front line soldier. For any pilot who, after bailing out or crash-landing behind enemy lines, was trying to make it back to friendly territory, the blue uniform was death, while the khaki was survival.

Gator drawled, "Yeah, the Wingco filled us in pretty good. But about this Rommel bit, Myles. D'you really think this is his headquarters? I mean it's what? 200 or 250 miles by road to the front. And hell, man, we have almost total air superiority. Every time he goes to visit his troops opposite the Americans in the St. Lô area or across from us at Caen or anywhere in Normandy he has to be on the road four or five hours just to get here, let alone get back, and he risks getting knocked off by us or our Spits or American Thunderbolts or whatever. Doesn't make sense. My guess is his headquarters are right up close, somewhere in Normandy in a great goddamn chateau, and not in this castle at La

Roche Guyon belonging to . . . whose is it? Those French names get me."

"De Rochefoucauld. The duke is supposed to be in residence on the top floor while Rommel and his staff generals—Spiedel is his chief of staff — on the ground floor."

"Yeah, well, I'll bet this castle we're going to photograph is a decoy or something like that."

Myles Eadon smiled, "Dear boy, that's why we need your pictures. Let me answer your doubts. I'll tell you what the intelligence people have told us about why they think Rommel chose La Roche Guyon and why they think he's still there. Early this year Hitler appointed him to command Armée Gruppe B, responsible for all forces from Holland south to the Brest Peninsula including the Normandy beaches. With that wide a geographic responsibility he had to find a headquarters location where he could drive to Holland or Belgium as easily as he could to the Brest Peninsula or Caen.

"When he took over Armée Gruppe B it was headquartered at Fontainebleau. The story is that Rommel decided to move the HQ from the opulence of Paris and into the field, closer to the two armies under his command. Rommel believed Paris had a bad effect on his men. They patronized the restaurants, cabarets, brothels and theatres. And, of course, Paris also offers an extensive black market. A man like Rommel doesn't drink or smoke, doesn't swear or countenance rude jokes of the kind you two and your pilot colleagues thrive on . . ."

"But not you army puritans," Mark roared, laughing.

"Of course not, dear boy. We're civilized. Anyway, Rommel decided to get out of Paris. His first choice was Wolfsschanze Two at Margival north of Paris. It was a complete headquarters complex built so that Hitler could use it to direct the invasion of England. That place had never been used, but all its facilities, in particular its communications equipment, were and I'm sure still are in perfect working order. But Hitler turned him down. So Rommel went for his second choice, La Roche Guyon."

Gator grunted, "That all makes sense. But what doesn't make sense is that he hasn't moved his HQ to Normandy or close to the battle."

Eadon went to another map showing the entire English Channel coastal area from Holland down past the Cherbourg Peninsula. His pointer went to the Pas-de-Calais area of France close and opposite to southeast England.

"The reason is that Hitler, Rommel's immediate boss von Runstedt, and Rommel are waiting for the next shoe to drop. They're convinced—or so our intelligence people tell us—that the next assault will be by an even larger Allied force, this one under General Patton and it will hit right there in the Pas-de-Calais any time now."

"Will that Patton attack actually happen?"

"Who knows, Mark. I think it will. So you can see why Rommel isn't about to move his HQ out of the castle when he might have to run two battles in two different places with La Roche Guyon midway between them."

"So we're supposed to go and take pictures of what intelligence believes, probably knows, is Rommel's headquarters just to confirm he's there?" Gator's voice had a tone of disdain. "Bullshit. Monty's got something else in mind or I'll eat my hat, shirt or my aunt Lucy's alligator."

"If he has, dear boy, you'll be the last to know. Now let me tell you about La Roche Guyon, a little guided tour, if you like, and then I'll turn you loose. Right here in the centre of town is the village square, the usual thing. And on it is an inn, a lovely spot called the Aux Vieux Donjon. The village's war memorial is in the center of the square which is lined with shops and houses. North of the square you enter the Rue d'Audience—a drive that leads to the castle, only a short distance if you want to go and have an audience with the duke."

"Or Rommel."

"Yes, or Rommel. The Rue d'Audience has lovely sculpted lime trees whose thick branches form a canopy over the roadway. Tall, iron, gold-tipped gates at the end of the drive open on to the castle's courtyard."

"C'mon, Myles," Gator was impatient. "What's this travelogue got to do with this sortie?"

"Nothing, really," Eadon confessed. "I just got carried away. Such a lovely village. Such a magnificent castle."

"Yeah. We'll go and take a look at it when the war's over, maybe sometime in the next twenty years." Gator turned to Tyler saying, "Let's go. Let's get our maps organized, nav planning done and all that crap."

"Okay. And let's check that weather. Thanks, Myles. See you when we get back. We'll fill you full of all the details including whether Rommel shaved this morning."

As he went out the van door and down the metal steps to the grass, Gator added, "And we'll let you know what the menu is at the O Pew Donjon."

"Aux Vieux, not O Pew," Eadon shouted, a laugh in his voice. "You ignorant Americans! I tell you."

Forty-eight minutes later at 10:52 a.m. Double British Summer Time, Tyler's and Peters' olive and green camouflage-painted Mustangs with the broad Allied Air Force black and white identification stripes at the wingroot, were lined up for a formation take off. Their aircraft were on the metal mesh of the button at the west end of the airstrip, under the watching eyes of the two A Flight pilots who were not in the air that morning, Clem St. Paul and Jack Clarke. Those two were not in the least bit happy that Peters from B Flight had been tasked for the Rommel sortie when it should have been one of them. Which was the reason they both gave Gator the "up yours and screw you" signal of the clenched fist with the extended middle finger thrust vigorously vertically as Peters taxied his Mustang by the chateau following his Number One, the leader, Tyler. Gator—somber in his leather helmet, goggles on his forehead, radio-microphoned oxygen mask covering his nose and mouth—returned the affectionate salute brandishing his gloved left fist enthusiastically.

Tyler in his Mustang with the large letter S on the side of its fuselage by the roundel and Peters in Mustang P had completed their pre take-off checks. The Allison engines of the long-snouted fighters ticking over smoothly in idle. The green Aldis lamp signal came from the airfield controller's hut halfway down the airstrip. They were cleared to go.

Palm facing his head, Tyler moved his right hand forward three times, the signal to his Number Two that the leader was opening his throttle. Peters, his aircraft's left wingtip tucked inside Tyler's right wingtip, began opening his throttle, his left hand easing it forward, carefully controlling it so that wingtip stayed exactly in position as the two big fighters accelerated down the airstrip, lifting smoothly into the air as if they were one, undercarriages coming up and retracting, engines and propellers making a thundering roar that could be heard for miles across the golden grainfields and fruitful orchards of Normandy under lowering gray solid clouds that blocked the rays of the summer sun.

At 2,000 feet Tyler gave the signal for Peters to move out into battle formation—out to the right about 200 yards and slightly behind the leader. That way they could keep a watchful eye on each other's tail against any enemy fighter that might attempt to attack them from the side or behind, the usual approach route.

They climbed up to the base of the clouds at about 6,000 feet and levelled out just below the clouds. They crossed the frontline to the north of Caen and ran through the expected gamut of 88s by twisting and turning—roller-coasting knowing if they flew straight and level the radar-directed 88s would stand a good chance of a hit. Then they descended to the deck, treetop level. Now it became Tyler's job to do the difficult navigating and Peters' task to watch for enemy fighters.

As they flashed by farms, villages, German installations and vehicles, the people and troops on the ground couldn't hear them coming until the powerful aircraft were almost overhead. Then their astonished faces looked up just as the aircraft swept by with a frightening roar.

Approaching the Seine and maintaining radio silence, both pilots could see that the ceiling, the cloud base, was moving much lower. It was solid, unbroken and probably no more than 1,000 feet above the ground. They had not seen any German fighter or other aircraft and had not experienced or seen any anti-aircraft fire.

But as they finished their turn to the right at the Seine, Peters reported, "Peco Leader. There's a Junkers transport ahead of us at two o'clock just under the cloud at about three miles. Heading same as ours. Probably going to Paris. He won't see us coming."

"Peco Leader. Got him. I'll take the sonofabitch."

"Hey, goddamn it!" Peters shouted into his microphone. "I saw him first and I'm right behind him!"

"And I'm leading this sortie. I'm in charge and I'm going to shoot him down. Got that?" Without waiting for an acknowledgment Tyler went ahead.

"Throttling back to 150 now so I won't overshoot him. He's probably doing 120 maximum. Maintain battle formation."

Tyler pulled his throttle all the way back after moving his leaned fuel mixture handle to full rich. At his cruise of 240 mph he had to cut his airspeed back to 150 or even 120 in a very short distance. Keeping his eye fixed on the tail of the lumbering, low-wing, all-metal, tri-engined Junkers as soon as his airspeed hit 180 mph he selected 10 degrees of flap down. That move cut his speed dramatically. At about a mile behind the target his speed was 150 and falling. Through the illuminated ring of his gunsight he was now keeping the center dot on the Junkers' tail. At his estimate of 500 yards he was still closing. Speed 130. Now closing gradually. Tyler wanted to be at 250 yards when he opened fire. That was the exact distance at which the six .5-inch-calibre machine guns, three firing out the leading edge of each wing, converged to maximize the Mustang's deadly fire power along with the two .303 machine guns that fired through the three-bladed propeller.

A final split-second check to ensure all gun switches were on and armed. Airspeed 120. Buffeting now from the prop-wash of the Junkers—250 yards right on the money. Gunsight dot right on the rudder halfway down.

Fire!

The index finger of Tyler's right hand gripping the control column squeezed the trigger. The noise of the guns firing and the immediate shaking of the Mustang as the vibrations shook the aircraft startled him.

But he wasn't prepared for the immediate violent disintegration of the Junkers. The concentrated salvo of the .5s and the .30-mms shredded the tail empennage, then moved forward to sever the left wing and engine which flew past, barely missing the Mustang's port wing. A smaller piece of the debris—Mark had no idea what it was—hit his right wing's leading edge with a jarring thump.

He immediately shoved his throttle to full open and selected flaps up, climbing to escape the shower of bits and pieces flying off the shattered Junkers like paper falling out of a loaded, fast-moving garbage truck. Its left wing gone, the Junkers started to do a quickening horizontal cartwheel as it arced slowly toward the ground just a few hundred feet below.

Suddenly it was all over. The remains of the Luftwaffe workhorse slammed into an open field just south of the Seine, exploding into a massive ball of orange and yellow flame plumed with black smoke. An appropriate funeral pyre for those Nazi bastards, Tyler thought as he looked back one last time at the inferno he had created.

"Okay, Peco two. I'm going down to the deck again. Back to your battle formation position on the starboard. Resuming 250. Should be at our target in 6 minutes." Tyler, euphoric over his first kill, asked, "Hey, Gator! How about that Junkers? Pretty neat job, eh?"

Seething with anger, Gator Peters did not respond.

When Tyler failed to get a response from Peters he became concerned that he might have lost radio contact. Being this deep in enemy territory was no time to lose communications.

He pressed the transmit button, "Peco Two. Do you read me?"

Peters would have liked to have said nothing. But his own safety was at the front of his mind. He didn't give a goddamn about Tyler's. He had to reply to the leader, upon whose eyes and voice he depended for survival if they were attacked. He had no choice but to respond, "Yeah."

They were back at treetop level again, both pilots watching for towers or wires, anything they could run into at that low level. Their heads swivelled constantly, turning to the left, straight ahead, up to the right and up to port, constantly checking to make sure that a Focke Wulf 190 or an Me109 wasn't moving in behind them ready to shoot them down. At the same time, Peters had to keep his station at that magic 200 yards to the right, while the leader, Tyler, did the navigating—which was much easier now because he simply had to follow the contours of the broad, winding Seine River as they flew eastward.

"Cameras on," Tyler said as he flicked the switch that

activated his Mustang's camera system. Peters did the same. Then both men pushed the camera button on the aircraft's control column for a final check. In the earphones clamped into their leather helmets, they could hear a "whiz, whiz" as the film was moved through the rapid exposure sequence in their planes' special oblique cameras.

The cameras were mounted at head level aft of the protective armor plate behind their seats. Pointing out to the left, their lenses faced out and down behind the wing, depressed at an angle that matched a black marker at the trailing edge of the wing, just inside the aileron. What the pilot had to do was put the black mark on the target as he passed it, turn on the camera, then let the target "move" into the open space behind the wing. The whizzing that the pilots heard was a comforting sound. Coupled with the movement of the numbers on the face of the exposure counter on the instrument panel, the whizzing told each of the pilots that his camera was working and ready to go.

Field Marshal Rommel's Headquarters at La Roche Guyon on the Seine River

Peters caught sight of the pointed, slate-covered towers of the castle straight ahead just as Tyler's voice sang out, "The target's at twelve o'clock, two miles!"

As they had planned, Peters immediately left his battle formation station to move his Mustang into a position close to Tyler's machine, but out and behind at the same level by two aircraft lengths. They would fly by the target at low altitude in that fairly close formation both with their cameras working rapidly. The reason for the relatively close formation was simple: If they had to run a gauntlet of flak, and if Gator's aircraft was a hundred or so yards behind Tyler's, then Gator stood an excellent chance of running into the anti-aircraft shells that were being fired at Tyler but shooting behind him because of the high speed of his aircraft.

"Climbing now," Tyler advised. With full power on, both aircraft moved up from the surface of the Seine to the cloud base at 1,000 feet, leveling out there for about 30 seconds.

"Through the gate!" Tyler shouted, moving his throttle lever through the wire stop, breaking it to give emergency maximum power to the engine. The plan was to get as close as possible to 400 mph, the faster the better in order to avoid the flak as they made their photo run.

"Okay, going down again. Probably max 350 from this low altitude." That was the speed Tyler guessed they would be able to achieve because of their low cloud base.

The castle was coming up quickly now. The Donjon Tower, perched on the cliff like a beacon watching over the village of La Roche Guyon, was getting bigger by the second. It looked just like the images presented by the maps, photographs and the loving description by Myles Eadon.

"We're half a mile back, 200 feet and tracking 200 yards south of target." The huge towering castle was looming large now. The hearts of both pilots were pounding hard as the adrenalin shot through their cardiovascular systems.

They were both thinking, "Still no flak," just as Tyler

under the leading edge of their wings. It quickly emerged under the black mark of the trailing edge with the cameras rapidly clicking away in both aircraft.

Both pilots could see steel helmeted soldiers standing in the castle's courtyard around two huge staff cars with their tops down.

Keeping his camera perfectly aimed as they rocketed by the castle, Peters checked his airspeed: 348 mph. Not bad. The faster the better to avoid any flak that might come at them. They were just at the finish of the photo run with the castle moving out of camera range when all hell broke loose. The German aircraft gunners were finally at their weapons and opening fire.

An absolute blizzard of 40-mm. flaming white tracer shells were flying at them from behind and ahead. "No 88s because we're too low," Peters thought as he switched off the camera. He shoved the nose of the aircraft forward to get down to treetop level and lower as quickly as possible.

Tyler did the same thing as Peters broke formation. The anti-aircraft shells were flashing and exploding above and behind them like a fireworks cascade. Just as he was getting his aircraft below treetop level and across a long farm field and thought he was clear and out of it, Peters felt a split-second vibration in the tail of his Mustang and saw a loud flash and heard the bang of an explosion behind him. No question about it, he had been hit somewhere in the tail area. If he couldn't control his elevators just a few feet off the ground, he would be a goner. As he pulled back gently on the control column to stop the aircraft's descent—he estimated he was only 30 feet above the ground—the Mustang immediately responded and leveled out.

Having survived that crisis, Gator immediately pushed slowly on the right rudder pedal. Normally that would have moved the tail to the left and the nose to the right. No response. The same thing with the left rudder pedal. Still no response.

"The bastards have knocked out my rudder, but I can live with that," Peters radioed to Tyler.

"Okay. Let's get our asses out of there, I can't see you, but I am now turning starboard 90 degrees. Go!"

F/O Ashdown by Peters' damaged tail

As his aircraft popped up above the trees, Peters could see Tyler's aircraft to his left turning toward him. That meant he would have to do a crossover turn above the oncoming Mustang in order to wind up on Tyler's left 200 yards out, and just behind Tyler when he finished that 90-degree turn. No sign of flak now, thank Christ! Gator's Mustang was responding just fine to the ailerons and elevators even though there was no rudder control.

Just as he finished the crossover turn and was in position, Peters saw them. "Two bandits at four o'clock, a thousand yards same level. They're 190s," he reported, his voice high pitched with apprehension.

"Got 'em. They're closing fast. Prepare to break right and head for that goddamn cloud." Tyler's voice sounded calm. "Break right, break right. Go!"

Peters slammed the control column hard to the right, automatically shoving his right foot against the rudder pedal. The objective of the "break" maneuver was to turn his aircraft toward the oncoming aircraft to present the attackers with the most difficult deflection shot at 90-degrees to the track of the Focke Wulfs.

The rudderless Mustang was slow to respond. But respond it did, flipping on its side into a steep turn as Peters hauled on the control column. His head was turned back over his right shoulder, eyes glued to the looming large noses of the two 190s. Their cannons and machine guns were winking out of the leading edges of their wings as they opened fire at their closest target, Tyler's hard turning and climbing Mustang. He was desperately trying to avoid the fire of the attacking aircraft and get his machine into the protective blanket of the solid cloud just a few feet above.

It was a life or death situation for the Mustang pilots. Either get into that cloud or be shot down by those much more maneuverable Focke Wulfs.

Suddenly they were enveloped by the cloud but still within close sight of each other. Had they lost those goddamn Focke Wulfs?

* * * * * * * *

"Terribly sorry, old boy. That's really bad news about Tyler." Myles Eadon was visibly upset.

Peters heaved the parachute off his shoulder into a corner of the ALO van, threw his helmet and goggles on top of the chute and put his maps on the table Eadon would use for the debriefing. He raised his hand to take off his sunglasses but decided it would be better if his eyes were covered while he went through this ordeal. "Awful. Just awful. I can't believe it. But it happened so fast."

"Yes, well. Sit down, Gator. The Wingco ops and your C.O. will be here any minute. They want to hear what happened. I say, would a shot of scotch or gin help? I have a bit of both tucked away. Medicinal purposes, you know."

"Scotch, please. I could really use a shot, Myles."

Eadon was just finishing pouring when Waddell came up the steps into the van followed by Chesters.

"Afternoon, sirs," the ALO greeted them as Eadon put the full glass of golden liquid down in front of Peters, who stood as the senior officers entered the van.

"Good afternoon, Myles," Waddell replied taking off his wedge cap. "Sit down, Gator." He put his hand momentarily on Garth's shoulder, a silent gesture of compassion. "Rough trip, eh? Your C.O. and I thought we should hear the debriefing. We're both going to have to file written reports, so . . ."

"Not a problem, sir."

Motioning for Waddell and Chesters to sit, Eadon pulled his chair up to the table. Pen in hand, maps spread out, he made his starting notes on the debriefing pad and began to record the usual preliminaries—takeoff time, track, altitudes, anything unusual seen en route to target.

Peters went through the details of Tyler's shooting down of the Junkers. The news of that "victory" was a pleasant surprise indeed. It was the first "kill" for 430 Squadron. "Jolly good show!" Eadon exclaimed as he wrote. Peters was careful to give no hint of his anger when Tyler had stolen the Junkers, taken it away from him. That anger still hadn't gone away.

Next came the photo run by the castle at La Roche Guyon, details of what he had seen and expected to see on the photographs. "It is being used as a headquarters, no question about that. Two big staff cars in the courtyard, tops down just as if they were ready to take off for somewhere."

"Any motorcycles?"

"Yeah. As a matter of fact there were four of them near the front gate, you know, leading to that street you told us about."

"The Rue d'Audience."

"Yeah. That's it. And lots of soldiers in the courtyard with those funny steel helmets, blue uniforms and jack boots. Then flak. The flak started just after we passed the castle. All 40-mm. No 88s. We were too low for the 88s. But the 40-mm stuff was heavy, heavy as my aunt Gert's guts. I got a hit on the rudder."

"You sure did," Chesters said. "Holed the fin. You were lucky your whole tail didn't come off."

"And lucky I could still fly without the rudder working."

The next phase of the debriefing covered the FW190s. He described their attack, the break to starboard as the enemy aircraft opened fire at Tyler, and the climb to get into cloud.

"I had a shot at one of them as he went by me. Tyler was on my right during the break about 150 to 200 yards and these guys had decided they'd concentrate on him. One of them sort of overshot and went through my gunsight, went past me. So I had a good shot at him."

"Think you hit him?" Eadon asked.

"No idea. I didn't see any hits. But I might have hit

him. I don't know. Anyway the cine-camera film may answer that question. I took it to the photo section myself. So they should have it developed fairly soon."

"They'll bring it here with prints of your photos," Waddell said. "I told them not to bother drying them. Bring them wet. Go on, Gator."

"Okay. Well, we both made it into the cloud. I was right behind Tyler and had closed up to maybe seventy-five yards when we entered cloud. Anyway, I was close enough to see him. I told him where I was. He throttled back slightly so I could come up and formate on him. That's what I did—on his right but not tight. I stayed about fifty yards out so I could check my flight instruments myself to make sure we weren't in some sort of steep turn or upside down." He looked at Waddell and Chesters. "You know what I mean."

"We sure do," Waddell agreed.

"Well, I'm sitting there with Tyler in this goddam cloud and I'm thinking we've seen the last of those Jerry bastards when all of a sudden there are hits all over Tyler's aircraft. I mean sparks flying, pieces of the aircraft coming off. One of those goddamn 190s had found us in that cloud. Unbelievable, but he'd found us. Like a needle in the proverbial haystack. And here we are flying straight and level. Sitting ducks."

He took another long gulp out of the Scotch glass, his hand shaking as he lifted it to his lips.

"Then he slumped over. I could see the strikes around the cockpit. He must have been hit. He slumped over and his aircraft nosed down. I mean all this took only a few seconds. Christ!"

"Then what did you do?" Eadon asked softly.

"I got Gator's ass out of there fast. I did a steep turn to starboard. Like, I was out of there. I mean, I couldn't see the 190 and for all I knew the other one was right up my ass or the one that got Tyler was about to get me. So I got my butt out of there fast."

"You didn't follow Tyler's aircraft down? You didn't see it impact?" Chesters asked.

"No way, sir. I didn't leave the cloud until I was three-quarters of the way back."

"I wouldn't have either," the C.O. agreed. "What d'you think Tyler's chances of survival were?"

"Zero. Absolutely zero, sir. The cockpit was hit. He was slumped over. The tail was damaged and, God, we were only 1,500 feet above the ground. He's gone, sir. There's no way he could have gotten out of that one alive. I called him several times immediately after he was hit but there was no response and I didn't expect to get one. He's dead, sir."

Eadon kept writing. No one said anything. Peters finished off the scotch.

The silence was broken by the sound of feet on the van's metal steps. It was the sergeant in charge of the photo section delivering the prints and the cine film.

He laid them out on the wooden table after Eadon had removed the maps and his debriefing pad.

"Here you are, sir. There are thirty-two photos in the run. I'll just lay them out in sequence. They're excellent quality. But there's nothing on the cine film. The whole thing was exposed but there's nothing on it."

Waddell observed, "It wouldn't have shown us very much, anyway. The important thing is the pictures. They're great. In fact they're beautiful. Monty will love them."

"Look at this shot of the courtyard," Eadon exclaimed. "The man standing in the doorway, the French doors on the east wall. He's standing looking up, no hat on. D'you think that could be Rommel himself?"

"It sure as hell could be." Waddell agreed. "Have you got a magnifying glass? Let's have it. Yes, it sure looks like the Field Marshal. But we'll have to wait until the APIS boys confirm it. God, what a coup if it's Rommel! Gator, I swear Monty will want to kiss you on both cheeks for this one!"

Peters smiled for the first time. "Rumor has it he has bad breath. But I'll take whatever he's offering."

Chesters turned to Bunt Waddell. "Sir, could I speak with you for a minute? Outside?"

"Sure."

As they went out the van door and down the metal steps, Chesters said to Peters and Eadon, "We'll be back in a minute chaps." Then he said to the sergeant, "That's all. Thank you for the photos, they look good."

"Yes, sir."

Standing on the grass under a broad-branched apple tree a few steps from the van, Waddell offered Chesters a cigarette, which he took. As they were lighting up, Chesters said, "We have to think about Julie. This is the first time we've lost someone who has a British bride."

Surprised, the Wingco said, "Julie, of course." He'd only met her once—at her wedding to Tyler. "What a sweet girl. This is going to be a terrible shock for her."

"That's what I've been thinking. Mark was with her for a four day leave last week . . . I have a suggestion to make, Bunt. There is a Dakota due in here in an hour with a load of supplies. He's out of Croydon Airport and'll be turning around and going back as soon as he's unloaded. Gator knows Julie fairly well. Remember that dust-up he and Tyler had in the bar at the Stafford?"

Waddell drew on his cigarette, nodding, "I sure do. I thought you handled that very well."

"Rather than have some stranger appear at her door, why not send Gator across on the Dak? He can give her the bad news personally."

"Sounds like a good idea—if it's not too much for him all in one day."

"And he can take Mark's personal effects and a copy of

his Will, not the original, just a copy. He made a new one just before they were married. My adjutant has the original. You know, it's one of those handwritten things, the Royal Air Force form. I haven't looked at it, but I know it's there."

"You better look at it before he takes it with him," Waddell cautioned. "If he has left everything to her or a big chunk, that's one thing. But if he made no provision for her, I think the Will should be left for another time."

"You're right. So it's okay to send Gator?"

"If he is willing to go. You better try him on for size first. But somehow I think sure he will. Give him four or five days' leave. I'll confirm it with Second TAF Headquarters. I will probably speak to Air Commodore himself to tell him what's gone on and that we've got the pictures Monty wanted."

"Thank Christ for that. Okay, sir, if you'll leave it with me, I'll talk to Gator and get things organized," Chester said.

"Where does she live?"

"Julie? I'm not sure, but I think it's just to the west of London, that's where her mother is. The last I heard Julie was still living with her."

"He shouldn't have any trouble getting to her, finding her?"

"No, he shouldn't have any problem."

"I'm going back to my van," Waddell said. "Frank, apart from this thing about Tyler, which is bloody awful, those photographs are just excellent. And if that's Rommel in those pictures—and I sure think it is—they'll be worth their weight in gold. I think you should put Gator up for a gong. I think a Distinguished Flying Cross would be the ticket. If you do a citation, I'll be happy to support it."

"Great. I was going to run that very idea by you. I'll get it done immediately."

Chesters went back into the van and sat down as he put

the proposition to Peters, finishing with, "You'll have a four- or five-day break. The pressure's been pretty tough here on everybody and you're at the top of the leave list after this sortie. You'll get to see Julie, do your thing there, then nip into London for three or four days. It depends on what we can arrange for you by way of a return trip, but the Daks are coming back and forth every day."

The C.O.'s proposal caught Peters totally off guard. Like any athlete who had just won a major heavy physical event against tough competition, Gator was pumped up after that action-packed, highly dangerous sortie. His emotions were still running high, the adrenalin coursing through his young fit body and agile brain. Any of the guys in the squadron would kill for the chance at four or five days' leave in London. But the business of having to see Julie after what she had done to him, then to have to tell her about Tyler and deliver his stuff to her—his immediate reaction was that he did not want to have any part of that.

"Sir, I am really not sure I want to do this. That means I am the one who's going to give Julie the bad news. I wouldn't wish that job on my worst enemy. I know her pretty well. In fact, I know her very well, maybe too well. Shouldn't it be somebody who doesn't know her, doesn't know Tyler, just takes the message?"

"We could do it that way. It would be easy to arrange. But it would be a lot easier on Julie, a hell of lot easier if you were to do it." Myles Eadon added, "You really should do it, Gator, you owe it to Mark. We all know that you didn't see things eye to eye from time to time, but somehow I think you owe it to him—and Julie."

Peters hung his head as he listened to Eadon's persuasive words. Then he looked up at him and then at Chesters and said, "I must be right out of my fucking mind. But okay, I'll do it. Sir, would you get somebody to go through Mark's stuff and put it in a box or something like that? Just make sure there aren't any letters from some girlfriend back in Canada, that kind of thing."

"Sure," Chesters said. "I'll get Dick Manser to do it."

"What about Mark's parents?"

"He only has his father. No brothers or sisters. His father's had a stroke. He's not expected to live any longer that two or three weeks."

"Yeah, the Wingco mentioned that when he briefed us this morning or something like that. Mark could have had compassionate leave, but he didn't want it." He shook his head. "Mark was a very secretive guy. I don't think anybody in the squadron knew anything about him except that he was a farmer from some place north of Toronto. Somebody thought his Dad was worth a few bucks, but who knows."

"Well, I know," Chesters said, "and so does the Wingco, but that's not important at the moment. So if you go and get changed, get your best blues on . . ."

"You mean my only blues."

"Your only blues. I'll get Tyler's stuff packed up, get your leave documentation done, and I'll get a copy of the Will made for you to take to Julie—we'll keep the original here in case something happens to you. I have to look at the Will first to make sure it's not a bad news document for Julie. The Dak will be here in about an hour and ready to leave in about an hour and a half, so we'd better get going."

6

The trip due north across the English Channel in the back end of the droning, slow-moving empty Dakota transport aircraft was a bouncing bloody bore for a twenty year-old fighter pilot spilling over with nervous energy. Apart from looking down from the Dak's mile-high altitude at the surface of the choppy Channel which appeared to be filled with hundreds of toy ships—some heading south to the Normandy beaches, others heading north to Portsmouth, Plymouth and the host of other English harbours—there was little amusement during the two hour and twelve minute flight from the dusty B8 airstrip to the smooth, paved Croydon Airport runway.

After clearing customs (he couldn't believe that the Brits would require him or anybody else returning from the Normandy battle to go through customs!), he got advice from the little Cockney customs inspector on how to get to Slough. According to the squadron's records, that's where Tyler's next of kin, Julie, resided. Actually, it was a small place called Farnham Common on the northern outskirts of Slough. "Take the train. The station is right close by here, lad. Take the train into London. Transfer to Paddington Station. The trains run from there to Slough and the West more often than George Formby plays his banjo." Garth Peters knew he was getting good advice.

When square boxy, black hearse-like taxi rattled to a squealing stop at Paddington Station, Peters was trying to decide whether he should telephone Julie to make sure she was at her mother's home in Farnham Common before he made the trip out there. He decided he should go anyway.

His reluctance to telephone was strong. At close to seven in the evening of that long, exhausting day, his decision-making switches weren't functioning with their normal, swift-moving precision. After all, he had told himself more than once after he boarded the train at Croydon, here he was in Blighty heading for Londinium when just a few hours earlier he had been having his ass shot off over Rommel's headquarters, and been bounced by two FW190s. Hard to believe. And then the shoot-down. The image of Tyler's Mustang being torn to shreds would be in his memory forever. When it happened, Peters had felt no sense of remorse, regret, or responsibility. He had been ice cold about watching the man's machine become his instant coffin. Maybe it had to be that way if you were going to keep going, keep fighting, keep attempting to survive in an environment where whenever you flew someone was trying to kill you, trying to shoot you down by firing thousands of anti-aircraft shells at you or getting his fighter right up your jaxxy and letting you have it. Just as Tyler got his.

* * * * * * * *

To telephone Julie at Slough, or not to telephone? He would do it.

If she answered he would simply hang up. Then he'd get on the train for Slough knowing she was there. If Mary answered—she couldn't because she'd be at the Vine—then he'd find out from her where Julie was, without telling Mary what was up about Tyler. Julie had to hear it first. If he failed to get an answer at the Farnham Common number, he'd try Mary at the Vine. And if that didn't work, if she wasn't there, he'd head for the Stafford, have a few drinks and dinner, a good night's sleep and try to track Julie down in the morning.

He was lugging his brown canvas parachute bag (it doubled as every pilot's suitcase), with his few traveling items: extra shirt, underwear, shorts, socks, toothbrush and paste, and a razor that he was now having to use every day instead of every second day on his blond, still almost invisible soft beard. His bag also contained a box full of Tyler's things, his 'personal effects' as the military liked to call them. Dick Manser had gone through Tyler's stuff, throwing some of it away, giving the cigarettes and chewing gum to Mark's tentmate, Clem St. Paul, and packed the remaining things—money, wallet, keys, photos and an unfinished letter to Julie—in a small box he'd scrounged from the cook, Stradiotti. At the bottom of Peters' bag was a sealed envelope for Julie containing a letter of condolence from Frank Chesters and a certified copy of the original of Tyler's handwritten and duly witnessed Last Will and Testament. Peters had not seen the letter or the Will. Nor had Chesters told him the information about Tyler's father that Bunt Waddell had given the C.O. in confidence after Peters' debriefing session.

Tyler had worked hard and successfully at keeping secret his private life and his family background. He cultivated his hayseed, farm-boy appearance because he wanted to be one of the boys—which he was afraid he couldn't be if "the boys" found out the truth about him.

All that Peters knew about Tyler's father was that he was a farmer in North York and, as of the briefing session that morning, that the father was in a coma and not expected to live.

Inside the bustling, cavernous Paddington Station in the midst of crowds of people heading home to points west of London or coming into the big city, Peters finally found a pay telephone—a monstrous English invention created for the purpose of gobbling up shilling and pence coins while ensuring that the innocent user was rarely successful in completing his call, particularly a long-distance call. Having been defeated by the Brit telephone many times, Peters was determined to win that evening. Marshalling his large coins and with the telephone number in hand, he lifted the bell-shaped telephone receiver from its hook and began his friendly confrontation with a facelessly pleasant operator. To his astonishment after two of the British double rings, he could hear Julie's voice. He hung up immediately.

An hour and ten minutes later he was in the Slough train station in combat again with another pay telephone which was more easily defeated this time because his call was not long distance.

"Julie, it's Garth Peters . . . Gator."

There was a pause then happy surprise in her voice. "Gator! How wonderful to hear your voice. But you're supposed to be in Normandy with Mark. Where are you?"

"At the train station in Slough. Can I come and see you? I have something . . . something for you."

"From Mark?"

"Yeah."

"Of course you can come. Take a taxi. There should be one right outside the door. Just tell him to take you to The Little Close at Farnham Common. He'll know where it is. This is a marvelous surprise, Gator. It's been such a long time."

"Since the wedding."

"A long time. You'll be here in ten minutes. I'll put on some tea. Have you eaten?"

"I had a bite just before I got on the train. But I'm going to need a scotch, Julie, not tea."

"Right. Forget the tea, and I'll have a gin martini."

"Great idea. Martinis do wonderful things for you."

She giggled. "Now don't be naughty."

"That's like telling Churchill not to suck on a cigar," he retorted with a nervous voice.

"Are you all right, Gator? You sound a bit different."

"It's been a long day, Julie, and by the time it's finished it'll have been one of the toughest I've ever had. I'll tell you all about it. That scotch is with water please!"

The taxi, an ordinary car and not one of those specially built London black boxes, pulled into the narrow, opened white-painted iron gates set between heavy hedgerows, up a slight crest of a driveway past what appeared in the long, late-evening shadows to be a garage, then by a blacked-out house to the left of the driveway with trees and a walled garden on the right. At the end of a two-storeyed house, the driver swung his taxi round to the front door.

Peters paid the driver, asking, "Are you sure this is it, the Roberts house?"

"Not to worry, sir. This is it. I usually bring Mrs. Roberts from the station off the last train every night. She manages the Vine in Piccadilly don't y'know?"

"Yes, I do know. I know her quite well. Well, well enough."

"Lovely lady, she is. And her daughter. Just got herself married. Say—are you Julie's husband? You're Air Force and all."

Peters hauled himself and his parachute bag out of the back seat of the taxi as he replied. "No. I'm on the same fighter squadron as her husband, that's all."

"Well now, there's Julie now." He pointed to the glass-topped white front door sitting under a small vine-covered roof canopy. The dim light from the hall behind the blackout curtained door silhouetted Julie's slender figure.

Peters stood still, parachute bag in hand, his flat hat under his left arm, waiting, not knowing what to do as she walked hesitantly, then ran to him throwing her arms around him and kissing him fully and hard, her soft wet mouth opening on his.

"Gator. This is marvelous. It's so good to see you. What a delicious surprise! Your scotch is ready." She took him by the arm and steered him into the house.

"How's your mum?" It was a feeble question from a young man who was feeling extremely uncomfortable and ill at ease but at the same time encouraged—perhaps even stimulated—by the unexpected physical warmth of her welcome.

He was experiencing an emotion that was rare for him. Guilt—because she was going to be devastated by what he was going to have to tell her. Guilt—because he didn't have enough guts to stop her in her transparent, open happiness that he, Gator, was there with her. Later. He would tell her later after he had that false-bravery-producing scotch or maybe two under his belt. And when she had two or maybe three blow-softening martinis in her tummy.

"Mum's fine. But what I want to know about is Mark. How is he?"

He dropped his hat and the parachute bag in the small entrance hall and followed her into the spacious living room, which he really didn't see because he was concentrating so hard on how to answer the question he had known very well she was going to ask him.

She sensed his hesitation. "There's something wrong isn't there?" Her eyes were staring, challenging him.

"Yeah. Something's wrong. We lost Mark." He had no choice, no way to soften it. "He was shot down. I was with him. He's dead, Julie."

Her hands flew to her face, eyes rolled back as she half moaned, half screamed, her mouth wide, as the impact of what he had said seared into her young mind. "No, no, Gator! This is a cruel joke. It can't be true!"

He shook his head, "I'm sorry. I'm truly sorry, Julie, but he's gone. That's why I'm here. To tell you."

The tears burst through her eyes. She began to sob, "Oh, God. What am I going to do?" She buried her face in her shaking hands as Peters moved to her to take her in his arms and comfort her.

"You'll be all right, Julie. You'll be fine. It's just going to take time."

"I can't believe it. I can't. He was so wonderful, so handsome . . . and he was so good to me. What am I going to do, Gator? What did I do to deserve this?" she wailed, her face buried in his shoulder.

"You'll work it out," his arms held Julie tightly as her body shook with her sobbing. "You've got your mum and this house and you'll have money from the government, the Canadian government. A pension and they're quite generous, much better than the Brits."

She pushed away from him, her hands wiping away the tears from her flushed red face as she fought to control herself and regain some of her composure.

"There's your drink, Gator, on the table by the door. Mine's over here." She went to the mantel over the fireplace and picked up the glass filled to the top with a gin martini. Taking it in both hands she looked at him and said, "I fixed these as soon as you called from the train station. Doubles they are. Don't know why I poured doubles. A premonition perhaps."

He lifted his glass to hers, touching it gently. "Here's to . . ."

She interrupted, her eyes on his, "Here's to us, Gator. We're alive and young. And to my Mark." The tears welled up again.

"And to you, Julie."

He threw back his entire scotch in long gulps. She downed her martini almost as quickly.

"Warms the cockles of your heart but fast." He smiled at her.

"My martini's already warming more than that," she managed a faint smile in return. Then it was gone. "God, Gator, everything happened so quickly. The whole thing. And now it's over."

"Yeah, I know."

"All so fast. I married Mark only three weeks after meeting him. And all we had was a Saturday to Monday honeymoon, four days last week on that special leave he had. I scarcely knew him. I mean . . ."

Peters sensed he should break her thought train. "Here. Let me get you the other martini wing. You can't fly on one wing, y'know."

He took her glass, went to the bar of gin, vermouth, scotch she had set up on the tea wagon and mixed a drink for each of them. Julie threw herself on the couch, shoes off, feet and long legs up on its cushions, skirt well above her knees. "Gator, I have a confession to make."

He handed her the martini. "You sure you want to tell me?"

She lifted her head sharply to throw her hair away from the side of her face—beautiful, long, dark hair, gorgeous face, Peters thought as he looked down at her. He undid the brass buttons of his uniform jacket, then sat on the carpeted floor beside her, his elbow on the couch cushion next to her flat stomach.

"My confession is . . ." She hesitated. "I don't think I really loved Mark. It was wonderful marrying him. He was good looking and charming. All I thought about was marrying a Canadian officer and then going back to live in that fabulous country of yours with the Indians and Mounties and Eskimos and all that."

He snorted, "That isn't my country! That's the frozen

north. It's Canada. I'm from alligator country, Florida, where it's warm all the time. The US of A, remember?"

"Of course. How silly of me. Anyway, I have to tell you, on top of all that Mark wasn't half the man you are . . . in bed."

Peters was speechless. He looked away, taking a long drink from his glass. "Jesus. You sure know how to put it on the line, Julie. Now my ruptured ego is almost totally repaired."

"Ruptured ego?"

"Yeah. When you went for Mark and actually married the sonofabitch, my male ego was ruptured all right, broken into a million pieces like the dumb egg, Humpty Dumpty. I mean, I was shattered."

She was surprised. "You. Jealous? You've never shown it."

"I've never had any chance. After our night at the Stafford . . ."

"That was bloody marvelous, wasn't it?" As she sipped on her relaxing martini the shock of the news of Mark's death began to fade rapidly.

"It was. Marvelous. I haven't forgotten one second of it. After that night I didn't see you until the wedding and the reception. I mean there's no way I'd've let you tell I was jealous or cared for you one goddamn bit."

She stroked the back of his head, her fingernails gently tingling his scalp. "Do you care for me one bit, Gator? Do you?"

Peters replied, saying it exactly the way it was with him. Tyler was gone, out of the picture forever. It was just as if he had never existed. There was no feeling of regret, remorse, not a pang of guilt, nothing in Peters' soul or mind about Mark's death. In Florida, Pompano Beach terms, he didn't give a shit.

But as to this long-legged, stimulating woman who had

given her body to him first before all other men, a woman who made love with him in such an uninhibited, wild way that aroused him to ecstasies he had never experienced—he had no way to say anything but, "I care for you a lot. I love you, Julie. I have from the moment I saw you at the Vine."

"And Mark?"

"He's gone. He's out of my mind."

* * * * * * * *

When an exhausted Mary Roberts arrived at The Little Close at 12:47 a.m. in her usual taxi, she was surprised to see the lights on in the kitchen. Julie was usually long in bed by this time.

Instead she was waiting at the front door, and as soon as Mary stepped out of the taxi and it moved off, Julie, sobbing and crying, threw herself into the arms of her bewildered Mum.

"'Ere, now. What's all this, my pet?"

"Mark. He was killed yesterday. He was killed, Mum. He's gone!" she wailed.

"Oh, my poor luv," was all that Mary could say, her mind reeling with the shocking news and the sight of her grief-racked daughter clutched to her bosom.

She calmed and soothed Julie, leading her into the kitchen and sitting her down at the table where they did so much of their family talking. And while Mary made a cup of tea, Julie told her the story between brief sessions of crying when her mum, tears of sympathy running down her own cheeks, would come to her and console her.

The kettle had whistled and Mary was pouring the tea. "So where is Gator?"

"He's in bed. I put him in the spare room. He talked

about getting a room at a hotel but I told him you'd have none of that."

"You had that right, luv. He must be worn out, poor lad with everything that happened yesterday, the traveling and all. So now, my poor sweet," Mary looked at the puffed face and red, tear-soaked eyes of her wretched child, "It's time for bed."

"The Will, Mum. I want you to look at the Will. It's right here."

Peters had given her the sealed envelope that the C.O. had handed him just before Gator climbed on board the Dakota, saying, "It's the will. A copy. It's okay. She gets everything. So—give it to her at the right time."

She picked up the single sheet of paper from the kitchen table and handed it to her mother. "He's left everything he has to me."

"But what's he got to leave you?" Mary wondered and asked at the same time. "A farmer's son out in that place where there's nuffing but snow and Indians and the Mounted police! Well," she huffed as she read Mark Tyler's written words copied by someone in a clear, vertical hand, "he's done that all right. Everything to you. The whole bloody lot—probably of nothing. I mean, after all, he was only a boy. Never been in business. Did he ever talk to you about his mum and dad?"

"Yes. But he never said they had money or anything. His mother died a while ago. No brothers or sisters, nothing like that. And his dad, well, he didn't say much about him, except they didn't get on too well together. His dad was a domineering old bastard. They weren't close. Never were."

Mary was searching. "Didn't he ever say anything about his dad? Like whether he was poor or rich?"

Julie shook her head. "No, nothing. He really didn't like to talk about his family, his mum and dad. And we were together such a short time, Mum!"

"Sure. And you had other things on your mind." She reached down to stroke her baby's hair then drew Julie's head to her ample bosom.

"Gator said the C.O. told him to tell me I should talk to the family lawyer about the will, what to do with it, the pension and all. Do we have a lawyer, a family lawyer?"

Her mother gave a chuckle as she released her loving hold and turned to go to the teapot. "Blimey. The last time we needed a lawyer was when somebody else died. Your dear old dad, that's who. Your dear old dad, who left me when you were born. And we had to break his bloody will because he tried to leave this house to his filthy mistress."

"He did?" Julie was shocked, her mouth hanging open as this horrible news sank in.

"Indeed he did, my sweet. Ten years ago he up and died. You were only eight so you wouldn't remember none of this."

"So what did you do?"

"I hired the meanest sonofabitch in Windsor, the meanest solicitor in the shadow of Her Majesty's castle, that's what I did. Colin James. And he broke that will just like he was snapping a dried-up chicken wishbone in half. That he did."

"But there's no fight here, Mum."

"And maybe nothing in the estate either. But Mr. James knows the law of wills and estates."

"Even in Canada?"

"Humpf. Canada? It's nothing but a British colony. The law here'll apply there for sure."

"D'you think Mr. James will look after Mark's will, his estate? There may be nothing in it, Mum. And the cost . . ."

* * * * * * *

Mr. James was terribly busy. What with dealing with the estates of the young men from the Slough area who were perishing in the Normandy battle, the Italian campaign and the navy's unending fight against Hitler's U-Boats in the Atlantic, Mr. James couldn't fit Julie into his appointment book until the morning of the fourth day after Garth Peters' arrival at The Little Close.

The late mornings, the afternoons and the evenings of those three days (up until Mary's midnight arrival home after closing the Vine) were filled with walks around the walled grass lawns and gardens of The Little Close. And there was a daily late-afternoon saunter up the main road to the local shop where smokes and newspapers and magazines could be bought.

The day before the appointment with Solicitor James, during their late afternoon visit to the village smokeshop to buy Julie's daily ration packet of cigarettes, Gator picked up the *Times* newspaper. He wanted to see the listings of the military awards that had been gazetted, announcing the decorations that had been granted by His Majesty King George VI. It was only the Air Force gongs he was interested in. He knew there might be something there for him some day as a result of that Rommel headquarters mission—if luck would have it and the C.O. got off his ass and wrote a citation. But it was always interesting to look at the list to see who among the Canadian bomber and fighter squadrons had made it. The awards announcement was usually on page five or six of the prestigious *Times of London*.

However, on this day, Peters did not get beyond the front page because his eyes caught a brief news report at the bottom right-hand corner which he quickly read. It was an item covering a death in the family of Canada's wealthiest entrepreneur, well known in the United Kingdom because of his extensive newspaper holdings in England and Scotland. Peters bought the paper, paying the shopkeeper for it and for

Julie's two packs of Players cigarettes. He would be careful not to let her see the front page. Very careful.

They were on the deserted side road, almost at the gates of The Little Close, walking slowly hand in hand, Julie puffing contentedly on a cigarette but not letting it hang from her mouth the way her mum did. She had been questioning Peters about the way he and his squadron mates lived. The tent life in the orchard, the food, what they did on their time off, the flying. But not one question, not one word about Mark. While they were chatting, Peters was making his decisions about what moves he would make. He would have to act quickly. He had only two days left before he was to be back at B8 and there was a lot to be done.

Garth stopped and pulled Julie to him. As he looked down into her eyes, she flicked the cigarette away then lifted both her arms up to lock her hands behind his neck. She was expecting to be kissed, not to hear the words he was about to say.

"Would you consider marrying me, Julie? I know it's such a short time after Mark, but . . ."

She was shocked but happy. Jaw dropping, her face coming into an astonished smile, Julie replied, "You must be joking!"

"No. I'm not joking. No goddamn way I'm joking."

"When?"

"Now. Tomorrow. Today if we can arrange it."

"But it's such a short time after Mark. What will your people, your squadron mates . . . what'll they think?"

"Screw them. It's you. You're the only one who counts. They'll know—eventually. Couldn't matter less about them. I'll look after you, Julie—not them."

She pressed herself against him, arms around his neck, her lips against his ear. "Thank you, Gator. Thank you, my darling."

"God, I love you, Gator. Honestly I do." She kissed him

open-mouthed on the lips, murmuring, "If we weren't in this fucking public place I'd make your wingtip fly at a speed, a slow excruciatingly wet and sucking speed it's never flown before."

"It'll be better if you take it out of its hangar, give it a gentle massage."

"Let's get into the house," she gasped as she turned to run up the driveway, pulling him by the hand.

Julie couldn't wait. She threw open the kitchen door and as soon as they were inside she turned on him, frantically undoing the brass buttons of his uniform jacket then his belt. Her fingers clawed open the buttons of his fly and reached gently in to guide out his red, pulsing penis. "My god, it's so hard," she moaned as she knelt to kiss and stroke it, then take it softly in her mouth.

Just as he could feel the magical surge mounting inside his groin he reached down to pull her away and lift her to her feet. Mouths locked searchingly together they slowly removed each other's clothes. When they were naked, writhing bodies pressed tightly together, he picked her up arms under her knees and shoulders and carried her into the carpeted living room. When he started toward the sofa, Julie hook her head, "Not there, darling. We might make a mess. The floor, on the carpet."

Their love-making done for the moment they lay contentedly exhausted, Julie on her side against him, her head on his shoulder while her hand lightly cradled his testicles.

"Gator, how soon do you think we can get married? Will we have to wait until your next leave?"

"No goddamn way, sweetheart. We'll do it now, before I go back to France on Sunday."

"That's only two days from now!"

"I know. There's got to be some way of getting it done. But not here in Slough. We'll have to go to London. They'll know, someone at the Red Cross or Canada House will know how to get a marriage license quickly, and where to find some reverend or somebody qualified to do the marriage ceremony."

He looked at the only thing he was still wearing, his watch. "It's twenty to ten. We can catch a train and be in London by noon. What d'you think, Julie? Shall we try it?"

"Let's have a go. Why not?"

Their train pulled in to Paddington station at eleven minutes past twelve. A rattling taxi took them to the Red Cross center near Piccadilly Circus. Yes, the Red Cross ladies knew exactly what to do—happened three or four times a week now that the fighting was really on. By three o'clock Julie and Garth had their wedding license and were taking their marriage vows before an elderly, pince-nezzed magistrate who was happy to interrupt his boring Friday court session to perform a happily urgent marriage ceremony —for a special fee of course.

By 3:30 the newlyweds were at the Vine to break the good news to Julie's Mum. She was miffed at first because they hadn't included her in the wedding. And it was such a short time after Mark. What would people think and all? But after a couple of glasses of celebratory champagne that she insisted on pouring, Mary had mellowed and was smiling.

"Well, with the war on and all and you having to go back to your squadron, you have to live your life to the full while you can. Right, Gator?"

"Right, Mum. No question about it." Peters clinked his glass against hers and smiled.

"So what are your plans, you two?"

Julie replied, "We're going back to the house for our honeymoon." She looked at Peters and giggled.

"I have to go back to the squadron on Sunday—out of Croydon."

"That's fine," Mary announced. "I'll stay here at the

Vine so you can have some privacy. There's a room up on the third floor, a bedroom I use when I'm too tired to take the late train home."

"Or if you've got some interesting young man in the bar you'd like to entertain after closing time?" Gator jokingly suggested.

It was Mary's turn to giggle. "Now don't get cheeky just because you're me son-in-law now."

"One thing, Mum," Gator looked serious. "I'd like to make a new Will before I go back. You understand. I'll get Mr. James to do it tomorrow and we'll get him to do one for Julie, too. It's very important."

Mary nodded. "It sure is, luv. I'm sure Mr. James'll do it for both of you. If he won't, I'll give him what's for." She laughed.

At ten o'clock the next morning Julie and Gator were in the musty law-book and file-filled office of Colin James, a wispy, gray haired, thin-faced, diminutive man, probably in his mid-fifties although to the twenty-year-old Garth Peters he looked to be at least seventy-five.

James had finished asking both of them all the questions necessary for him to prepare simple crossing wills. In the event of the death of either, the whole estate of the deceased would go to the survivor. Or if both died at the same time, the estates of both would go to the children of the marriage or, if there were no children, then everything would be divided evenly between the surviving parents of the deceased.

"We can't go much beyond that sort of distribution and still keep the wills simple, can we?" the solicitor asked rhetorically as he scratched out his notes. "That should do it," he announced, looking up at his clients across the file-littered, large carved oak table that served as his desk and that of his father before him.

"My secretary should be here any minute now. I'll dictate

the wills to her. They'll be ready by noon. Now what's this business about a power of attorney?"

"Well, sir," Peters replied after a sideways glance at his wife, "Julie and I thought . . . well we thought it would be a good idea because Mark's estate . . . there'll have to be dealings with the Canadian Air Force authorities, dealings on Julie's behalf to settle the estate, her widow's pension and allowances and that sort of thing and whatever assets—there probably aren't any—whatever assets he has back in Canada. Just to give you an example. I brought her a copy of the will. The C.O. wouldn't let me have the original because everything has to be processed by the squadron and wing admin people, then everything has to go to RCAF headquarters in London, and then there's whatever has to be done in Canada. It just seemed to Julie and me that it would make things easier for her if I had her power of attorney so I could sign for her, make things go faster, that sort of thing."

"What d'you think of that, Mrs. Peters?"

Julie was startled on hearing herself called Mrs. Peters. "Oh. I think it's a good idea. Really I do, just as my husband said."

"Very well. I'll draw a standard form, a general power of attorney so he can sign just about anything on your behalf. That shouldn't take long. If you'll come back after lunch, say three o'clock, then everything should be ready. Ah. Here's my secretary just arriving on time—fifteen minutes late as usual!"

After a ploughman's lunch at a pub near James' chambers and a bicycle ride back to The Little Close, they made love, until Gator suddenly said, "Hey, it's twenty to three. We'll be late if we don't get going!"

Like James' secretary, they arrived at the solicitor's office on time—ten minutes late.

The wills were signed in the presence of Colin James and his secretary. Julie had designated Peters to be executor of her estate, or her mother in the event Peters died first. In turn Peters designated Julie and chose his father to be the backup.

The wills being executed, Colin James excused his secretary, then said to Julie, "Now here's the power of attorney. I want you to read it before you sign it. You must understand this document gives your husband power to do any and all things on your behalf, hold assets on your behalf and to conduct business and other matters for you and to sign on your behalf any document he considers appropriate. He does this for you in trust, so to speak. The power of attorney is irrevocable unless the court orders it terminated or until your husband returns it to you. Do you understand what I'm saying to you?"

"Yes, of course I do. Really, I don't have anything, any money, just what I might get from Mark's estate. And, anyway, this will help Garth to, as he said, get the paperwork and the like finished quickly for me—won't it, Gator?"

Peters didn't look at her. He merely nodded his head, eyes on James and the sheet of paper lying on the ancient desk in front of Julie.

James was satisfied. "Very well. I'll get my secretary to come back in to witness your signature. I've prepared three notarial copies of the original—a copy which I certify under my seal to be a true copy—so you can have the original and two copies, Flying Officer Peters. I'll keep one in my files, and I have a plain copy of the power for you, Mrs. Peters."

As the solicitor went to his office door to call in his secretary, Gator took Julie's hand and in a church-like whisper said, "This'll make things so much easier to get the paperwork done, the estate paperwork. I'll start on it as soon as I get back to the squadron tomorrow."

"But tomorrow's Sunday!"

"On the beachhead all the days are the same. The fighting doesn't stop because it's Sunday."

7

Peters was uneasy as the Dakota transport aircraft crossed the Normandy beaches over the huge Mulberry port at Arromanches and descended through 2,000 feet toward the B8 airfield base of 430 Squadron. Uneasy because there might be a stray Focke Wulf 190 or Me109 whose pilot was either stupid or brave enough to cross into Allied territory to attack anything he could find—troops, vehicles and particularly juicy, easy-to-kill transport aircraft like the slow-moving Dakota, just like the Junkers that Tyler shot down.

Peering out a window, Peters took a good look at the Mulberry port. He hadn't seen the huge manmade harbour since D-Day plus ten when 129 Airfield, the support unit for 39 Recce Wing, had arrived at B8 with all its trucks, vans, tents, repair shops, kitchens and all the mobile equipment required to support three fighter squadrons in the field. From that day, June 16, onward, Peters and his fellow recce pilots never flew their fighters north over the beaches, but only south and east over enemy territory through the flak-filled skies around Caen, the focal point of the assaults of the Canadian and British armies.

When he had been in the Dak that carried him to Croydon a week earlier, Peters had no interest in what was down below in Normandy and on the beaches. But in the last few minutes of the return flight he sat with his face glued to the window as he took in the sights a thousand feet below.

The Mulberry port, one of Winston Churchill's inventive

concepts, was teeming with activity as it had been from shortly after D-Day, when its massive floating concrete sections had been towed across the English Channel and sunk off Arromanches, its sections locked together by bridges to form an instant port.

Peters could see at least a dozen freighters docked at the Mulberry, cranes lifting cargo off onto trucks, tanks, heavy guns, crates being moved onshore, men in motion everywhere like players on a soccer field as they handled the massive tonnage of equipment and supplies required to sustain the three Allied armies under Montgomery in their unceasing attacks against the Nazi forces under Rommel.

As the Dakota moved inland above the flat, crop-filled farm fields of Normandy, Peters saw the roads leading away from Arromanches filled with trucks, armored vehicles and marching troops moving south toward the increasingly distant frontlines, the Americans in the St. L area, the British due south past Bayeux in the Mont Pinçon sector, and the Canadians around the hinge point of heavily defended Caen.

What a contrast to what reconnaissance pilot Peters had grown accustomed to seeing on the enemy side of the lines. In daylight nothing moved on the roads. Trucks and battle tanks might be found lurking under trees hiding from the searching eyes of the recce pilots who might find them then call in the Spitfires with their bombs and cannons or the Typhoons with their deadly armor penetrating rockets.

The difference between the scenes on the Nazi side of the frontlines—furtive hiding—and the Allied side—teeming openness—was caused by a single factor: near total air superiority in the hands of thousands of Allied fighter aircraft backed up by thousands of heavy bombers.

Garth Peters and the aircrew and groundcrew of the three Canadian squadrons of 39 Recce Wing were but a small cog in the huge wheel of Allied Air Forces that by day and night battered away at Rommel's panzers, artillery and troops. A small cog in the wheel but an exceedingly important one because the pilots of 39 Recce Wing were the eyes of the British Army in the field and received its daily tasking from its commander general and the headquarters of the divisions under his control.

The British recce wing—two Mustang I squadrons and a Bluebird (unarmed) high-level photography Spitfire unit—was assigned to support the Canadian Army. No one could sort out the perverse logic of putting the RAF with the Canadian Army and the RCAF with the Brits. Probably another eccentric Montgomery decision was the general consensus among the low-life pilots and their ever-suffering ground crews.

The Dak pilots up front in the cockpit had only one thing in their minds—get this aircraft on the ground as quickly as possible. They didn't want some stray Jerry up their large vulnerable jaxxy any more than their lone passenger did back there among the cargo, two crates each containing a brand new Allison engine that would fit snugly into the snout of a Mustang I.

The copilot announced on the loud speaker system, "We're going straight in. Make sure your seatbelt's done up back there."

"You asshole," Peters thought, "of course it's done up." Nevertheless he gave the belt a tightening tug as he heard and felt the undercarriage lock down and the Dak slow perceptibly as the flaps went down and the engines were throttled back. The captain was in the final approach to landing at B8 and Gator Peters' mind was retracing and reworking the plan of action he had been developing from the moment he'd seen that news report in the smoke shop in Farnham Common.

He had only one objective in mind—to get control, complete control of the situation in Canada. He wasn't exactly sure how he'd do it. He'd have to adapt his plan of action to the circumstances, the barriers he knew people would throw up to prevent him from getting his hands on the estate.

The guys on the squadron, the C.O. and the Wingco were bound to be pissed off at him for marrying Julie when Mark had been wiped out only five days before. "Screw them. They'd do the same thing, all of them if they had the chance," Peters told himself. He lifted his hand to touch the inner tunic pocket below the wings on his left chest. The original and one certified copy of the power of attorney were in an envelope in the pocket. That piece of paper was his ticket to power, money and a one-way trip to Canada.

The lumbering Dakota landed and taxied to the airfield's maintenance area where its engines were shut down. Peters shouted his farewell to the pilots. Then he was out the rear door and down the steps. Once again he was walking the browning turf of B8. He headed for the van of his commanding officer Frank Chesters to do two things—report in and get phase one of his plan started. "Poor old Chesters is going to get one helluva shock," Peters thought happily. "He won't know whether to shit or wind his watch!"

The baby-faced pilot was right. Poor Chesters' face registered shock and plain disbelief as he heard the story of Garth's week.

"So what else could I do, sir? I love Julie, so we got married. Just like that. And I really don't give a damn about what anyone on the squadron thinks. I really don't. All I care about is Julie and helping look after Mark's estate, I mean her money. D'you know anything about Mark's dad? D'you know he's probably the wealthiest man in Canada? I mean, we all thought his dad was a farmer, an ordinary dirt-poor farmer, and Mark was the poor son of a nothing farmer. But, son of bitch, his dad is the one and only E.P. Tyler. Has to be worth at least a hundred million bucks. Owns newspapers and breweries and radio stations and God knows what else!"

Chesters pulled himself together. Sitting behind his protective desk he leaned forward to pick a cigarette out of his package of Players, and as he lit it replied to the agitated Peters. "Yeah. I knew about Mark, about his father. The Wingco's from Toronto, old Toronto family, and he knows E.P. Tyler. He told me about him when Mark joined the squadron. Mark asked the Wingco to help him keep his identity secret. He was just a farm boy from North York, that's what he wanted. He didn't want to be treated differently. He wanted to be one of the boys. So how did you find out?"

"There was an article in the *Times*. Front page. Saw it in a smokeshop near Julie's house. We went there to buy cigarettes and there it was. Just caught my eye. I was looking at the paper while she was buying the cigarettes. It said that the son of the Canadian tycoon E.P. Tyler had been killed in action just hours after his father had died from a stroke. It said Mark was the only child. His mother died three years ago. No other family. That's how I found out."

"And Julie? How did she react to that news?"

Peters looked down at his own hands clamped tightly in front of him. He was going to say, "She didn't because I didn't tell her." Instead he said, "She was surprised. And I can tell you, sir, as Mark's wife and sole beneficiary she's really excited about the fact she might be entitled to a piece of E.P. Tyler's fortune."

Chesters nodded, "I can understand that. Julie and her mum are working people. A possible windfall like this one could put them on easy street."

"It sure could. So Julie gave me her power of attorney. You know, a document that allows me to sign for her, do business for her."

"Yeah. I know what a power of attorney is."

"I've got it right here. The original and a copy."

Peters reached into his tunic to pull out the envelope. He handed the copy to Chesters, who read it slowly as his memory reviewed the Will of Mark Tyler lying in the squadron's safe, leaving all of Mark Tyler's estate to his wife Julie Roberts Tyler. If E.P. Tyler's Will left all of his estate to his son, even Chesters could figure out that Julie Roberts Tyler had unwittingly hit a monster jackpot. And that Gator Peters already had his hands on it.

"You know What Mark's Will said?" Chesters asked.

"She showed me the copy I delivered to her."

"So you know there's a possibility she might be entitled to the whole of E.P. Tyler's estate?"

"Yes, or at least a piece of it, a big piece or a little piece."

Chesters stubbed out his cigarette butt. "I have to talk to the Wingco. You go take your stuff to your tent and get changed. Be back here in half an hour."

Chesters knocked on Bunt Waddell's operations van door and got an immediate, "Come in." Waddell could see the 430 Squadron commander was operating at two or three notches above his usual phlegmatic, unflappable demeanor. Something was on with Frank Chesters.

"Sit down, Frank. Cigarette? What's up?"

Chesters took off his wedge cap and tucked it under his left shoulder epaulette. He took the offered smoke saying, "Gator Peters is back, and, Bunt, you won't believe what I'm going to tell you, not a fucking word."

"Try me." Waddell tried to be as nonchalant as possible knowing that Chesters was about to tell him something he really didn't want to hear.

"You won't believe this, but that little asshole married Julie the day before yesterday."

"He what?" Waddell shouted.

"He married Mark's widow, that sweet little thing you gave away at that wedding. Remember?"

"He married Julie? Jesus Christ! Mark's body isn't even cold, wherever the hell it is."

Chesters shook his head. "That's only the beginning. Gator found out our best-kept secret—that Mark was the son of E.P. Tyler. He found out sometime during the week. Saw a front page news item in the *Times* about E.P. Tyler's son being killed and E.P. dying just a few hours before."

"Old E.P. died?" Bunt Waddell was astonished. "Why didn't someone try to send word to Mark? A telegram or something. It would've been too late but . . ."

"Maybe the people in Toronto didn't know how to send the message across."

"Bullshit," Waddell retorted. "Whoever the executor is or the family lawyer, all they had to do was call Mackenzie King's office and the old fart would've called us himself. Anyway, there was no message, no word."

"And it wouldn't have changed a goddam thing even if there had been. So the question, sir, is what in hell are we going to do with Peters?"

"What d'you mean what are *we* going to do?"

Chesters pulled at his lengthening mustache. "We have to . . . I guess *I* have to decide what to recommend to you."

"What's the problem?"

"It goes this way. I have to put on my half-a-lawyer's-hat for this one." Chesters had two years of University of Alberta law school under his belt before he had enlisted in the RCAF in 1940. "Mark was the only child of E.P. There were no other relatives, at least according to Mark. Mark's mother died some time ago. So it follows that E.P.'s will would leave everything to Mark. I mean everything. In turn, Mark's will leaves everything to Julie. We know that."

"So what you're saying . . ."

"What I'm saying is—E.P. died before Mark did. That means Mark inherits all of E.P.'s estate—if my guess is right as to what E.P.'s will says. Which means that Julie through

Mark's will inherits E.P.'s entire estate. Add to that the fact that Julie's now married to Gator who also has Julie's wide-open power of attorney."

"Which means that Gator has his hands on the estate of old E.P. Tyler, the richest man in Canada."

"He sure as hell has. And we have to handle what happens to Gator Peters as though we were handling a flimsy crate full of rattlesnakes."

Waddell snorted, smiling. "Yeah. We're up to our asses in alligators. Alligator Peters, to be exact. What d'you think we should do?"

"Get him out of here and fast. There'd be all hell to pay if we let him back on operations and he got shot down after you and I knew that Julie is or should be entitled to E.P.'s estate and Gator's married to her. This is what I'm recommending, sir."

A quarter of an hour later Chesters was back behind his own desk with Peters across from him. Gator was now in his bought-from-the-Yanks, summer khaki flying clothes, his Smith & Wesson revolver on his right hip, knee-high escape boots with his dagger sticking out the top of the right boot. The ever-present, beaten-up blue officers' flat hat jauntily on his head, Gator Peters was ready to go flying on operations again.

He wasn't ready for the C.O.'s words, although he knew he'd shaken Chesters up. No doubt about it. Peters had sorted out in his mind that he'd fly with the squadron for a week or so, let Chesters and the Wingco digest the news he'd dropped on them. Then he'd ask for compassionate leave to go with Julie to Canada to begin to sort out the details of the Tyler estate.

That's what Gator had in mind, but that wasn't Chesters' plan.

"Gator, the Wingco's grounded you."

Peters sat bolt upright. "He's what? He can't do that! I'm fit and ready to fly!"

"Sure you are and we're going to miss you, Gator. The squadron won't be the same without you, our number one," he smiled, "shit disturber. But that's the way it is. The Wingco's cleared it with the Air Officer Commanding. The AOC's authorized your immediate return to England. RCAF headquarters in London, Lincoln-in-Fields, will get you and Julie organized on a flight to Canada, I mean, God, Gator, Julie's the richest woman, the richest person in Canada and she hasn't even been there. And you're a goddamn Yankee. Unbelievable!"

Peters shook his head in agreement. "It sure as hell is. When you get right down to it, it sure as hell is."

"And what you're going to have to do is get your ass over to Toronto as soon as you can, you and Julie. You'll have to deal with the estate's lawyers, get the will probated and get everything transferred to Julie. That's your first responsibility now."

"What about coming back to the squadron later on?"

"When the time comes, we'll be glad to have you back. I haven't any idea how long it will take to get through all the legal stuff, probate, transfer of title and all that stuff. Maybe a couple of months."

"Then I could get back here?"

"Sure. You could keep your flying current on Harvards. Camp Borden's probably the closest or Trenton."

"I can make those arrangements." Peters then asked, "The guys on the squadron, do they know who Mark was? Have you told them?"

Chesters shook his head. "No. They still think he was an ordinary farm lad from North York, wherever the hell that is."

"You'll tell them, of course?"

"Sure. After you've left. I'll give them all the full gen."

"Including my marrying Julie?"

"Natch. Better to do it after you've gone. And I want to get you out of here as soon as possible. I mean like right now."

"What's the hurry, sir? I'd like to see the gang, have dinner, have a few drinks with them tonight. Then I can be outta here tomorrow. There'll be a Dak in here or one of the other airfields."

"No way." Chesters was adamant. "The guys are gonna flip when they hear this story and some of them aren't gonna like it one goddamn bit. If you'd like to know, I don't like it one goddamn bit. The marrying Julie thing's pretty hard to take so soon after Mark died."

"Listen, sir." Peters' voice was hard. "I love Julie. She loves me. She was mine before that asshole Tyler got his filthy fucking hands on her. We got married and I don't give a shit what you or anybody else thinks—sir."

Chesters' tone matched Peters. "You got married after you found out about E.P. Tyler. You've got her power of attorney. And I'll bet a year's pay you haven't said one goddamn word to her, not told a fucking thing about E.P. Tyler. You said she's excited about being entitled to a piece of the Tyler estate, but you're lying. You haven't told her anything, have you?"

Peters shot back, "What I have or haven't told my wife, sir, is none of your goddamn business."

The C.O. shrugged, "You're right. It isn't. Take my jeep. Go and get your things packed and report back here in fifteen minutes. And keep your mouth shut about Julie until you're off this airfield. That's an order that is part of my goddamn business!"

Peters was back at Chesters' tent twenty-five minutes later, with his kit and parachute bags loaded with all his worldly possessions on the jeep's back seat.

"I've made arrangements for you to spend the night at

an army field hospital halfway between here and Bayeux. It's Canadian. Corporal Levine'll drive you there. He'll come back in the morning to pick you up at eight and drive you to the Spit wing at Beny-Sur-Mer. A Dak is scheduled out of there at ten for Croydon. When you get to Croydon go straight to RCAF headquarters at Lincoln-in-Fields in London. Report there to Wing Commander Wright, Caesar Wright, the senior administrative officer. He'll look after all your arrangements from that point, getting you and Julie back to Canada and all that sort of thing."

Chesters picked up a large, bulky brown envelope from his desk and handed it to Peters, saying, "Here are your personal records. Do not, repeat, do not open them. Just hand them to Wing Commander Wright."

"Is that all, sir?" Peters asked, his hostility unmasked.

"Yeah. That's all. Except—you've been a contributor to 430 Squadron, Gator, a hell of a contributor. You're an outstanding pilot, one of the best I've ever run across. When all this has blown over and . . . well, in spite of this difficulty, you'll be, as I said before, welcome back in 430 Squadron anytime."

He held out his hand. Peters refused to take it, demanding instead, "I want the original Mark Tyler Will. I'll take it with me."

Taken aback, Chesters reacted. "No way. I'm going to send it back to RCAF headquarters. They can handle it from there."

Peters stood his ground. "I demand to have that Will. It is the rightful possession of Julie. It's hers. I have her power of attorney. In her name I want you to give it to me."

"You've got a certified copy."

"I need the original. If you think Julie and I are going to go all the way to Canada to do battle with E.P. Tyler's lawyers without having the original Will in our possession . . ."

Chesters hesitated. "You're right. And why would I want

to keep the goddamn thing anyway. Levine'll have it with him when he picks you up in the morning."

Peters smiled. This time it was he who offered his hand. Chesters, unsmiling, took it as the younger man said, "I hope I'll be back. But if I don't, remember there'll be a place for you in the Tyler organization. Yes, sir, you're a straight shooter. A senior place, sir. Remember that."

Gator Peters turned and walked out of the hot tent of the flabbergasted Commanding Officer of 430 Fighter Recce squadron of the Royal Canadian Air Force in Normandy.

8

Corporal Levine, the squadron's administrative clerk, a frail, black-haired, sallow-complexioned older man of about thirty-five, stopped the jeep in front of a tent that carried a sign reading: "10th Field Hospital, Canadian Army Service Corps, Headquarters."

"This is the place, sir," Levine told his passenger. "You're supposed to find the head nurse, Major Osborne, or something like that."

Peters looked at the headquarters tent and the dozen or more much larger tents standing in the mature apple orchard behind it.

"Okay. Just let me get my bags out," he said as he jumped out of the vehicle and turned to hoist his two bags out. "The 10th Field Hospital. Weren't they in a Brit hospital near Gatwick last winter? I was in for a week with bronchial pneumonia."

"Yeah. That's the same outfit. You'll probably know most of them. At least the good-looking ones anyway," Levine smirked.

"Could be," Gator agreed, his memory suddenly filled with the smiling, beautiful round face of nurse Captain Jane Knight and her naked, long, full young body as she lay in his arms. Where was it? Yes. The tall, thirteenth-century four-poster bed in the Hind's Head Hotel at Maidenhead. "Yes, could be—if I'm lucky."

"See you at eight in the morning. Have a great night, sir. Sleep well."

"And don't forget Tyler's original Will or I'll have your balls for bookends!" Peters threatened.

"Yes, sir!" the corporal shouted as he gunned the jeep's engine and took off in a cloud of mid-July Normandy dust.

Peters walked to the tent which had its flap tied back to let air in. He put his bags down on the grass and stepped inside the khaki canvas structure, his eyes straining to adjust to the sudden darkness.

"Can I help you?" came a strong female voice to his left. There was a woman sitting behind a table-desk that was covered with paper and files. "You must be Flying Officer Peters, right?"

"Right and I'm supposed to be billeted here tonight."

"We're expecting you. I'm Major Osborne, the chief nurse. Something tells me we've met before."

"That's right. I was a patient last winter when your hospital was at Horsley."

"Of course. You had bronchial pneumonia and your nurse, Captain Knight, all at the same time."

"Not quite. Bronchial pneumonia first. Captain Knight second. I mean I had no idea you people were here. Is she here?" There was hope in the way he said it.

"She's here working her tail off, like all my girls. Casualties have been really heavy in the last week." Major Osborne looked at her watch. "She should be in the mess tent having her dinner just about now. She's just gone off shift. I'll show you where you'll be sleeping. You're in luck. You'll be in a two-holer tent with one of our doctors—except he's at one of the other hospitals on TD, temporary duty, for a couple of days. So you're on your own. C'mon, I'll show you."

Peters followed the slender, dark-haired Major Osborne, watching her hips move up and down like small round pistons in a pump. She could certainly turn him on. Pretty face but a bit old. God, she must be close to thirty, Gator thought. Then his mind was back to Jane Knight. What a gorgeous creature and, boy, did she ever know what to do with his wingtip and bombs. An unforgettable night with Jane and that tight, soft, wet hangar of hers. When was it? Back in March. He'd lost track of her after he got back to the squadron. During a spot of sick leave he returned to Gatwick and telephoned Jane but she was away at a course for six weeks. The duty officer's voice at the other end of the scratchy English phone wasn't sure where she'd gone but said if he called back the next morning the adjutant would be able to tell Gator where she was.

Peters never got around to calling the next morning or any other time. His attention then had been diverted by a young thing called Emily. He met Emily at Crackers Club, a downstairs pub near the Regent Palace Hotel where he was staying during his one-week sick leave. He got so worn out by little Emily and his drinking time at the Crackers Club and other fighter-pilot watering holes that he was ready to go back to the hospital to recuperate. By that time Jane Knight was history, except when her image would come alive in his memory as his mind, enveloped in pre-sleep darkness, would conjure up with soft clarity a selection of the most exciting of his sexual exploits with the many girls who had been with him in his short life.

"Here's your tent. Looks like that cot's empty. Make yourself at home." Major Osborne pointed to her right. "The mess tent's down there. If you have any problems, give me a shout. My tent's here, right next door to yours. I hope you don't snore."

As she turned to walk back to the HQ tent, Peters said, "Thanks. And I hope you don't snore, too."

Peters threw his bags on the cot then headed out. He was hungry for food and anxious to see Jane Knight. He stepped into the vast mess tent filled with uniformed men and women eating, drinking and chatting at the two long dining tables in the center of its space. The enticing smell of cooking food was cut by the pervasive smoke of cigarettes, the clattering of silverware and metal dishes, and the muted cacophony of talk across the table broken occasionally by a high-pitched female laugh.

His eyes searched for Jane looking at the khaki-uniformed nurses, rank epaulettes on their shoulders, distinctive downturned-at-the-back white caps squarely on their young heads. Almost as one the sea of faces stopped its chatter and turned to look at this interesting young Air Force officer intruder, two dozen sets of lusty female eyes sizing up the attractive male body in its blue battle dress and crumpled "operational" peaked flat hat.

Peters grinned self-consciously saying, "Hi, ladies. I'm looking for Jane Knight." Might as well be up front.

A small voice came from the far end of the tent. "She's right here!" A hand waved in the dim distance pointing down.

Gator moved. There she was. Smiling, blonde, tanned-face, young Jane Knight, her wide blue eyes watching him approach. She didn't attempt to get up. Just waited for him to come to her. Something told him "that's not like Jane—she should be on her feet and coming right at me." But no, she sat glued to her chair even when he was close enough to reach out to touch her, to take her hand, as she smiled at him, white teeth gleaming, joy written on her upturned, tanned face.

"Hi, Jane. Long time."

"Yes. Four months. March wasn't it?" The welcoming smile disappeared as he stood over her still holding her hand. "I thought you would've kept in touch. I mean . . ."

Gator shook his head slightly, "I tried, Jane. Really I did. But you were off on some sort of course. You know." He could see all the inquisitive listening ears around him. "Can I buy you a drink or a cigarette or something? Outside?"

"Sure." He helped her as she moved her chair back and stood up. As she straightened, Peters thought, "Christ, she's put on some weight around the middle. Not that flat, hard, kissable stomach. Looks like a bit of a pot. I think I can take that. Won't bother me when we get down to the short strokes."

On their way out of the mess tent, Peters stopped at the honor bar, a rickety bridge table carrying a bottle of gin, one of scotch, some glasses, a jug of water but no ice, and a plate to put coins amounting to two shillings a drink. He poured doubles. Outside they walked deep in the orchard away from the tents. The sun was down but the sky was still lit, its orange pinkness glistening off the shiny green leaves of the gnarled apple trees growing heavy with their summer fruit.

"Cigarette?" Gator offered when they stopped their saunter to sip on their scotch. She took it and as he held the flame of her lighter to the tip of the cigarette hanging from between her pouty, unpainted lips, he said, "I've missed you, Jane. I really have."

She sucked in a strong draught of smoke, felt it, then blew it slowly out her nostrils and mouth while she thought about his stupid remark. "I could say 'bullshit.' In fact, I will say it. That's bullshit. If you missed me, you could've found me—if you really wanted to."

"Look. I tried. But you were on a course somewhere. And, then, we moved out of Gatwick way over to Odiham." He shrugged lifting the glass of scotch to his lips. "Anyway, you look great."

"I feel great, I really do, but a little sad tonight."

"Why. Because I'm here?"

"No, of course not. I'm being sent home. Back to Canada. I leave tomorrow."

Peters was astonished. "Why? I mean, they need you here."

"It's because I'm pregnant."

"You're what?"

"Pregnant, Gator. With child. Can't you see it's beginning to show? After all, it's five months since we had that weekend at the Hind's Head."

Peters couldn't believe what he was hearing. "C'mon Jane. You've gotta be kidding. You're pregnant and I'm the father? How the hell do I know I'm the father? I mean how many guys were you with? I wasn't the only one."

"You sure were. You can try to tell yourself anything you want, Gator, but you're the only one I was with. The only one. You didn't have any safes. Remember I asked you? So we had no protection, right?"

His tanned face was pasty white as his mind reeled as he thought about the consequences. "What about an abortion? Christ, you're in a hospital. You know what to do. Somebody could've helped you!"

Jane took another deep drag on her cigarette. "No way. I'm a Catholic, a good Catholic. And I want to have this baby. Can you understand that?"

"No, I can't. And let's get one thing straight. I'm not going to marry you. No way I'm going to marry you. No way." He wasn't about to spew it out that he was already married. That would only give her more ammunition.

"Marry? I didn't say anything about getting married. Marry you?" She threw her head back and laughed. "You're just a boy in a man's uniform. You couldn't earn a living if you had to. I really don't know anything about you. You're from Florida. Probably haven't got a pot to piss in. You've got a lean hard body and you can make love by the hour, hour after hour, with that huge beautiful thing of yours. Your wingtip as you call it. But marry you? No fucking way!"

Peters didn't know whether to be angry or relieved. He was like a young dog trying to choose between two big juicy bones. He chose the relieved bone, which was tainted slightly by Jane's unexpectedly coarse language. Didn't matter that Peters and his fellow pilots used the "f" word at least once in every sentence, the use of it from the mouth of a pretty woman was jarring to him.

"Okay. So the marriage isn't a problem." He smiled. "I like that. And you're right. I haven't got a pot to piss in. I will—some day. The biggest goddamn pot you can imagine. But your parents, what'll they think about this? In Florida unmarried mothers are hung out to dry, socially. And money. How're you going to support yourself and . . ."

"My baby? Don't worry, I have lots of money. Piles. My father and mother were killed in a car crash two years ago. Left me everything. That includes not having to worry about what they think."

Peters was impressed by this woman who was obviously prepared to have her baby. Not his baby. He might be the father—and he really had no reason to think he wasn't—but the child would be her baby. Just as if Peters didn't exist.

He could scarcely hide the pleasure he was feeling. One minute his stomach was knotted in a ball of gut-wrenching panic as Jane hit him head on with the news of her pregnancy. The next minute the pain was gone like a disappearing card in a magician's hand. The card, like the baby-to-be, was still there. The new life was unseen but present, a thing to be dealt with in the future, some day, somewhere, but no longer the immediate life-twisting trauma that had come out of nowhere at the unsuspecting twenty-year-old pilot.

"God, Jane, I have to hand it to you."

"No. For heaven's sake no! You've already handed me enough as it is." A light smile crossed her lovely face. Lovely and attractive in the penetrating eyes of Gator Peters. His glance went down to her rounding belly past taut breasts capped with hard, stand-up nipples he remembered so vividly.

He reached out to put his hand on her bare arm. A delicate test to probe the possibility of more touching, to find out if Jane would respond positively to his gentle signal that sex with her now, tonight, would be a pleasure for him if she was willing. He thought about Julie as he touched Jane. But his wife was in his mind only momentarily, not long enough to trigger even a hint of guilt. He watched her face intently, waiting for a reaction. Her green irises twitched ever so slightly as she assessed his unmistakable intention. Gator moved toward Jane to take her in his arms, his face coming down, his lips about to touch hers.

He could feel her arms tense. She dropped her glass. Instead of leaning to meet his body, Jane pulled back abruptly, the palms of her hands shoving hard against his chest, her head turning away to avoid his kiss.

"What's the matter?"

She broke away. "I don't want this. I really don't."

"What d'you mean? Nothing's changed. I want you now just the way I wanted you when we were together at the Hind's Head. That was fantastic!"

"Yes, it was. But that was months ago and everything's changed. You don't turn me on now, Gator. You turn me off. That may be hard for you to take, hard on that ego of yours, but that's the way it is."

"I don't believe you." He moved toward her again.

"Don't you come near me. If you touch me I'll scream," she snarled, teeth gritted.

He was astonished. "Christ, you really mean it!"

"You're goddamn right I do." She stopped to pick up the glass, saying, "We'd better get back. It's almost dark and I have to get up at six in the morning."

"Yeah, well, so do I. Sure. Let's go."

As they began to walk back to the mess tent Peters said, "I'm sorry, Jane."

"It's okay, Gator, really."

"So what about the baby? You'll go home to Montreal? Have it there?"

"Yes. My sister's there and the family house. My father was a doctor, a surgeon. And that's what I plan to be."

"A doctor?"

"Sure. I'll try to get into McGill this fall."

"McGill—what's that?"

"I forgot you're from Florida. McGill's a university in Montreal. Has a great medical school."

"Sounds good. With your nursing background . . ."

"I already have a bachelor of science degree from McGill."

"You shouldn't have any trouble. Great idea."

"What about you? You told me you're on your way back to Canada, but you didn't say why."

Peters thought about how he should handle that one. This with-his-child woman (he really didn't doubt it was his since she was too straight and believable) didn't have to know.

"Well, they want me to do a Victory bond drive tour. You know, the American fighter pilot in the Canadian Air Force. DFC and that sort of thing."

"Distinguished Flying Cross? Wow, that's marvelous." She stopped him, smiling with pleasure. "That's wonderful, Gator, absolutely wizard."

"Gee, thanks Jane. They told me about it just before I left the squadron."

"You must be really happy about it."

"Yeah, I guess I am, for sure."

"So how long are you going to be back in Canada? Will you be in Montreal?"

"I'll be there for a month anyway. Sure, if I get to Montreal I'll look you up. But I have to have your address."

She reached into a trouser pocket for a slip of paper while taking a pen out of her shirt. "Here you are. Don't lose it."

"I may have lost you, but there's no way I'll lose your address."

"What happens if I change my mind?"

"About what?"

"About the baby. Suppose I want to go after you for financial support, name you the father."

"Remember, I haven't a pot to piss in. You said it yourself. On top of that, I'm nothin' but a temporary Florida transplant. Going after me won't get you anywhere. Thank God."

"What d'you mean, 'Thank God'?"

"It's just that I don't need to be somebody's dad. I mean, what the hell, I'm a fighter pilot, a recce pilot. One of the best. The last thing I need is to be worrying about my unborn kid."

She gave a ladylike snort.

"Which'll be when?"

"The end of November. Maybe a bit earlier."

"I should be back here long before that. Should be back by the end of August, if I'm lucky."

They were just a few steps away from the mess tent in the darkness of the calm warm Normandy night.

"You'll be lucky." Jane turned to him, took his arms in her hands and reached up to kiss him lightly. "Goodnight, Gator, and good-bye. I know how to find you. I'll let you know when the baby arrives."

"Thanks, and big thanks for not putting the noose around my neck."

"Not yet, anyway."

"Is that a threat?"

"Of course not. It's just reality that a virile, very young father with no responsibilities has to face. Again, good night Gator. If you go into the mess tent and the bar . . ."

"I'm going, believe me. After this session with you, sweetheart, I need a drink."

"If you go in there, put a padlock on your fly." She giggled. "Sweet dreams, Gator." Then she was gone, disappearing into the night like a swift, agile bat, seen for a moment then gone into the infinity of the deep blackness.

Peters, his mind still boggled by Jane's revelations, could hear the chirpy, busy nurses talking in the mess tent. A drink with those lovely creatures was exactly what he needed. And put a padlock on his wingtip's hangar? No fucking way.

Major Osborne intercepted him when he had walked only two paces into the mess tent. "Buy you a drink, Gator?"

He threw his hat on the closest table, saying, "Yeah, thanks, Major. A scotch. Double if you don't mind. And how can I get something to eat?" He followed her to the bar, his squinting eyes watching her small bum undulating in the tight-fitting trousers. He was nearly, not quite totally, oblivious to the suddenly quiet gaggle of young nurses admiring his face and body but standing aside in favor of their boss-lady Osborne. No way any of them would interfere with her interception of this special prize. No way the chicks would try to lure him away from the mother hen.

Two fried egg sandwiches and two more double scotches later, Gator Peters' fogged mind told him he had to get some sleep.

"I have to get to bed, Major. Sorry." The words were slurred, "But how the hell do I get to my tent from here? Christ. It's blacker than you know what out there."

"Don't worry," she assured him "I'll get you there." Grace Osborne emptied her third gin and tonic, put down her glass, stubbed out her cigarette, and started out of the empty mess tent. Like an unsure-on-its-feet puppy Peters grabbed his cap off the table, plunked it on his head and followed that Osborne posterior, a bum he could enjoy and appreciate even through his increasing alcoholic haze.

As they walked through the tent flap, she took his hand to lead him through the baffling blackness. "C'mon, Gator, it's not far."

"Haven't you got a flashlight?"

"I don't need a flashlight. I'm a cat in the darkness."

"Hey, nothing I like better than a pussy." He laughed and threw his arm over her shoulders, his hand landing cupped on her right breast. "Sorry," he exclaimed but as he started to lift off his hand she grabbed it to keep it firmly in place.

"Holy shit. This is the best walk in the dark I've ever had."

"It can get better," her voice promised. "Here we are. Mind the tent pole. Here's your cot. Can you feel it?"

"Yeah. My sleeping bag's somewhere. In my parachute bag."

"Here, hang onto the post. I'll get it for you."

"Hey, there's something else you could get out for me."

"Sure. It's bigger than a flashlight, isn't it? Now just hang onto the post."

He could hear her rooting around. Then she announced, "Okay. Your sleeping bag's on the cot. All you have to do is just get in. Can I help you get undressed?"

He didn't answer. He didn't have to. Her hands quickly worked the buttons down the front of his jacket which she slipped back over his shoulders and off onto the ground. His necktie she loosened and lifted over his head, his cap with it. The shirt buttons unfastened easily, allowing her to run the palms of her hands against the nape of his neck gently, slowly down the soft skin of his chest to his flat belly. The belt buckle needed a moment's assistance from Gator. The top button of his fly went, followed in swift succession by the rest. He could hear her gasp as she took the measure of his fully extended, rock-hard manhood. It was his turn to gasp and clutch the tent pole even tighter when she took the tip of it into her soft, wet mouth.

* * * * * * * *

Corporal Levine was right on time at seven the next morning with Tyler's original Will in a brown envelope, which was the first thing Peters asked him about. Gator, looking the worse for wear, had been up in time for a shave and breakfast. He didn't see Jane but as he threw his bags into the Jeep, Grace Osborne stepped out of the admin tent looking fresh and flushed in her neatly pressed working uniform.

"Safe trip, Gator." She smiled. "Look us up when you get back. We can always find a cot for you." She held out her hand.

"Yeah. You've been great, Grace. Too bad I couldn't see more of you."

"There are advantages to keeping things and people in the dark. It forces people to be in touch, right?"

"Depends on how you feel—and you certainly know how to do that." He laughed as he let go of her hand and turned to get into the jeep. "Say goodbye to Jane for me, please. Tell her I'll find her in Montreal some day."

"How about finding me instead of Jane? We could try the Hind's Head at Maidenhead. Wouldn't that be fun?"

Gator's head snapped around. He looked at her in surprise, then grinned. "Yeah. That would be fun. It sure would. Only one problem," he announced as he settled into the passenger seat next to Levine, who was gunning the engine, anxious to get going.

"What's that?"

"I broke the legs off the four poster bed the last time I was there."

"Just the way you broke the legs of your cot last night,

right?" Grace Osborne laughed. Levine threw the jeep into gear and hit the accelerator.

"Right!" shouted Gator as the vehicle lurched forward. He turned to wave goodbye as the jeep disappeared in a billowing cloud of Normandy dust.

9

Half an hour later Corporal Levine dropped Gator and his bags off at the headquarters tent of 411 Squadron, a Canadian Spitfire unit that had been operating out of B4 airfield at Beny-sur-Mer since the 19th of June. "Here's Tyler's will, the original, sir."

The Dakota aircraft was already on the ground off to the side of the airstrip, its cargo being unloaded. Peters reported to the squadron C.O., Squadron Leader Bob Hayward, who received him cordially, and made a few joking remarks about Peters' unfortunate plight in having to fly the dreadful Mustang instead of the superb Spitfire.

In short order, Peters was strapped into the long seat that ran down the fuselage wall of the Dakota, and the workhorse machine was airborne. Garth Peters was on his way to Canada, his marriage certificate, Mark Tyler's last will and testament, and Julie's power of attorney all in a heavy brown envelope tucked securely in the inside pocket of his uniform jacket.

Peters' passage through Croydon customs this time was free of hassle. He caught the train into London without telephoning Julie to let her know he was back in England. He'd do that later. No sense in letting her know until he had the Lincolns-Inn-Fields situation under way. If he could be there by two o'clock, he'd be able to find out what the arrangements were for the trip to Canada, assuming that the approval signal had arrived from Ottawa. It would be best to be able to tell Julie the whole story. The news that she was the richest person in a country she'd never visited and, for that matter, one of the wealthier people in England, would be a shock in itself. And the news that they would be leaving for Canada would be another jolt for her. He knew that her image of Canada was typically British. In her mind's eye it was a place of perpetual snow, savage Indians and the Royal Canadian Mounted Police, where everyone lived in log cabins in never-ending wilds of remote forest beyond any hint of civilization. Yes. Much better to give her all the news at one go after a couple of martinis and a session of lovemaking.

Peters arrived for the first and last time at RCAF headquarters at Lincolns-Inn-Fields at 2:09 pm. From the reception desk he was immediately escorted (still carrying all his worldly possessions in his parachute and kit bags) up one flight of stairs and along a dark, windowless, many-doored corridor to the office marked 'C.Ad.O., Chief Administrative Officer.'

He was left in the C.Ad.O.'s reception room to cool his heels for fifteen minutes until the occupier of that exalted, non-flying post, Wing Commander Caesar Wright, sent out his pert typist corporal to fetch him.

"Have a seat, Peters. Cigarette?"

"Thank you, sir."

"You are from Florida, aren't you?"

"Yes, sir," Peters replied.

Lighting his cigarette—Peters noticed it was from a pack of American Camels—the Wing Commander's smoker's cough got the better of him for a moment. He was older, probably in his middle thirties, with thinning combed-straight-back brown-grey hair, sallow complexion, thin mustache, close-set blood-shot, green eyes, thin lips, tobacco-stained teeth in a long, narrow face that reminded Gator Peters of his hound dog, Sam.

Wright finished coughing, saying, "Sorry about that, Garth."

"They call me Gator, sir."

"Yes, well, Gator, we've got to get Mrs. Tyler and you to Canada and I'm here to help. When Minister C.D. Howe says jump and the Minister of Defence says jump, we do exactly that."

Garth was about to correct Post to tell him Julie was Mrs. Peters, not Mrs. Tyler, but he decided that since the Tyler name had such power in Canada, why not let it ride—for the moment.

"That's pretty high-powered stuff," Garth said. "You mean the two of them, they've both had something to do with the business of getting us to Canada?"

"That's for sure. Here, read this." Wright shoved a long piece of paper across the desk. "It's a signal from Powers."

"Who is Powers?" Gator asked, picking it up.

"You mean you don't know?" the Wing Commander was incredulous.

"How the hell would I know, sir? I'm just a lowly flying officer. I don't know the first goddamn thing about politicians except for Roosevelt and Churchill and Patton."

"Patton's a general, not a politician."

"To hell he isn't."

"Chubby Powers is Canada's Minister of Defence. He's our big boss. Howe is the Minister of Industry—the production of fighters and bombers, guns, tanks, everything. Aside from the Prime Minister, he's the most powerful politician in Canada."

"So who's the Prime Minister?"

Wright couldn't believe what he was hearing. But he gave no hint of his surprise.

"A portly, pince-nezzed old bachelor who wears a homburg and a vest and lives with his dog in whom he confides everything. His name is Mackenzie King. I'm sure he's as famous and beloved in Florida as he is by the Canadian troops over here."

"Oh, yeah." That turned Garth Peters memory on. "He's the old crock who got booed by the Canadian troops he was inspecting over here."

"That's right. So read the signal."

Peters picked up the paper and read it. It was addressed to Breadner.

> You are hereby authorized and instructed (with the concurrence of the Prime Minister) to provide the earliest possible air passage to Toronto for Mrs. Mark Tyler, the widow of F/L Mark Tyler, DFC, and with her F/O Garth Peters, DFC, and to extend to her all appropriate courtesies. F/O Peters is granted indefinite compassionate leave to accompany Mrs. Tyler in order to assist her in the handling of the administration of the estate of her late father-in-law, E.P. Tyler. Report to the undersigned the travel plans with particular reference to date and time of arrival at Malton (Toronto).
>
> Signed
> Air Chief Marshal
> Chief of the Air Staff
> RCAF: Ottawa

"Jesus Christ, sir. That's pretty impressive. And I can sure see why Julie's going to be Mrs. Tyler on the public record."

"You'd better believe it." Wright coughed again. "A piece of free advice, Gator. Don't let anyone know you and Julie are married. Not a goddamn soul. It'll just confuse the issue. You're Mark's great pal. You were with him when he was shot down. I'm sure Julie trusts you and has asked permission for you to help her through this difficult, extremely difficult session coming up in Canada. Right?"

Peters nodded his head. "Yes, sir. I hear what you're saying. It's okay with me. When are we leaving?"

"Day after tomorrow out of Prestwick up in Scotland. You'll be in a Lancaster bomber. To Iceland then across to Goose Bay, Labrador. Then on to Toronto. It's a cold, long uncomfortable trip but it beats the hell out of going by ship and running the U-boat hurdle."

"How do we get to Prestwick?"

Wright threw a large thick envelope across the desk. "Here's everything you need. Train tickets. Special passes. Everything. Just be sure to take warm clothing with you on the aircraft. You'll be flying at about ten thousand feet and it'll be cold, really cold. There'll be somebody to meet you at the train station at Prestwick."

Garth Peters was suspicious by nature. When things were going so well, you couldn't believe it was so good, then it was time to wonder what or who was wrong.

"Sir," he said, "that's great. I'll go and collect my wife. Sorry, Mrs. Tyler. We'll get ourselves up to Prestwick. We'll get on the Lanc bound for Toronto. But what's going to happen when we get there? Who's going to meet us? I mean, after all, we have to deal with the estate of E.P. Tyler, the wealthiest man in Canada."

Wing Commander Wright smiled, his tobacco-stained teeth showing themselves briefly like a row of khaki-clothed dancers on a seriated stage. "So you will, Garth, and you'll do so with the advice and counsel of the best law firm in Toronto, the firm of Fasken and Wright. They're the executors of the estate of E.P. Tyler. Walter William is old E.P.'s personal lawyer—he's young, in his middle thirties—the partner in charge and he's named in the will as executor and trustee."

"Walter Williams. He's the key man, is he?"

"Yes. He'll meet you and Mrs. Tyler at the airport in Malton, near Toronto. It's an RCAF training airfield."

"Just outside Toronto to the northwest, right?"

"Right. He'll have a car to take you into the city. You'll be put up at the King Edward Hotel on King Street just east of Yonge Street. It's very central. Not far from the Fasken firm's offices on Victoria Street. I understand the estate is a little complicated."

"Not complicated at all, sir. The estate went to Mark, who left it to Julie. Couldn't be simpler."

"And you have her power of attorney, according to your squadron commander."

Peters touched his jacket under the pilot's wing and beneath it the newly sewn-on, coveted ribbon of the Distinguished Flying Cross, white with distinctive diagonal purple stripes. "And I have the original Will right here. What's the name of the law firm again, please?"

"The Fasken & Wright firm. They're large. About twenty lawyers. Even have two women in the firm."

"You seem to know quite a bit about them."

"Well, if you must know, I'm a Toronto lawyer disguised in a wing commander's uniform."

Peters snorted and laughed. "I should've known. My dad's a lawyer."

"Yes, I know. I have your personal file in my drawer. Quite a record for such a young lad. And that DFC. Congratulations."

"Thank you, sir." Peters touched his jacket under the pilot's wing and beneath it the newly sewn-on, coveted ribbon of the Distinguished Flying Cross, white with distinctive purple stripes. "Is that all?"

Caesar Wright stood up and offered his hand across the desk. As Peters stood with him and took the hand, Wright said, "Yes, that's all, except for one thing. If you have any problems with anyone in the Fasken firm, particularly with my dear young friend Walter Williams—let me know. Here's my card, my law-firm card. I've written my London phone number on it."

He handed it to Peters who immediately read it, a broad smile on his face. The words printed on the card were, "Caesar Wright, K.C., Fasken and Wright, Barristers and Solicitors, 50 Victoria Street, Toronto."

Less than half an hour later, Peters, lugging his baggage, walked through the pulled-back blackout curtains of the Vine to be greeted happily and loudly by a surprised Mum Roberts.

"It's our own Garth! Bloody 'ell. You're a sight for sore eyes, luv," she shouted as she ran from behind the bar to clutch Garth to her ample bosom. After kissing him she asked, "Does Julie know you're back?"

"No, she doesn't. They shipped me out on short notice. I tried to call her but those goddamn payphones of yours. No way I could make it work. So I thought I'd come and visit Mum, get her to ring through, and have myself an American martini."

"Ooooh, and that lovely DFC." She touched the ribbon. "Bloody luvly, ducks. Congratulations. We're so proud of you, Garth."

"You're wonderful, Mum. Now get me that martini on the rocks and Julie on the telephone and be quick about it." He laughed, giving her a pat on her ample bottom as it waddled back behind the bar. Garth had decided there would be no telling Mum what was going on. She'd have to hear it later from Julie. What excitement there'd be when that happened. 'Cor luv a duck,' or however the Cockneys said it. He'd keep his mouth shut. Hard to do but he was learning. Words passed in sworn secrecy had the inevitable tendency to be heard by one's own ears from the lips of some unexpected third party.

His arrival at The Little Close in Farnham Common was immediately celebrated on the living room floor by a frantic clothes shedding, followed by a languorous lovemaking. It was at the after-moment when Julie returned in her gorgeous nakedness, a crystal of champagne in each hand, that he decided he would tell her.

"Julie," he began, "I have a happy story to tell you that's going to change your life and mine forever. It's a happy story that has an unhappy part to it. The unhappy part is the tragic death of Mark Tyler. Mark was not who you and I and the guys on the squadron—except the C.O.—thought he was, the son of a poor farmer from a farm just north of Toronto."

Julie sat transfixed as he continued, eyes wide with unbelieving astonishment, little shrieks punctuating parts of the story as it unfolded.

Garth threw back his head to take the last sip of champagne. "So there we are. We're going to Canada the day after tomorrow where you'll be the wealthiest woman in the land. So what d'you think of that?"

Julie had been speechless, dumbfounded through his recital, her mind trying to get itself even partly around the significance of what he was telling her.

"Let me show you what I think. I'll tell you later," she murmured, throwing her glass into the dark maw of the fireplace. "I seen someone do that in a movie once."

Reaching for her, he nevertheless couldn't help himself from correcting her English. After all she was the richest woman in Canada. She'd soon be moving with him in high society. "I *saw* someone, sweetheart. I saw, not seen."

10

After a tearful, joyful, kiss-filled leave taking from Mum Roberts at the Vine, Julie Tyler and Garth Peters had left London on the train to Prestwick on the evening of August 19. That same evening and on the following day, Garth Peters' squadron mates and the British, Canadian, American, Polish and French armies and air elements were in the final stages of the bloody destruction of the Nazi troops and their equipment that completed the closing of the Falaise Gap. The German defeat marked the end of the Battle of Normandy.

Peters was by now oblivious to what was going on in Normandy, the fighting there or anywhere else. His total concentration was on getting his and Julie's asses out of England, getting to Canada and taking control of the massive fortune of a man he'd never even heard of until a few weeks before.

Garth had persuaded Julie to not use his surname, at least for the time being; it would only confuse the lawyers, politicians, the executives running the Tyler industries, and the media—the newspapers and radio stations. Julie had to be solidly and unmistakably identified in Canada as a Tyler. The Peters name could come much later. And their Canadian lawyers, who would have to know they were married, would be so instructed.

Garth Peters' presence at her side (out of his Air Force uniform) could be explained away by his being her financial and public-relations advisor. Everyone in Toronto would know they were living together, but in the veddy British high-society structure of that place among the Eatons, the Phillips, the McDougalds, the Taylors and their ilk, Julie Tyler with Garth Peters, DFC, would (wink, wink) be accepted.

The flight across the Atlantic had been excruciatingly long, uncomfortable, cold and noisy. Garth Peters couldn't believe how cramped the space was in the small passenger cabin area of the four-engined Lancaster. There wasn't any vacant seating space in the huge Canadian Ferry Command converted bomber. Between the extra fuel tanks lashed down inside the fuselage, there were three generals, two colonels, an admiral and five men in civilian clothes and fedoras who looked as though they'd just left the Casbah.

It had been warm and balmy when all the passengers had been herded on at Prestwick but by the time the Lancaster was at its cruising altitude of ten thousand feet with its course set for its first stop, Iceland, they had begun to penetrate the unpressurized aircraft. Coats, scarves and gloves were quickly put on. Julie, who had never been in an aeroplane before and was terrified, snuggled against Garth, her arms wrapped tightly around his midsection, her toes wiggling in the oversized, sheepskin-lined flight boots the crew had loaned to the passengers who were wise enough to accept their offer.

Iceland, then on to Goose Bay, Labrador and finally (almost twenty-two hours after the Lancaster had left Prestwick) past the glittering multitude of buildings of the metropolis of Montreal far to the south of the aircraft's path as it began the final hour-long letdown leg into Malton, the main Toronto airbase of Ferry Command.

The ordeal was over at 12:15 p.m. The exhausted captain who had taken over the aircraft at Goose Bay taxied his aircraft onto the ramp of the Malton control tower and passenger terminal and shut down the four Rolls Royce engines and propellers that had pulled them all safely across the Atlantic.

In later years Garth Peters would be reminded of that moment of stepping down the Lanc's ladder, putting his feet on the tarmac and turning to look at the Malton terminal building. It was a gray two-storeyed wooden structure, perhaps a hundred feet long with wide entrance doors in the center. Perched above the doors was Malton airport's state-of-the-art air-traffic control tower. The heads and upper bodies of the controllers, radio earphones clamped to their ears, were clearly visible, moving about like birds in a glassed-in aerie.

He would be reminded of that moment whenever he would fly his private turbo prop aircraft into the Toronto Island Airport starting in the 1960s. The reason was that the Toronto Island terminal building was an exact duplicate built from the same plans at the same time as that long-gone Malton Terminal where Julie and he arrived at noon on the 22nd day of August, 1944.

What a fateful day.

After a cursory clearance of customs and immigration—the way had already been smoothed by the two members of the Fasken firm who were waiting for them—Julie and Garth were greeted by Walter Williams and his junior, John Stewart.

The curly-haired, bespectacled, dishevelled-looking young man in a rumpled suit, stained tie askew, perspiring in the over 90-degrees temperature, held out his hand to Julie as she was waved through customs. "Hi. I'm, I'm Walter Williams," he stuttered. "I'm with the Fasken firm, the solicitors for the E.P. Tyler estate and this is, this is my junior, John Stewart. Welcome to, to Canada, Mrs. Tyler."

"Charmed, I'm sure," a confused, disoriented Julie, a cigarette already hanging from her full lips, responded as the two lawyers shook hands with their firm's most important client.

Walter Williams instantly sized up Julie's long, full-breasted body then turned his attention to Peters. Williams and his assistant thought they knew everything about Peters. The day before, Williams had described the situation to Stewart over a cheap, quick dinner without booze (there was no restaurant that served alcohol in puritan Toronto) at Stoodleigh's in the Toronto Star building, "We don't know the first fucking thing about this woman! She's a fucking teenager from London who probably doesn't know where to go to buy a fucking stamp. And this fucking fighter-pilot asshole who's obviously married her for her money . . ."

Stewart had asked, "Even though he didn't know she was heir to a fucking fortune?"

"Heir*ess*, for Christ's Sake, John. Heiress! No. Somehow this Peters guy knew Mark Tyler was loaded. Somehow he knew. Which is why he married Julie within a week after Tyler was killed. Plus he knew that E.P. Tyler had died first. I'll bet my bottom fucking dollar on it."

"It doesn't matter," Stewart replied deferentially but determined to make his point. "Julie Roberts Tyler is the sole heir . . ."

"Heiress, for Christ's sake!"

"Heiress of Mark Tyler's estate."

"– If the original will that Peters is supposed to have in his possession is validly executed and says what it's supposed to say."

"And if Mark Tyler survived his dad, which he did, and if E.P. left everything to Mark."

"Which is the way it happened," Williams glowered through his thick glasses as he cut a piece off his gristly Stoodleigh steak.

"Then whether or not you know the first fucking thing or not about Julie Roberts Tyler or Flying Officer Gator Peters, the fact is she is the sole heir—heiress. She's it. She's the client. She's the richest woman in Canada. And Julie Tyler and the Tyler estate are going to pay the freight and overhead and profits of the Fasken firm for the foreseeable future."

Williams thought about that. He reached down for the hidden Canadian rye whiskey bottle at his feet. From it he poured a full tumbler under the table without looking, lifted the 'ginger ale' to his thin, pouting lips, tossed half of it back, then acknowledged, albeit reluctantly, "You're right, John. You're right. I hate to admit it to a fucking junior, but you're right!"

"And, Walter, sir. I don't care what she looks like, you'll have to, you absolutely must, keep your hands off her. No moves. Nothing. You understand what I'm saying?"

Williams huffed and puffed, smiling. "Understand? Of course I do. It's just that women can't keep their hands off *me*! Okay, John. OK. I hear you." He downed the bottom half of the tumbler of rye, muttering, "I promise. And you follow the same rule, or else. What's good for the gander is good for the junior gander. Right, John?"

"Right. But that depends on who's going to get the goose or give it."

"We're talking about fucking, John. Not goosing. And no matter, what both you and I are going to be like eunuch monks when we're with Julie Tyler. Let us pray."

"Don't worry, Walter. She'll be crossed-eyed, bucktoothed, fat, bad breath, bad underarm and elsewhere odor, balding, six-foot eight, and make bad smells at the dinner table."

Williams belched. "Even so, to keep Canada's wealthiest woman as a satisfied client there is no sacrifice that I consider too costly to make. But with Julie Tyler, Mrs. Mark Tyler, I am as cold as stone. Some rye, John?"

* * * * * * *

Looking back now at Julie, Williams cursed the pledge he had made the night before. He remembered his manners, though, and quickly introduced his colleague to Julie, "And this is John Stewart, my junior." Stewart shook hands, his eyes glinting with pleasure behind his glasses, a crooked smile under his mustache. Thank Christ he'd extracted that promise out of Williams! But he, Stewart, hadn't sworn off anything. What a gorgeous bird. Probably about twenty, twenty-one at the most. None of the sketchy information the law firm had received about her gave any indication of her age. She had to be young because Mark Tyler had been in his early twenties. But that she was as young as she obviously was came as a bit of a surprise. Her age would also create some legal problems if she was under the age of majority, twenty-one. Nothing that he and Williams couldn't solve. John stroked his mustache, an involuntary sign of delight.

Williams again looked past his smashing new client to the young Air Force officer standing tall behind her, watching and listening, obviously sizing up him and Stewart. This time the arctic blue eyes of the handsome brown haired pilot told the perceptive lawyer that this kid might be intelligent and probably ruthless. Just a first impression.

"Hi, Mr. Williams, I'm Garth Peters," he said, moving past Julie to shake hands. Then to Stewart. It was time to take charge. "We've had a marathon trip, really tough, twenty-four hours in that goddamn flying coffin called a bomber. We'd like to get to our hotel as soon as possible."

"Yes. Of course." Williams replied. "We have a limousine. The driver's right here. Are those all your bags?"

Garth Peters nodded. "Yeah. Those three bags contain all our worldly possessions. One is Julie's. The other two are mine."

Williams quickly observed, "All of your worldly possessions might be in two bags, but Mrs. Tyler's are across all of Canada."

To which Stewart added, "With a few baubles in the United States and Britain."

After heading east out of the Malton airport on a recently paved township concession road, the limousine turned south on King's Highway No. 27 down through open farm country past Highway No. 5. They were still in open agricultural terrain until the limo, a pre-war Packard, crossed the Queen Elizabeth Way on the overpass. This new, an ultra-modern divided highway had been finished in time for its dedication by Queen Elizabeth when she and her husband, King George V, visited Canada in the summer of 1939 just weeks before the outbreak of the Second World War.

As the huge automobile entered the Queen Elizabeth Way heading east toward Toronto, Julie pointed ahead, asking "What's that tall building? See it—the one straight ahead in the distance? It looks like a cathedral towering over everything by itself. Is it a cathedral?"

Stewart, in the jump seat in front of Julie, answered, "No, Mrs. Tyler, that's the Royal York Hotel, the tallest building in the British Empire."

"A hotel? Is that where we're staying?"

"No. We've put you up at the King Edward."

"Why not the Royal York?"

"Because the King Edward's about a hundred yards from our office building on Victoria Street. The Royal York's about half a mile away. And your suite at the King Eddie is the King's suite, every bit as nice, if not better, than anything at the Royal York. You'll like it."

Stewart's judgment proved (as Peters was to find out many times) to be good, right on the money. Except when it came to the matter of women.

The conversation on the way in from Malton Airport to the center of Toronto was mostly strained, largely a guided tour as the legal greeters described points of interest: the

Humber River, the Palace Pier dance hall, the Sunnyside roller coaster and entertainment area, the Argonaut rowing club, and the massive grounds of the Canadian National Exhibition that had been taken over by the Royal Canadian Air Force as its Number 1 Manning Depot to receive and indoctrinate new recruits.

"Don't tell me about this place," Peters admonished Stewart. "I went through it at the beginning of '42. Lived in the Cow Palace when I arrived here as the lowest of the low, an eighteen-year-old Aircraftsman Second Class. That's a private, in case you didn't know."

Williams and Stewart, both physically unfit and unacceptable for military service, knew but said nothing.

As they passed by the Maple Leaf ballpark at Lakeshore and Bathurst, Williams remarked, "Down there beyond the ballpark is Little Norway, the Toronto Island Airport. That's where the Norwegian Air Force have set up their flying training school."

The limo went past the Toronto harbour waterfront with its warehouses, ocean and lake freighters, dock areas and grain elevators, then turned north up Yonge Street. "We're going under the tracks, a whole series of them, at Union Station," Stewart announced. "It's our biggest railway passenger station. And it's connected directly by tunnel with that tallest building in the British Empire you saw, Mrs. Tyler."

"The Royal York!" She was so pleased to have remembered its name.

When the Williams, Stewart team had seen them to their King's Suite, it was arranged that Stewart would come to the hotel the next morning at ten to escort them to the Fasken offices just a few steps away.

* * * * * * * *

At ten o'clock sharp the next morning, Stewart called from the house phone off the King Edward's spacious, elaborate Victorian-style, high-ceilinged lobby. "Be there in a minute" was Garth Peters' terse response.

When Peters walked into the lobby, Stewart didn't recognize him. The lawyer's eyes were watching for the long legs and full breasts of Julie Tyler. Instead he was confronted by a tall, slim brown-haired, handsome young man in a double-breasted dark blue suit, white shirt, plain gray tie, a white handkerchief puffing out of the jacket breast pocket. With his shiny new black shoes glinting in the lobby's lights, Garth Peters could have been a professional clothes model.

He stopped in front of Stewart, who was still looking for Julie, and said, "Good morning, John. I'm Garth. Remember me?"

The startled Stewart's jaw visibly dropped. "Jesus Christ! I didn't recognize you! Where did these clothes come from? All you had on yesterday was your uniform."

Peters grinned. "Easy. After you people left, I put Julie to bed. She was out like a light. Then I went over to Eaton's. One hour and a hundred dollars later I was completely outfitted out of the five hundred you'd left with us. So here I am, the ultimate civilian, lean and mean."

Uncharacteristically, Stewart was nearly speechless. "Where's . . . ?"

"Where's Julie? We had breakfast in the room. Then we had a little mutual comforting, if you know what I mean. She went back to sleep. She won't be joining us."

"But we need her," Stewart protested. "Julie Tyler's the heir to the E.P. Tyler estate."

"The heiress."

"The heiress. We have to brief her, tell her about the will, go over the assets with her, get instructions from her. We can't do what we have to do without her."

"The hell you can't. Look, Julie is a naive girl from the outskirts of London who knows nothing absolutely nothing about business, estates, shares, assets, balance sheets. She didn't even know where Canada was until we got here and I doubt she knows even now. So you're going to have to deal with me John—you and Walter—with me."

Stewart started to pull himself together. "I think we'll have to take this up with him. I'm just the junior. Let's go."

In Williams' office Garth Peters restated his position, adding, "You should know that I have Julie's power of attorney. It's a general power of attorney. Covers everything. Here's a notarial copy of it."

Williams glowered as he read the document. "How old was she when she signed this? If she was a minor, under twenty-one, it wouldn't be worth the paper it's written on."

"She was twenty-one on the eighth of June, weeks before the power of attorney was signed."

Williams gave a muted "harrumph," a noise he characteristically made when confronted with a fact or proposition he hadn't anticipated.

"So she's twenty-one. You're her husband—and you're also twenty-one. Right? I'm sure you've got proof documents with you . . ."

"You bet I have."

"And you have her power of attorney. It looks as though you're calling the shots, Garth."

"You've got that right, Walter. Don't worry, I'll keep Julie fully informed and get her verbal approval for everything we're going to do and the decisions I'm going to take."

Williams offered his opinion, with Stewart nodding his agreement. "It would be better if you had her approval in writing—you know, as important decisions have to be made."

"Better for you, maybe. But not for me and not necessary in law because of the power of attorney, right?"

There was a pause. Then Williams admitted, "Yes, you're right."

"So where do we start? My daddy says E.P.'s and Mark's wills have to be probated. Here's the original of Mark's. I also have certified true copies."

"What's your dad know about these things?"

"He's a lawyer in Florida. He says as far as he knows the laws in Ontario and Florida are probably similar since they both have their roots in English law."

Williams harrumphed again. "You can tell your dad, your daddy, he's right. We're about ready to file for probate in E.P.'s estate. It's complicated because we have to pay succession duties and get releases. But we're almost set. And because Mark's estate is a straight-through devolution to Julie, we can go for both at the same time."

"Sounds good. If you're that close to filing, you must have a list of all of the assets, all the holdings and their evaluations, right."

"Your daddy tell you that, too?"

"Yeah. We talked on the phone for about an hour this morning."

"I have the asset and evaluation list—two copies for Mrs. Tyler."

"Julie."

"For Julie. Right." Williams shoved two copies of a thick loose-leaf book across the desk. "If you look at the first five pages, they give you a summary and total of the value of the assets. The following seventy-four pages provide details of each of the estates' holdings, cash, stocks, bonds, real estate, corporations wholly owned or controlled by ownership of a majority of shares or by less than a majority, boards of directors on which Mr. Tyler sat either as a member or as chairman and on which Julie or her nominees will be entitled to sit."

Peters broke in, "You've got that wrong. They're boards

on which *I* will be sitting and, where appropriate, chairing, not Julie. And *I'll* do the selection of the people to the boards. Let's get that straight right now."

Stewart wouldn't keep quiet. "But, Christ, Mr. Peters, you don't have any business background. I mean, how can you be chairman of the board of a trust company, an oil company, a major brewery, Canada's largest trucking company—just for openers?"

Peters was supremely confident. "I'm a fast learner. And I'll have one or both of you guys with me. You'll be on the boards of directors and my lawyers, right?"

He watched Williams and Stewart look at each other and smile. At that moment, Peters knew he had them both by the shorts and in his pocket.

"Well, with the two of us as your team, as your advisors, I don't think you'll have any trouble," Williams said. "It'll be a learning process the first six months or so. Learning for you and . . ."

"For you as well. You haven't been sitting on any of E.P.'s, boards have you?"

"No, I haven't," Williams admitted. "One of our senior partners has been on a couple of the boards, but E.P. really wasn't anxious to have his law firm people as directors of his companies."

"There wouldn't be any conflict of interest problem, no reason why you can't sit on a board and your firm be the lawyers?"

"Not really." Williams turned to Stewart and asked, "What d'you think, John?"

"I agree. But maybe it's something you'll want to take up with the partners."

Williams harrumphed. "You're right. Right." He turned back to Peters. "Assuming it's all right with the firm, we'd be pleased to be your team."

Peters smiled, "For a reasonable fee of course."

"Of course."

There was no smile when Peters added, "My team must understand clearly from the beginning that they are not the decision makers. I am. The team advises, it does not direct. It does not give the orders. Understood?"

"Of course," Williams agreed. "Now, can we advise you how to attack the assets book?"

"Sure. No liabilities?"

"Read the book. It'll give you the answer. You'll find the assets exceed the liabilities, for tax purposes . . . Are you ready for this?"

"Why not! The number I saw in the newspaper in England was $60 million."

"You had the currency wrong. That was in pound sterling, round figures. The number in this book is $126 million. And we've tried to keep the values to a minimum because of succession duties."

"How much will they be?"

"I don't have that figure yet. Several million. Probably five or six."

"Enough cash to cover that?"

"Plenty. E.P. liked to have liquidity. My advice is to take the books back to the hotel. Go over them carefully. Make a list of the questions you and Julie have. Then we'll meet again tomorrow to talk about the situation."

"What about the farm?" Peters had to ask the question. The answer was undoubtedly in the book, but it would only be in the form of a statistic.

"The farm? John's been there recently."

John Stewart had till now felt as though he'd been left out of the conversation. That was a junior's job: keep quiet unless spoken to and asked or allowed to speak; assist your senior and make him look good. Here was the chance to show how competent he was, what an excellent to-the-point raconteur, a person well worthy of the Peters team. Well, he would try.

"The place is huge. It's a two-hundred-acre spread on the east side of Leslie at Wilson. It's way out there in the country. Actually it's a horse farm. Old E.P., like his friend Eddie Taylor, got into the breeding and raising of horses. In fact, there's often confusion between the stables and the enterprises of E.P. Tyler and E.P. Taylor, Eddie Taylor. But, believe me, the two men are, or rather, were quite different in appearance, achievement, philosophy and fame. E.P. Tyler has always been low-profile, secretive, a non-public person. Nobody on the street knows who he was. But everyone knows Eddie Taylor. Everybody.

"Anyway, E.P. Tyler, like his friend Eddie who has a big farm on Bayview Avenue just north of Lawrence, E.P. bought his place much farther north of Taylor's and built a magnificent huge house facing west and set back from Leslie by about a quarter of a mile. It's called Windacre Farm. The house looks like a porticoed, classical southern mansion right out of Gone With The Wind. The house is probably about 15,000 square feet. Twelve bedrooms, fifteen bathrooms, indoor swimming pool. It even has its own theater. And the house is filled with old master paintings, sculptures and artifacts E.P. collected from all over the world. Fantastic things."

Peters asked, "What about Mr. Tyler's personal stuff, his clothes, his wardrobe, what's in his bedroom drawers?"

Stewart was nonplused. "It's all still there. The executor hasn't done anything about it yet."

"That's one point you haven't told me about. Who's the executor?"

"It's our senior partner and E.P.'s closest friend and confidant, Alex McIntosh. He's the executor along with the Canada North Trust Company—which of course, E.P. owns, the estate owns."

"Perfect. Since I haven't met the executor yet," Peters put the request to Williams, "I'd sure appreciate it if you'd ask him to clear Mr. Tyler's things out of the master suite or wherever they are in the house. Put it all in the attic or some storage space. And tell the house staff that Julie and I will move in tomorrow. I assume there's a house staff."

"Ten of them, at last count, including the chef and his wife," Stewart answered.

Both Williams and his junior were taken aback by Peters' instructions. It hadn't crossed their minds that these two non-descript, unsophisticated, foreign strangers were actually the new owners of everything of E.P. Tyler's. Everything including his mansion, and that they could *actually take physical possession of it and the master suite!*

Williams muttered as he picked up his pen to make a 'must do' note, thinking, "Jesus Christ, poor old McIntosh is going to have a fucking stroke when he hears about this." He said to Peters, "I'll give Mr. McIntosh the message as soon as he gets in. He's in his seventies so he doesn't get into the office until about 11:30. I'll set up an appointment for you to come and see him. What would be a good time for you?"

"Three o'clock this afternoon. I'm not coming to see him. He's coming to see me. Julie and I are the clients. It's not the other way around, although that seems to be the way your firm likes to treat people who use their services."

"No. That isn't true," Williams protested. "It's just that Alex is used to dealing with clients in his office. I mean everybody he acts for comes to his office."

"Oh really? When was the last time E.P. Tyler was in the office of Mr. McIntosh?"

There was no way Williams was going to be caught out in a lie on this one. "Eleven years ago, about two weeks after I joined the firm as Alex McIntosh's junior."

"I will be happy to receive Mr. McIntosh at our suite at

three. Ask him to bring a copy of E.P. Tyler's will, please. If that time isn't okay, then let us know what time would be convenient. If you come with him, I'd be happy to pour you a drink." He looked at both lawyers when he extended the invitation.

"Yes, well . . ." Williams nodded. He had no other response.

"I'm sorry, John," Peters apologized, "I think you got cut off in the middle of telling me about the Tyler estate. Sounds fabulous. What about the horses?"

"What I can tell you is there are six or seven stables. Beautiful buildings. Room for about ten horses each. Built in 1938 and 1939. E.P.'s been breeding horses but, as I understand the situation, he hasn't done any planned breeding since the war started. There are about fifty horses in residence at the moment."

"I suppose I can find the horse operation in this asset book and whether or not it's been profitable." Peters didn't wait for an answer. "One thing you haven't told me about is where Mr. Tyler's head office is. I'm sure he didn't run his vast holdings out of his back pocket.

Williams was feeling more and more uncomfortable by the minute. Peters wasn't the docile, dumb, naive, inexperienced Florida fool they'd been expecting. And there was that goddamn lawyer daddy of his coaching him from his Pompano Beach sidelines.

"Garth, I think we've misjudged the situation pretty badly, the firm and Stewart and I. We can serve you and Julie a hell of a lot better, a hell of a lot, if we do some proper preparation now we have a bit of a handle, a handle on who you are and where you're coming from." Williams' tendency to stammer and repeat increased when he was under unexpected pressure. The lawyer leaned forward continuing earnestly, "If you don't mind, Garth, I'd like to have a word with John. We'll go, we'll go into the library for a few minutes. I have a proposal for you I want to talk over with him. Is that okay?"

"Sure. Go ahead. Take your time. But remember I have to know about E.P.'s head office, how he's been operating and no screwing around as if I was a dumb twenty-one-year-old."

"That's exactly the point. I think we've inadvertently shortchanged you and I want to fix that, okay?"

"Go ahead. I'll give Julie a call on your phone, if it's all right with you. I'll tell her I'll be there for lunch at 12:30, in half an hour. Will that give us enough time to finish things off for today?"

Peters was still talking to Julie when Williams and Stewart returned less than five minutes later. He got off the line quickly, speaking loving words to her in the process.

When they had settled into their chairs again, it was Stewart who led off. "Garth, we think we should lay on a full-scale rundown, a briefing, sort of like a military briefing, on the whole Tyler empire. We'll give you a picture, literally photographs of the plants, the office buildings, the head offices, the breweries, the trucking companies, all the companies, everything. We'll prepare charts showing the holding companies, the operating firms, who's on the boards and a biographical sketch of each of them."

Williams had a thought. "And we'll also give you our opinion, the firm's, on who's who in Toronto society, the upper crust."

"Great. I like what you're telling me. Particularly that upper-crust stuff. When?"

"We're going to need two days to pull all this together and do it properly," John replied.

"That's fine. Two days are okay. We'll do it in the theater at ten in the morning at Windacres Farm. You might even invite the top people from each of the Tyler companies based in Toronto and Montreal or wherever. I'd like to meet them."

"Three days."

"Why not? But we move into the house tomorrow. There's a chauffeur and cars? Right. Julie and I will study the books, go to Niagara Falls for the honeymoon we never really had. And we'll see all of you—whoever all of you may be—at Windacres at ten. Lunch will be served after the briefing."

Peters stood up. The lawyers respectfully followed suit. "In two minutes, Walter, tell me where the Tyler business headquarters offices are located and who the head man is."

"Try 'woman.'" Williams showed his perfected macho male smirk.

"That will change," Peters promised.

* * * * * * * *

Julie's menstrual period was scheduled to begin three days later. It did not arrive. Julie Roberts Tyler Peters was pregnant. Her daughter, Louise, was born prematurely on April 1, 1945.

*W*hen I left you in 1944 so many important happenings were about to take place for Julie and me as we (sorry, "I") took control of the then enormous E.P. Tyler estate.

I went on to consolidate, buy, sell, finance, refinance, acquire new companies, expand and generally build the basic Tyler holdings into a massive multi-billion-dollar empire. My holdings were rivaled only by the hugely successful achievements of Ken Thomson, who built on the newspaper publishing, media and oil/gas fortune that had been left to him by his father, my friend, Roy Thomson, Lord Thomson of Fleet.

I tried to tell the story of my life in Canada from 1944 to 1998 but it was simply too much. I couldn't handle the detail. Instead, I'll talk about the events that have occurred since 1998. Central to that short period was my battle with Louise Peters, who may or may not be my daughter. I tell you, Senator Louise Peters is one tough lady. But I'm tougher than she is, as you'll find out.

But before I take you to the war with Louise, let me tell you how I myself got a seat in the Canadian Senate and I'll tell yet another flying story.

I finish all this off by telling you why I'm in this goddamn penitentiary instead of languishing in the Mediterranean on my 150 foot yacht with a least four beautiful, nubile young secretaries to respond to all and every of my physical and intellectual urgencies.

Garth Peters
Author/Caged Eagle
10 September 2001

11

Senator Garth Peters was alone in his suite at the venerable Chateau Laurier Hotel close by the Parliament Buildings in Canada's capital city, Ottawa.

The room was dark. It was three minutes after five in the morning of October 2, 1997, five days before the seventy-fifth anniversary of his birth in Pompano Beach, Florida. He had been awakened by a signal from his bladder. That relieved, he was back in bed, now wide awake and trying to get back to sleep. But his roiling mind, full of past images and memories, wouldn't stop.

Suddenly he was back in London at the Vine. He could see the blurred image of the pert, cute, little and young, very young—eighteen to be exact—chick at his side under his protective arm, her full breasts pressed against him ready for the dreamworld night of sex that was to follow. It was the image of a person who still lived but, for him, had long since ceased to exist except as a pathetic, booze and cigarette-ravaged unintelligent, uninformed frump. It was the countenance of his bride, Julie Roberts Tyler in the summer of 1944. The smile on his face in the darkness was replaced by a sour twist of his mouth as the pictures of that long gone moment passed through his teeming brain. Then there was a fleeting glimpse of Jane Knight but, thank God, after the war was over she had tracked him down and let him know she had a miscarriage in Normandy.

He shook his head trying to get rid of what he was seeing. There *had* to be something pleasant to think about. Like the many-moons-ago October telephone call from the man who owed him for a whole bunch of reasons, mostly money—the Prime Minister. Or that Order of Canada investiture.

Ah, yes. The Senate story. His mind decided to review that story yet again.

In 1990 it became apparent that then Prime Minister, Brian Mulroney, was going to stack the Senate with Progressive Conservative loyalists (and with a few token bodies who were not politically tied but were prepared to pledge support if appointed to the Senate). They would give the Government a majority in the Senate and would be prepared to ram the dreadful, and universally despised, Mulroney-Wilson Goods and Services Tax, the GST, happily named as the Gouge and Screw Tax by that robust bombastic PC, Don Blenkarn, Member of Parliament. The need to stack the Senate became clear, including the Prime Minister's willingness to use a hitherto unused section of the British North America Act that would allow him to create (subject to Her Majesty's personal approval, which, of course, she would never refuse) an extra additional eight senators. Peters had decided to go for an appointment. He wouldn't use any intermediaries, no Cabinet contacts, no old buddies of the PM who used their St. Francis Xavier at-school-with-Mulroney connection both for access to the party leader and for the means to earn a substantial "I have influence with you know who" living as a lobbyist. None of that. He would go directly to the PM and lay it on the line.

Which is exactly what he did. The gravel-voiced Mulroney, smiling through his thin-lipped mouth, had greeted him with his usual reserved-for-supporter-friends Irish warmth, then listened to Peters' list of reasons why he should be appointed to the Senate. One of the most persuasive was the suggestion that Mulroney needed someone other than the usual hacks and bagpersons. He needed a business leader with a rags-to-riches track record, a Canadian achiever who was both credible and independent.

In addition, there were the super-large campaign contributions Peters' corporations had made and his unflagging high-profile support for the North American Free Trade Agreement. Mulroney had made all manner of circumlocutionary noises that sounded like a positive response but, typically, the supplicant wasn't quite sure what the conclusion was, except that there were dozens of worthy people out there whose names had been put forward. "You do understand, don't you, Garth? So, leave it with me. And for your loyal support in good times and bad, and putting your mouth where your mind is, both in the Free Trade fight—and that isn't finished yet—and now with the GST (I've been reading excerpts of your positive speeches in the *Financial Post*, and in your own paper, the *National Planet*)—so, not to worry, Garth. I know what you have to offer, where you're coming from and, believe me, I like what I know. But there's no way I can give you a commitment. You do understand, don't you? I'm sure you do. I don't know anyone in Canada more perceptive, shrewd and analytical than Garth Peters. I'm sure you wouldn't argue with me on that one, would you?"

Garth Peters couldn't disagree. All he could do was join the other "dozens of worthy people" and wait for the Prime Minister to make up his mind.

The first round of appointments was made within the week with no call for Garth Peters. Then the second round of names was announced. Still no call. Peters, all too often impetuous, was on the verge of calling Mulroney to tell him that if he was prepared to put the likes of that irrelevant hack so-and-so and that jerk what's-her-name in the Senate, let alone any one of the idiots he had already appointed, then surely he had to have a place for Garth Peters.

But Peters didn't make that call after the second round. The final list of the three who would complete the filling of the vacant Senate seats was due. Furious and slighted as he was to have missed the first two and after all he'd done for Mulroney and Canada—and dying as he was to pick up the phone and go right at that pompous asshole who called himself Prime Minister—Peters didn't call. He had been persuaded not to by a much less impetuous person who at that time had a soothing physical and mental influence over him, particularly during the long lunches they shared in bed two or three times a week at her conveniently situated Lonsdale suite across from Upper Canada College.

Beth. She was a calming, cooling young thing, except when it came to the passionate matter of lovemaking with a sixty-six-year-old who thought and almost performed as if he were in his twenties. He'd settle for thirties.

It was during those noontime trysts with Beth that October that she had talked him out of chasing Mulroney again. "Don't lower yourself," she had whispered. "You're one of the richest, most powerful men in the country. You're not a political hack. You're not a Conservative bagman. You've made your pitch. To hell with him. Besides, the people out there, the poor, dumb unwashed taxpayers are fed up with the government in general and these Senate appointments in particular. There's no prestige now in being a puppet Senator. So don't call him, Garth. Just think about being here with me for the next hour—if you have the strength." Which indeed he had.

However, when he arrived back in his office after his "lunch" with Beth, he had decided, "To hell with it. I'm calling the sonofabitch." Peters was reaching for the phone when his secretary rushed into the office without knocking, face flushed with excitement.

"It's the Prime Minister. He's on line one!"

"You're sure?"

"Absolutely, Mr. Peters. It's that voice. I'd recognize it anywhere."

Caged Eagle

Hand trembling, Peters picked up the telephone. It would be an offer or a refusal. But why would Mulroney call to tell him bad news?

"Garth, dear boy, you know I'm going for the final three appointments. Well, what d'you think—are you still interested? Because if you are I'd like to have you."

That was one instance when Garth Peters enjoyed being had.

Senator Garth Peters! He had made it. He truly had it made. If he'd been a Brit, it would have been Lord Peters, but Senator would be just fine—for now. Next year he would go after a peerage in the UK. After all, as the owner of the prestigious *London Times Telegram*, which he had picked up for a cleverly negotiated song in 1985, he had much-used access to the royals along with considerable editorial page and face-to-face influence with the British Prime Minister. If Roy Thomson, that irascible old reprobate whom Peters had known, liked and admired, could pull off an hereditary peerage, then surely Peters could negotiate a life-only honor. An hereditary peerage would pass to his first-born—his loathsome daughter, Louise, whom an admiring Prime Minister Trudeau had put into the Senate in 1983. No way would he leave anything to that superbitch—his favourite description of her—let alone leave her a peerage!

Senator Garth Peters. Stretched out on his bed he remembered savoring the moment of hearing Mulroney's deep voice giving him the senatorial benediction. That euphoric event was followed a few days later by another, the swearing-in ceremonies in Ottawa with the first entrance into the Red Chamber and the rowdy, Goods and Services Tax debates. Those events were capped by the Order of Canada ceremony at Government House, the Governor-General's residence, on October 24, 1990, when he was invested as an Officer of the Order of Canada. He was envious of the two invested in the highest rank as Companions of the Order—Bud Estey and Youssef Karsh—because he thought his accomplishments for Canada certainly equaled if not exceeded theirs. Grudgingly, yet in his own way happily, he had accepted the Officer honor made more palatable by the fact that he shared the same ceremony with the likes of Conrad Black, Galen Weston, and their entrepreneurial opposite, the trade union terror, Bob White.

His mind slipped back to the superbitch, his daughter, Louise. Or was she Mark Tyler's daughter? That question had never gone away from the moment in August 1944 when Julie had announced that she was pregnant. Peters had kept the question to himself and never raised it with Julie. Why rock an increasingly unstable boat?

But as Louise grew up, and even before her teen years, Garth thought he could see in Louise physical as well as personality traits that were suggestive of Tyler's genes. However, there was no certain evidence. So far as Peters was concerned, she was Louise Peters, his daughter and he treated her accordingly. Which meant that he was like his own daddy, a full blown martinet perfectionist in his performance demands of both Louise and her brother, Garth Junior, who had arrived in 1946.

Garth Jr. was a conformist child, bending easily to the wishes and dictates of his father, like the branches on a fullleafed tree give way to the wind. But not Louise. She was the non-conformist, the rebel who repudiated whatever her father tried to tell her to do, whatever the advice or order he gave her.

Then there was Louise's perceptive antipathy toward her father because of his increasingly rough treatment of her mother. As he pursued his international business objectives, Peters had increasingly left Julie out of his life and she had fallen more and more into the clutches of alcohol.

By the time Louise reached puberty, she deplored her father's disregard for her mother and for his frequent angry rants at Julie. Louise's teen years saw countless shouting matches between daughter and father. One became so intense that he slapped her in the face. That encounter arose because, at the age of eighteen, she had stayed out all night with her boyfriend.

That slap was the end for Louise. Supported by her mother, Louise left the family home, never to return. She went to Queen's University in Kingston that fall. There she majored in political science. From there to Harvard for an MBA. Then to the University of Toronto for her law degree. And wherever she went, the beautiful, brilliant Louise had her pick of men. As she would much later tell her despised father, "Thanks to you and your slapping women around, I had more affairs in my university years than you've had in your whole degenerate lifetime!"

Peters never regretted that slap. It got the insufferable Louise out of his house. As he recalled the image of that long ago moment, sleep took Garth Peters.

12

He had no choice. By statute law the Honourable Garth Peters was obliged to retire from the Senate at the age of seventy-five. On his birthday he would be gone. And he would be missed. At least that was what many of his Red Chamber colleagues told him. He believed them.

The Prime Minister told Peters that he would come to the retirement dinner if the Senator would foot the bill. Yes, a retirement dinner. Great idea. At the Chateau Laurier. Say, two hundred guests: Conrad Black, Hilary and Galen Weston, Frank Stronach, Jimmy Pattison, plus the Chief Justice, all the Cabinet ministers, of course, present and former, and the Senate colleagues who were on his favor. But not including Senator Louise Peters. Never.

As the retirement date approached, the editor-in-chief of the *National Post* decided that Peters would be a good interview subject. In addition, the interview would be of value when it came time to write Senator Peters' obituary.

When Christie Blatchford, the *National Post's* top-line journalist, called for an appointment, Peters immediately agreed. The interview was scheduled for nine o'clock in the morning three days before his birthday. His senate retirement dinner was scheduled for that same evening.

The morning of the interview began badly. Senator Peters, his thinning wispy white hair battened down by gel, arrived at his office by eight. There he took a call from a senior partner of his New York law firm. Peters was furious about the delays in the floating of a $4 billion US combined stock and debenture issue he urgently needed for the refinancing of the debt he had taken on in his acquisition of a North Sea oil field from the Sultan of Brunei. Delays, delays. Christ, those goddamn lawyers never get anything done on time except get their exorbitant bills out.

He should have been in his New York office today directing the financing documentation and Security Exchange Commission processing personally. But he had this interview with Blatchford, and on top of that the Senate leader had put the arm on him yesterday at noon demanding that he turn up in the Red Chamber for the crucial, emotionally charged debate on immigration.

So here he was in his Ottawa Senate office when he should have been in New York. Support the government's bill? No doubt about it. Cut immigration by fifty percent? Absolutely!

The interview by Blatchford had proceeded well, or so Garth Peters thought. Her tape recorder had functioned perfectly and Christie had asked him sharp, loaded questions. He enjoyed being interviewed by a feisty, intelligent young woman.

"Senator, when you and your wife arrived in Toronto in 1944 to take over the E.P. Tyler estate, how much money did you have—personally that is?"

"Julie and I didn't have a pot to piss in. I had maybe three hundred dollars saved from my measly RCAF pay. That was it."

"It must have been quite a shock to step into that Tyler pool of wealth."

"Yeah, it was a shock all right. But we were lucky. We had some really first-class lawyers in place ready to help us like the great Walter Williams, rest his soul. But we had a few problems with some of the executives who headed up Mr. Tyler's companies. They resented, deeply resented us upstart foreigners—Julie from England and me from the States. It took me about a year, maybe a little longer to sort them out.

No one was fired, at least not at that point. The war ended and I knew there would be a flood of people my age, or close to it, looking for jobs. It was important to keep my executive team—E.P. Tyler's executive team—in place, which I did."

"What were the main assets, operating companies you took control of?"

"A trust company, truck transport firm, a national brewery, five radio stations—it was before TV—ten newspapers. There were many other smaller units including forestry in British Columbia."

"The value then?"

"About $120 million—that was the value of the entire estate."

"And what's the value of your holdings now, the Peters Group, that is?"

"Our national and international holdings including our North Sea oil and gas, our Mackenzie Delta natural gas—the pipeline will be in place in the next ten years—our TV, radio and newspaper units, our airline and trucking ventures, total somewhere in the range of $8 billion US. That's not as much as Ken Thomson is worth, but I'm pretty close."

"Lord Thomson of Fleet."

"Yes. I knew his father well. Old Roy, the First Lord Thomson of Fleet, who put the initial family fortune together—and it has grown from there."

"Just as E.P. Tyler put yours together. What are your personal plans? Are you going to retire from business, turn over the reins to your son, Garth Junior—or are you just going to keep going until they put you in a box?"

The Senator snorted. "Listen, Christie, when they put me in my box, there'll be a hundred people there with matches to make sure I burn!"

"Try a thousand."

"Sure. Maybe ten thousand. I'm not the most popular bastard on Bay Street or Wall Street. I'm just going to keep going for the time being. I'm fit and healthy. Still have my flying license and I keep current."

"You have an amphibious bush plane, an old de Havilland Otter, the single engine plane, you fly yourself around in."

"Use it in the summer to get to my cottage in Muskoka out of the Toronto Island Airport, and for moose hunting in the fall. I can still fly my Otter with what I call 'great skill.'"

"Let's get to your women," Blatchford said. It was as much an order as it was a request.

"Nothing I'd like better but I'm not sure Julie Peters would be pleased to hear about them. So, I'm prepared to talk—off the record."

"Okay. Off the record. Who does the Senator have in his current stable in this center of carnal iniquity that's seen so many members of Parliament and indeed the Senate lose their—shall I call it moral virginity, once they have their seats in the hallowed House of Commons or the Silly Senate?"

"Moral virginity? Try any kind of virginity. Listen, the number of members of Parliament—let's talk about the men who have come to Ottawa from the boonies out there—who have left their young families at home because they couldn't bring them here and have found some delightful young thing with whom they've shacked up. Goodbye family. I'd hate to think of how many times that's happened over the last— well, since the Second World War. Give me a break. I don't want to talk about my ladies of the moment. It's sufficient that there's more than one. I don't possess them and they don't possess me. Mind you, there were times in my, how shall I put it, my extensive career, that I became deeply involved with this lady or that with or without husbands. I never got shot, although some husbands would have liked to have done it to me. So can we just drop the ladies for the moment? If one of them pops up during these interviews, sure, I'll be glad to talk about her but in the meantime can we just stick to business—on the record?"

Blatchford backed off. "Sure, why not. On the record. Let's go back to Garth Junior. Is he ready to take over when you step aside?"

"Or when somebody shoots me?"

"That's always a possibility."

"Garth Junior? He's as ready as he'll ever be. He's been involved at the executive level in the Peters Group since he got his MBA out of Harvard in 1972. He's been CEO of our air and trucking division and he's currently chairman of our Nationwide Trust Company, which every Canadian bank would like to buy."

"Like the Toronto Dominion Bank buying Canada Trust then shutting down half of its competitive small-town operations. For the government to allow that to happen is to screw the public interest."

"So Garth Junior is ready. And I have Brad Foster, he's president of my holding company and my right arm. He's there to support my son, if and when."

"What if something happens to Garth Junior?" Blatchford had to be gentle with this one. "What if he's not there to take over when . . ."

"When I get into that box?"

"Yeah. Where would control of the Peters Group go then—to your daughter, Louise, Senator Louise?"

Her name caused him to spit out a muttered, "That bitch!"

"She may be a bitch, Senator, but she's an extremely capable woman, an outstanding lawyer, a stand-out attender and performer in the Senate, and in the opinion of many people she can stand up to you in any debate any time."

His eyebrows furrowed and his face darkened, "Bullshit. I can whip her ass in a debate any time!"

Blatchford could see that Garth Peters was upset. She thought for a moment that he would say the interview was finished. But he controlled himself.

"To answer your question, there's no way control of the Peters Group would go to Louise Peters. Absolutely no way. There is simply too much animus between us. Put it this way, we hate each other. Off the record again?"

"Okay."

"She believes her natural father was Mark Tyler and that I'm in possession of everything that is rightfully Julie's and therefore to go to Louise." Senator Peters paused, then asked, "Still off the record?"

Blatchford didn't hesitate. "Sure."

"Assume theoretically that both my wife and Garth Junior were out of the picture, gone at the time of my demise or I became incapacitated, and Louise would get only a token as opposed to zero. Assume all that, then you might ask what would happen to the Peters Group, to my enormous fortune? Who would I will it or give it to?"

She shrugged. "How the hell would I know? To some university or hospital or something. Maybe a little piece for the Christie Blatchford Old Age Fund?"

He smiled. "Who knows. But, Christie, I have a relative, a close relative that I've never told anyone about. He's young, intelligent, highly educated. He would get all of it, except for a lousy crumb for Louise."

Blatchford just had to ask that question. "We're still off the record. Who the hell is this relative? You have to tell me, for God's sake!"

Peters leaned back in his chair, a contented grin on his face. "Not a chance, kiddo. My good friend President George Bush once said, 'Read my lips' and I say to you, Christie Blatchford—read my will."

"Thanks for nothing, Senator. You've got this big retirement dinner coming up tonight. Then what?"

"Moose hunting. My son and I are off on our annual hunt. We're taking Julie with us. Garth Junior thought it would be good for her."

Blatchford couldn't resist. "Moose hunting. You'll be shooting the bull—as usual."

"Right on, Christie. Right on."

13

It was in late evening when he had spotted the moose browsing in the shallow waters at the west end of the small lake. In Garth Peters' judgment the lake was rather short but, what the hell, he knew he could get his short take-off and landing Otter aircraft down without any trouble. He would do it quietly at the other end of the lake to the east well away from where the moose was standing. When he first saw the huge beast, the Otter was about fifteen hundred feet above ground. He made a snap decision and immediately pulled back on the throttle that sat between his left seat, the captain's, and the right hand co-pilot's seat occupied by his fifty-four-year-old son, Garth Jr.

Peters slapped down the carburetor heat and hauled the aircraft into a sharp left turn, while telling his son what he was doing. Getting ready to land he did the pre-landing check and put the pitch lever into full fine. As he swung the aircraft around and started his turn toward the west descending rapidly, Peters checked the moose. It was still there unmoved by the sound of the aircraft which was now almost silent in the distance. Peters was pleased to see that there was enough wind to cause a ripple on the surface of the water, making it easy for him to judge his aircraft's height while he was landing. That lake was far too short to attempt to make a glassy water landing using the Otter's flying instruments. Glassy water meant that there was really no way to judge the height of the aircraft above the surface of the water—so the pilot had to fly the machine on instruments descending slowly at a set speed with power on, cutting that power when the floats touched the water surface. Thus the little chop in the water was great.

About to complete the turn west on his final approach, Peters selected full flaps and checked them when they reached the full down position. He instinctively looked at the indicators to make sure that the amphibious wheels under the floats were not down. Wheels down landing on water would mean the aircraft would flip right over on its back, which more often than not meant curtains for the pilot and everyone else on board.

He was set up for his landing approach. A touch of power. Just a touch to have it available if he had to ram the throttle forward to abort the landing. Everything looked good. They were heading right into wind. Garth Jr. was comfortable. His hands on his knees, a good place for them to be in case, for whatever reason, he had to grab the wheel in front of him. He was an experienced pilot, particularly now on the Otter which his father had purchased fifteen years before when the high-winged, single-engined light transport aircraft became surplus out of the Canadian Forces Air Reserve. Peters knew that the surplus Otters—the Air Reserves were converting to helicopters—were in excellent condition even though they were over twenty years old. They had been maintained superbly by the military.

In the 1960s and '70s Peters had come to be an aficionado of moose hunting in northern Ontario. It reminded him of his hunting days long ago in the Florida Everglades when he and his father would go out in an airboat to shoot alligators—totally illegal but what the hell.

Peters had his right hand on the throttle, pitch full fine, mixture full rich, the carburetor heat now cold, his left hand on the wheel, his feet firmly on the rudder pedals. Check the speed, eighty knots coming down to seventy. His aircraft just clearing the tops of the trees at the edge of the water, tail down slightly, he held the stick back so that the rear portion of the bottom of the floats would touch the water first at the indentation of the step on the float bottoms. The speed was coming down to sixty knots. He checked the stick back slightly farther, nose a little higher. He was almost on the surface, maybe three or four feet above it. Then he could feel the water bite at the bottom of the floats. He was down. Power full off, the aircraft quickly came to a stop in the soft clutches of the lake.

The bull moose was still there. It had lifted its head probably to see what sort of a bird had landed at the other end of the lake. Judging there was no threat, the moose had lowered its antlers and snout into the reeds to continue feeding.

"There's a flat rock over there, Dad." Garth Jr., in the co-pilot's seat, pointed to the right at a piece of flat granite sticking about three feet out of the water with a perfectly flat table of perhaps thirty yards in length with no obstructions for the aircraft starboard wing, no trees or bushes or other rock.

"Looks good. I'll swing it around and put the starboard float up against the rock. You'll get out and handle the ropes. Make sure the bumpers are out. I don't want the metal and the rock rubbing each other. And be careful of the goddamn propeller." He knew that Garth Jr. was totally aware of the propeller danger but it was automatic that the captain would give that extra bit of caution, particularly to his son. "Tell your mother what we're doing."

Julie Peters was strapped into the removable canvas seat on the left side of the Otter immediately behind the metal bulkhead that separated the cabin from the cockpit. Her scrawny gray face was shrivelled by incessant smoking and the excessive use of booze—her favourite was vodka because it didn't smell and so it was hard for anyone (she thought) to tell whether she'd been into it. The face that had once been full, pink, unlined and unblemished, was but a harsh, creased cartoon of the beauty Garth Peters had first laid eyes on at the pub in London that summer of 1944 when he had taken her to bed at the Stafford Hotel. Or had she taken him?

Peters' recall often brought his memory of her and of their incredible couplings to life. Now a dreadful transformation had overcome her.

Get rid of her? That was something he would have given anything to be able to do. But there was that piece of paper, her power of attorney in his favor. His lawyers had long since advised him that a divorce would terminate the power of attorney and that the courts would likely rule that all of the family assets were in fact hers, subject to a pittance to him under family law legislation.

So, in a loveless marriage, Garth Peters didn't have a choice. There was no divorce, but he did have countless clandestine affairs including one in New York that had produced a secret child, a boy. That one had cost him a fortune until the lad was through university. Brilliant student. Doctorate in nuclear physics. No idea about his father. Thought he was long dead. Clandestine and secret had been Peters' marital modus operandi about his affairs since the late 1950s when he had his first encounter, and he had gotten away with it. If Julie had known of his extramarital activities, she never let on, nor he about hers in the 60s and 70s when she was still attractive enough to capture the speculative eyes of many a male.

Years ago when Peters first had been caught up in the annual foray into the northern Ontario bush by hundreds of macho moose hunters, Julie, still robust and vigorous, had insisted on going with him. She never hunted, never carried a rifle or shot one of the majestic animals. But she was enchanted by the few days of adventure in an environment so unlike the cities. It was rough tent life in the bush, primitive, cooking over a fire, listening for the crack of a rifle shot echoing in the distance, waiting for the hunting party to return. And it was a time when she didn't have a touch of alcohol, even when the triumphant hunters celebrated a victory.

It had been ten years since Julie had been on a moose hunting trip with Peters. She had acquired other interests, so she said, and declined his invitations to go with him. Julie then lacked the stamina and energy. And she had come to detest her power-hungry, inconsiderate, rude husband who treated her with indifference, without any love or affection and who spent so much time away "on business" as he called it, in New York, London, Paris, the Middle East or wherever. What he did as "business" she had no idea, but Julie had no doubt that much of it was done with one good-looking woman or another. She was content with the luxuries that were provided by the massive fortune he had built from the original Tyler lode. She had her car and driver. She was part of the Glitter Girls group of rich Toronto wives. She had her cigarettes and booze. And she could fly across to London to see her mum whenever she wished.

Garth Peters was delighted when Julie had given up the moose hunting trips. She was such a pain in the ass to have along. Just before the season of 1999 she had sent him a note through his office telling him that she was feeling fine; that the month at the Betty Ford clinic had been a success and she was "dried out." Could she please go with him and Garth Jr., "this one last time?" Peters wasn't sure why he relented. Guilt perhaps? Garth Jr. had encouraged him to bring her. She would be so much baggage but her son would look after her. Father wouldn't have to do a thing for her. And that's what father planned to do.

The docking went flawlessly. Garth Jr. tied the aircraft tightly and securely to the rock, bumpers in place. Then he was back in the Otter cabin to check with both his parents. His father said, "Let's get rid of the Mae Wests and get your mother on shore." The two men shucked off their lifejackets and threw them up on the net overhead shelf in the cabin.

Peters took pride in the special inflatable lifejackets (commonly known as Mae Wests) that he had designed for use in the Otter when it was in water service on floats. He had six made to his specifications with several pockets in the front of the inflatable vest. One of the six Mae Wests was fitted for himself and the other for Garth Jr., who was of about the same build as his father. The pockets were for maps, matches, wallets, money, Swiss knife, anti-bug stuff—whatever the wearer wanted to stuff into them, including the tags purchased from the Ontario government to permit the killing of moose.

They practically carried Julie down the steps, off the aircraft's starboard pontoon and onto the rock where she immediately fished a cigarette out of her purse and lit it. That purse would be with her even in the bush just like the Queen had her symbolic hand bag everywhere she went. Both men quickly set about untying the canoe from the port float and struts. They gently lowered the delicate craft into the water. Then Garth Jr. went into the cabin and handed the paddles out. Next out was Garth's favourite 303 high-powered rifle with its telescopic sight. There was no talking, no voices to carry across the lake against the light wind that might alert the sound-sensitive great beast.

The father knelt in the bow of the canoe, paddle in hand. The butt of the rifle was on the floor of the craft within easy reach in front of him, its barrel pointing forty-five degrees up toward the sky ahead. They paddled silently away from the Otter, Peters whispering curses when he heard Julie's cigarette cough. 'God, that woman is a mess,' he told himself for the several thousandth time that year. A smoking drunk, wizened shrivelled face, body as attractive as a starved female ape. And that Betty Ford thing hadn't really done anything for her. At least the cough had not disturbed the moose.

When Peters judged they were about a hundred and fifty yards away, the moose lifted his head and stared directly toward them. The beast was within range and might begin to flee at any second. Down went Garth's paddle and into his hands came the rifle, its stock against his right shoulder, the safety latch off, the telescopic sight against his right eye. The crosshair was steady on the moose at the head, right between the roots of the antlers.

He squeezed the trigger. The blast of the powerful gun shoved his shoulder back. The noise of the crack of the shot filled the air for miles, echoing back with the sounds of several shots instead of the single one.

To the great satisfaction of father and son and shouts of exultation from both of them, the moose began to stagger and slowly fell sideways into the water.

"You got him, Dad!"

"I got the son-on-a-bitch! Fantastic. Keep paddling, Garth. But be careful, we've got to make sure he's dead. I don't want him punching holes in the bottom of our canoe." He cocked the rifle, fitting another shot into the breach. He held the rifle ready to put it to his shoulder in a split second in case he had to fire another round. The canoe was about twenty feet away from the head of the moose when Peters held up his hand as a sign to stop. They sat motionless looking at the huge animal, watching for signs of life. Its head was lying flat on the surface of the shallow water. From it flowed a huge pool of blood, getting larger. The blood was the only thing moving. There were no signs of life, no twitching, no breathing, nothing.

"We'll wait another five minutes."

"Maybe you should give him another shot just to make sure."

Peters nodded, "Why not?" Still kneeling he raised the

rifle and put another safety round into the skull making sure it went in well clear of the prized antlers.

"Okay, son, let's go back and get the airplane. We'll bring it over here, put a rope around his neck off the cleat at the front of right pontoon. We'll tow him back to our docking rock and cut him up. Then we'll haul him out of there into the airplane."

The next half hour was spent carrying out that plan. When they had the huge carcass to the rock, they winched it up onto its flat surface, having tied the winch, a standard piece of equipment on the Otter, to a huge pine that was at the shore edge of the rock.

The next challenge, getting the carcass onto the airplane, required some surgery. They helped Julie into the aircraft so she wouldn't have to see what was going on. They put her in the cockpit in the right-hand seat, told her she couldn't smoke. The scene on the rock became instant gore as the men worked with sharp knives and equally sharp strokes, severed the hindquarters. The bowels and the stomach with its contents went into the water, now crimson red with the blood flowing from the severed blood vessels. Each man taking a leg, they lowered the severed rear body into the water to let as much blood and other liquids drain out. They then stood it feet up on the stone deck for more draining. The head was next. It was severed in short order but with some difficulty getting through the vertebrae.

"He won't be very good for mounting with that hole in the head," Garth Jr. observed.

"I don't want the head. The antlers, yes, they're beautiful. They're huge!"

"But we'll have to take the head with us, there's no way we can get the antlers off here."

"You're right," the father agreed.

There was concern in Garth Jr.'s voice, "We're going to have a hell of a load on the aircraft, Dad. Do you think we're going to have a problem with that? You know the amphibious floats with their wheels are heavy as hell as it is and we've got all kinds of stuff on board—our tents, the canoe, all the gear for the three of us."

Peters nodded, "Yeah, I've been thinking about that. But we should be all right."

"But, Dad, we've got almost a full load of fuel. We topped up at Wawa and we're only half an hour out. Maybe I should sit down and add up where I think we are weight wise."

This time, Garth Peters, the ancient pilot, shook his head negatively, "Look, don't worry about it. I can get this thing out of here with my eyes shut. I'll use just the right amount of flap. We'll be fine."

The son had great confidence in his father's ability as a pilot. And Garth Jr. had long since learned when to give up in an argument with the old boy. That point had been reached.

"Okay, son, let's get this beast on the aircraft. We've got enough plastic to wrap most of it. We'll tie the parts down on the starboard side of the aircraft floor and cover it so your mother, who will be on the port side, won't have to look at it. But before we do that, let's get her out of the cockpit and back up on this rock so that she can have a whiz or whatever before we get going. What time is it?"

"It's quarter to five. Still lots of light left."

"Good. It'll take us fifteen minutes to get George here on the aircraft and tied down and the canoe back on the left pontoon. Then we're out of here. I want to go back to Wawa. Got to report this kill with my tag to Natural Resources. Then we'll get George into a local butcher. We can spend the night in Wawa. I'll radio ahead for a couple of hotel rooms and the butcher, if they've got one. He can meet us when we land. We can head on north in the morning and we'll pick up the carved-up George on the way back down. Sound good?"

"Perfect."

It was 5:12 when Garth started up the huge radial engine of the Otter. There was much banging, clouds of grey smoke and a bit of a cough, then the powerful engine roared into life. The huge three-bladed propeller sprang from its hesitant turning into a blur of invisible silver as the revolutions per minute of the prop moved into its smooth-idle numbers. Peters gave his son the cast-off and shove-off signal by changing the pitch of the propeller from fine to coarse and back to fine. That meant that the engine was performing correctly, the oil pressure was up, and they were ready to go.

Garth Jr. untied the bow rope and pushed out on the starboard pontoon, jumping onto it as he did. Then he was up the steps into the cabin. He grabbed the yellow lifejacket out of the overhead rack and wrestled it on. He quickly stepped gingerly over the moose parts and past his mother strapped in her seat on the left side of the cabin immediately behind the bulkhead where his father was in the cockpit in the captain's seat.

The young Peters immediately sat in right-hand seat, buckled up his harness and put on his crash helmet with its plugged-in microphone and earphones. His father already had on his helmet, and the intercom was on. As Garth Jr. settled into his seat, his father moved the throttle forward and began to taxi away from the rock shelf. Both men had noticed that the wind had died and the water surface was flat. There was no head wind to help them lift the heavy Otter out of the clutches of the clear lake water.

It was on the younger man's mind that he should ask his father again about the heavy load. 'Shouldn't we wait until morning? Maybe there'll be a wind.' But he didn't ask. The subject was closed.

He sat back and watched his father skillfully handle the

aircraft in preparation for the takeoff run. He took it halfway down the lake to the west at near takeoff speed. The purpose was to create waves on the lake. Then he turned and ran east down the lake in a great arc heading close to shore. When the Otter was at the eastern end, where they had carved up the moose, and running at a speed of about forty knots, he selected fifteen degrees of flap in order to give more lift. Swinging as close as he could to the easterly end of the lake he then turned the Otter west for its takeoff. Using that forty knot speed, he then opened up the throttle to maximum power. He was in his takeoff run.

With no wind and a heavy load on board, the acceleration was ominously slow. Peters had the wheel back in his gut to force the tail down until the floats hit a sufficient speed that he could shove the stick forward and get them onto the step. Once on the step—which is the front part of the pontoon floats—the Otter would then begin to accelerate rapidly up to its flying speed then lift off and be airborne. Even when airborne, with the load they were carrying, the real question was whether they could achieve enough speed and lift to clear the tall trees at the west end of the narrow lake, where the moose had been feeding.

With the engine going full bore, Peters finally got the Otter on the step when the machine was more than halfway down the lake. He and his son knew it was too far. They had run too great a distance before liftoff. Their speed was just above stalling speed and not increasing as Peters attempted to pull back on the stick to try to get altitude to clear those trees. He was committed now. There was no way to cut the throttle and smash back down into the water. That option was gone. Both men knew that the moment of crisis had arrived. The father, with both hands on the wheel, felt his body involuntarily begin to shake from head to toe. The adrenaline was telling him that they were going to crash. It was inevitable. As the Otter flew into the wall of trees that stood like a fortress in front of them, Garth Peters shouted the word that aircraft pilots almost inevitably use as their last words on the recorder box when they are about to die. "Shit!"

In a few seconds the beautiful single-engine Otter, a spectacular piece of aircraft workmanship and strength was turned into a mass of twisted metal as the enormous sixteen-cylinder engine and its howling propeller drove straight into the trees. The wings of the aircraft were pulled off their roots by the clutching pine trunks like the wings being viciously pulled off a fluttering butterfly.

At the last split second before impact the right hand of the father and the left hand of the son came together on the master switch to turn it off. It was a near automatic last-ditch effort to prevent an all-consuming fire when the contents of the loaded gasoline tanks were spewed like a lethal rain over the red-hot engine parts and severed electrical wires.

It was to be the last touching of their hands.

As the Otter hit the trees, the two huge, heavy sections of the moose carcass broke loose like a battering ram, smashed through the cockpit compartment wall, going through it as if it were paper; while the last part of the enormous animal, the head and antlers, ricocheted down the left side of the cabin, impaling the frail body of Julie against the cockpit compartment wall.

14

On its location at the rear of the shredded Otter, an automatic radio signal, triggered by the force of the impact, began to operate. It was the Emergency Locator Transmitter, the ELT, whose pulsing transmission on the frequency of 121.5 MHz could be heard by passing aircraft and by search aircraft dozens of miles away. It would be the device that would lead the Search and Rescue, SAR, aircraft of the Canadian Armed Forces, a huge Hercules transport out of Trenton, Ontario, to the crash site. The SAR Herc was over the ELT and crash site by 2:45 a.m. At dawn from an altitude of 4,000 feet the orange, steerable parachutes of two highly skilled SAR airmen caught the first orange rays of the rising sun. At 6.18 a.m. the parachutists touched down in a small open clearing about 200 yards from the place where the cabin of the Otter, stripped of its wings and tail empennage had come to rest like a huge silver coffin.

It took the search and rescue men with their heavy gear some half hour to slice their way through the dense bush to reach the remnants of Garth Peters' beloved flying machine. They were shocked by what they found. Their radio report to the captain and crew of the still circling Hercules aircraft was immediately passed to the Search and Rescue Center at Trenton.

After taking all proper precautions and researching who were the next of kin, the duty officer at Trenton was on the telephone to Senator Louise Peters' office in the Senate building in Ottawa. It was 8.30 a.m. The Senator was not there, but her secretary gave him the number where she could be found that morning. It was in the apartment of Claude Mason, the most recent lover of the strikingly gorgeous (even in her fifties) Senator Peters. Mason, a heavy-set, square-jawed man in his early forties, was the Deputy Minister of Defence. He had caught Louise's eye at an embassy function three weeks before, and their chemistry had been immediate.

Mason was still on top and inside Louise, luxuriating in the euphoria of their shared coming together. It was as if each of them had been lifted to another level of other-world existence. It was a moment they wished would never end. But the ringing of the telephone by his bed immediately began to strip away the fabric of their fantasy.

"Don't answer it." Her voice was a low whisper from moist lips against his ear. He lifted his head, saying, "Sorry, sweetheart, I have to answer it. It might be my minister."

"Screw your minister!"

"I'd rather do that to my beautiful Senator." With that he reached to pick up the telephone. He spoke and listened. "It's for you. It's important."

"It goddamn well better be," she muttered as she took the phone and put it to her head. "Yes?"

A gruff male voice asked, "Are you Louise Peters, the daughter of Garth Peters?"

"Senator Louise Peters, yes. Who's this?"

"This is Captain Marc Lachance of the Canadian Armed Forces Search and Rescue Control Center at Base Trenton. I got your number from your secretary. I have some difficult news for you, Senator."

As she was listening, Mason lifted himself up and away from her, rolled over on his side, then left the bed to get a towel from the bathroom.

Louise sat bolt upright. "What do you mean difficult news?" she demanded.

"There's been a crash. It happened last evening northeast of Wawa. A single-engine Otter on amphibious floats. Your father and mother and brother were in the aircraft. I'm sorry to have to tell you, Senator, that your father and mother did not survive."

Her hand flew to her mouth, eyes wide in shock, as she began to grapple with the reality of what she was hearing. "Oh, my God! My mother, my poor, sweet mother—and my brother, what about him?"

"The information we have is that the survivor has a broken arm and suffered a severe concussion. He's still unconscious but alive. His crash helmet was split open. But it saved him."

Mason came back into the room, a towel wrapped around his midriff and a white bathrobe in his hand. He threw the robe around Louise's bare shoulders as he tried to piece together the situation from what he heard her say and from her reaction to what was being said to her. She was transfixed by the words on the telephone and her thoughts. She paid no attention to Mason.

In the control center in Trenton, Captain Lachance expected to hear more sobs, tears and sounds of grief. Instead he heard a now-in-control voice.

"When will you people get them out of the bush and where will you take them? I have to know, it's very important."

"It's hard to say, ma'am. Evidently they have the survivor out of the cockpit but the inside of the airplane is a real mess. They had a cut-up moose in the cabin. And, well, it's a real mess. We may have to send two more people in with cutting equipment to get the bodies out. It may take us a day, maybe two days, I don't know. The lift out will have to be by helicopter to the closest airport where a Hercules transport can get in."

"Where's that?"

"Sault Ste. Marie."

"Can I get my father's jet in there? It's a Challenger."

"Probably. I'll have to check on that and get back to you."

"Call me at my office in half an hour. You've got my number."

"Yes, ma'am."

"How long do I have before the press find out about this?"

"Probably within the hour. We have to report that a crash has occurred. We don't have to give the names of the people in the aircraft, at least not until next of kin have been notified."

"I am the only next-of-kin and you haven't been able to reach me yet. Is that understood, Captain? I need about two hours, maybe three. Yes, it'd better be three. Give me until 11:30." She would need that time in order to begin the daunting task of taking over hands-on control of Garth Peters' complex web of corporate holdings.

Even though Louise had been alienated from her father for several years in a bitter, unforgiving relationship of hate, in her Toronto law office she and her staff had kept a constant monitor of all of the companies that he controlled or in which he had substantial holding. Louise had the full details on every individual who headed up a Peters' corporation or organization: resumé, telephone and fax numbers, emergency numbers, cell phones, everything.

"I'll call you as soon as I get to my office, Captain. Give me your last name again and your telephone number, please?"

She put down the phone, pulled on the bathrobe and moved out of the bed as Mason, not knowing what to say, ventured, "Whatever it is, it sounds very bad."

She told him the gist of what Lachance had told her.

"My father and I—to put it mildly—simply hated each other's guts. I'll explain it to you some time. The fact that he's gone doesn't move my soul to tears at all. The only thing that would move me to tears is if he has kept me out of his will—whatever that says—or cut out my mother for that matter. He was a hard-hearted son-of-a-bitch. My tears at the right time will be for my poor mother. He treated her terribly. Drove her to drink. He had all kinds of affairs. A dreadful, simply dreadful man."

"And your brother?"

"Garth Jr.? A year younger than I and a lawyer. Straight as an arrow. Went into the family businesses because he could take my father's domineering attitude. Girlfriends. Plenty of them. But no wife, no encumbrances at all. Looks a lot like his father even to his gray hair."

"So who's going to take over the control of the Peters empire?"

She moved to him, put her arms around his waist, kissed him fully on the mouth, reached down to pull his towel off then gently massage his softness. "Senator Louise Peters will. I like to control everything—don't I? Or at least get my hands on everything."

The telephone rang again. "I'll get it," Louise said. "It's probably my secretary. I want to talk to her anyway." It was.

"Senator, I hope I did the right thing in giving that captain your phone number. He said it was of the greatest importance, absolutely necessary to reach you."

"It's okay, Betty. The call couldn't have come at a better time or a worse time. I'm not sure which. Let me put it this way. I've had death in the family, a flying accident. I can't tell you any more than that right now."

"Oh, I'm so sorry!"

"It's a disaster, an absolute disaster. Both my father and my mother . . ." She paused, pulling herself together. She just had to keep control. "We have important work to do, Betty. I want you to organize a conference call for an hour from now. Nine-thirty. There's not much time so you'll have to bust your butt to do it. You've got the list of the chief executive officers and chairmen of all my father's operating companies, newspapers, banks, trust companies, communications, radio, television, auto parts, and mining. I want you to find each one of them, no matter where he or she is in North America, Asia, Europe, wherever. I want them all on the line at nine-thirty. If you can't achieve nine-thirty in the short time we've got then stretch it to ten at the absolute maximum. Just tell them that Senator Peters is acting for her father and has called an emergency meeting of the utmost importance."

"What about the lawyers, Senator?" Betty knew she had made a mistake as soon as she stopped talking.

"I am *the* lawyer. My firm are the lawyers—Lang, Michener. I don't need any outside help from anyone on this." The edge in her voice made it clear that the suggestion was not appreciated. "I have my cell phone with me. It'll take me about twenty minutes to get to the office. Call me if you need me."

"I'll get on it right away, Senator." And the secretary added in her thoughts, "and there's no way that I'm going to call you unless I absolutely must. Bitch."

Louise loved Mason's bathroom because some prior tenant had conveniently installed a bidet. A quick use of that cleansing facility, makeup in place, pantyhose, brassiere and dress slipped on, everything back in her purse where she turned on her cell phone. She was out the door after a tight squeeze from Mason, who was still bare from head to toe. As he ran his cupped hand over the soft roundness between her thighs he offered, "I'm so sorry, Louise, about this terrible thing that's happened. If there's anything I can do . . ."

She smiled, "Just keep doing what you're doing to me the next time I get back here—whenever that is."

* * * * * * * *

From the office window in the Senate building, Betty kept a sharp lookout for the Senator's white Jaguar convertible as she worked the phones with the Bell conference-call operator organizing every aspect of the urgent meeting. First she gave all the names and telephone numbers to the operator, saying that the operator should try to reach the top five while she would try to reach the bottom half. Again it didn't matter where in the world they were or what time it was there. The experienced telephone professional immediately advised her to set the call for ten o'clock. Without waiting to consult with the Senator, the secretary agreed. It made good sense.

There was the white Jaguar speeding up the road from Rideau Street at high speed. Speed limits were not of concern to Senator Louise and particularly so with this special emergency.

When Senator Peters burst into the office, Betty was as ready for her as she possibly could be. "We've found six people. They have the message and they're standing by for ten. Nine-thirty was just too early."

"What about the other four?"

"I'm working on two and the Bell operator has the other two. Just give me another ten minutes, maybe fifteen and we'll have everything in place. They tell me that Brad Foster, the president of your father's holding company, is on his honeymoon. We can't reach him."

"Too bad. If he's smart, he'll have his cell phone stuck between his legs."

"I don't think his bride would like that."

"If it's shaped the right way she might like it even better."

By 9:25 the conference call was totally structured, with

one missing—Brad Foster, the man on his honeymoon. The Bell conference operator reported that he couldn't be found.

"When I'm finished with him, he'll wish he'd had his cell phone stuck up his yin-yang," was Louise's ladylike response to the report.

At four minutes to the hour the conference-call operator reported that she had all the participants on the line with the exception of Foster, then proceeded to do a roll call. It was time for Senator Louise Peters to do what she liked to do best—take charge, particularly when the persons being taken charge of were male. Out of the nine, two were women. With one exception, she had never met any of them but they knew who she was, make no mistake. The Senator had scanned the large up-to-date personal file she had in her computer on each of them, a fact that none of her listeners had any idea about.

Senator Louise Peters opened the telephone conference, her voice businesslike, cool, controlled. "I am Louise Peters, Senator Peters. I believe you all know of me and I certainly know about you. I wish to congratulate all of you in the capable professional manner in which you have acted in your senior capacities, your executive roles in the operations, yes, the profitable operations of my father's many companies." She hesitated for a two to three second count. She knew that every one of them was wondering what was coming next. "The news I am about to give you is not yet public, but when it is, and it should be some time today, the impact on each of you and your companies and on the value of those companies on the stock markets will be great. Late last evening my mother and father were both killed in the crash of a bush plane in northern Ontario . . . ."

The sounds of shock and dismay came garbled to her as her words sank in and each bright mind in the conference began quickly to sort out the consequences for himself or herself personally and for the corporation in that person's charge. And, of course, there was the effect that Garth Peters' death would have on the value of the shares and options on shares that many of them held in the principal Peters company or in the Peters spin-off corporations they respectively headed.

She waited for a few moments. "As you are all aware, the controlling and majority shares in each of your companies is held in a privately held offshore company based in Bermuda. My father was the chairman, CEO and, with one exception, the only shareholder. As you are also aware my father and I were deeply estranged and so I have no idea what his provisions are in his will as to the disposition of his estate. I know his solicitors are a Bermuda firm. I intend to be in touch with them immediately after this conference call is finished. In the matter of his will, I assume that with my mother and father both deceased at the same time, the entire estate will fall to my brother and me. And, of course, he is totally incapacitated—at least for the moment.

"The preliminary reports from the search-and-rescue people indicate that my brother has suffered severe head injuries in the crash. He's in a coma. So it falls to me to take charge until the question of his health and the matter of my father's will—if any—have been sorted out."

Much earlier Louise had had an elaborate legal plan worked out with the estate experts in her own law firm, Lang, Michener. It was a plan to be executed on the demise of Garth Peters. The objective was to set aside the Garth Peters' will if it was unfavorable to her—set it aside on the grounds of her questionable paternity. But that was not something she was going to open with this crowd.

She then answered questions about the circumstances of the crash to the extent that she knew them. "I have asked the Search and Rescue coordinator at Trenton to withhold the announcement of the victims of the crash until eleven-thirty. At that point he will officially notify me as the next-of-kin and then he is obliged to go public with it. So obviously I wanted to have all of you heads up because the press will be all over you when the announcement is out. I want you all to be in a position to say that continuity of the management of the Peters' corporations is secure. It's in my hands and the succession should be clear and straightforward. My secretary will forward to each of you my personal resumé so that you can get up to speed on the details of my background if you're not already there. But I think it will be important for you to have that information in the next hour."

"Allan Price here, Madame Chair." The president of the mining corporation had things right to begin with. "Will you be in touch with all of us in regard to the funeral arrangements, the memorial service or whatever you're going to do?"

"Absolutely. And I will go down to Toronto this afternoon. We'll get the company Challenger in here. I plan to move into my father's offices in BCE Place and I'll do the same in the New York offices . . . ."

"After the funeral?"

"After? No way. I'm going to move in on them just the same way as I'm doing Toronto, and it will be before the funeral. The way things are going it may be two or three days before the bodies are released and down to Toronto. I'll have them taken care of by the Humphrey Funeral Home organization. We'll do a joint service at the St. Paul's Anglican on Bloor Street. I'll get the archbishop organized immediately."

She checked to make sure that her telephone recorder was working properly. She wanted to have a full audio record of this conversation.

"Now, ladies and gentlemen, as you know, I'm fundamentally out of the loop of my father's business activities although I have kept very close track of what's going on. What I'm going to ask you is to report to me now about any major acquisitions or divestitures that are in process in the company that each of you heads. All I want from you at this moment, if there is something going on, is a report. Give me the basic details, the amount of money involved, how the acquisition is being financed if it's a purchase and the same details if it's a sale. Then by tomorrow at noon I'd like a written memorandum giving the details of the transaction, who in your corporation is looking after the transaction, who the lawyers are, accountants, and if appropriate the underwriters. And you will have to be prepared to put a hold on any of those deals for ten days unless there is a closing in which the other party will not give us such a delay because of the circumstances."

There were only two transactions on the table. The first was an acquisition by the Transportation Group, a mixture of coordinated courier services combined with air parcel and freight. "Madame Chair, it's Fred Kite here—and no I'm no relation to the golfer. The Peters Transportation Group has signed a deal to purchase the Buffalo-based Bison Airex Corporation that serves the dedicated air freight and parcel carrier for several ground couriers in New York, New England and the eastern seaboard. The purchase will be a tactical fit with our Chicago-based Mid-West air operations which will put us in a good position to compete directly against Fed Ex."

"How many aircraft and what type?" Louise Peters began a string of questions.

"Twenty-two aircraft, basic fleet of Boeing 727 freighters, purchase price of the shares we're buying is $820 million."

"How is the consideration broken down?"

"Two hundred million cash and the rest in shares."

"Shares of what?"

"Peters Airex."

"Nothing else? No other collateral?"

"No other collateral. The cash of two hundred comes from a private placement."

"Terms?"

"A five-year pay-out at eight per cent interest."

"Put a hold on that private placement until I have done a complete check as to what cash is available from one of the companies in the Peters group," Louise stated. "If I can find the cash rather than borrowing it, that's the way I want to go."

"But your father had approved of the private placement deal."

"Oh, really. His approval was obviously conditional on his staying alive. Can I have a complete memorandum from you in the morning. Fax it please to the Toronto office and I can deal with it there." Louise was through with that subject. "Broadcasting, television, anything there?"

"Jane Persons here. Your father had been in negotiation with the Waters family in Toronto to take over the entire CHUM group, radio and television, including CITY-TV."

"That's Allan Waters and his family, right?"

"Correct. Allan is the dean of Canadian private broadcasters, an outstanding, straight-as-an-arrow person. He and his kids hold about eighty percent of the CHUM stock."

"Negotiating value?"

"Well over a billion."

"Are the Waters interested in selling?"

"Absolutely not. But who knows."

"Okay. That doesn't seem to be very solid at this point but give me a full report on it anyhow."

Louise had been scratching notes for questions she wanted to ask.

"Next topic is publishing."

"Grant Ross here, Chairperson. As you probably know the Peters publishing group has forty-eight daily newspapers, thirty-eight in the U.S. and ten in Canada and about seventy community newspapers in the United States. We have no major purchase or sale transactions going on at the moment but I am aware that your father was keenly interested in picking up the *Globe & Mail*. Its profitability has been hammered by Izzy Asper's *National Post*. In recent weeks he had been negotiating directly with B.C.E., the new owner. As I understand the situation, the way it was left was that in the event there was some idea on the part of BCE to sell, they would be in touch with your father first."

"A first right of refusal?"

"I wouldn't say that. Just a sort of we'll let you know if we change our minds."

"Well, it sounds to me as though there isn't anything to get excited about there. What about mining. The gold mines?"

"Nothing to report, Louise, except that your father has been talking with Peter Munk of Barrick Gold about a possible joint venture in China."

The voice of the suave Adam Zolt immediately pulled memories of her relationship with Zolt into her mind's focus. Their affair ten years ago had been one of her best. He had come to Ottawa as a Member of Parliament. Louise remembered that he had physical drive and staying power beyond any other of her many relationships. The affair had lasted for weeks until his wife in Winnipeg finally became suspicious. And it was his wife, with ties into the great Richardson family, who had all the money. He needed access to his wife's family treasure, so when she heard about Louise Peters through the courtesy of *Frank* magazine, Mrs. Zolt gave a *prenez-garde* tug on his chain. In the end the lures of Louise's voluptuous body were no match for his lust for Richardson loot. So much for Adam Zolt. But here he was, now the prosperous Peters Group mining engineer who had assembled a clutch of producing gold-mining companies (no exploration or development please). Each mine had to be a producer so that Peters could borrow from financial institutions at one percent interest against his gold production. Better still, with proven annual production he had been able to borrow gold from a bank at around one percent in interest, sell that gold and replace it out of production. It was really a marvelous mineral manipulation that Adam Zolt had worked so well for and on behalf of Garth Peters and, of course, for himself.

"Where are you, Adam, in Nevada?"

Nevada was the location of the main Peters gold mine northeast of Peter Munk's fabulous Goldstrike open pit mine.

"No, I'm in Toronto today. Actually I'm in my office at your new headquarters at the BCE Place, Madame Chair."

"I'll talk to you tomorrow when I get there," Louise said.

There was nothing of interest from the other heads of companies.

"So we can wrap up this conference call now. I'm grateful to all of you for the marvelous work you're doing for the Peters—what should I call it—empire. What my father was able to put together from the time he arrived in this country in 1944, arrived to stay that is, is nothing short of phenomenal. As you know, he and I have had our differences, very strong differences that have prevented us from having any association with one another over many years. We have gone our separate ways and that suited me very well."

Zolt added, "And you've done very well doing it your way, Senator. You've become one of the wealthiest and most influential women in Canada—and are about to become even more so."

What he said was true, but Louise chose not to encourage him with a direct response. "Be that as it may, the reality is I will need the support and loyalty of all of you in the days ahead. I look forward to meeting all of you, most of you for the first time, during the funeral visitation and the ceremonies themselves. But before we go there is one point I want to emphasize. I am in charge of the Peters corporations. No lawyer, no trust company, no person outside of myself has any authority whatsoever to make decisions for the Peters group or any part of it, and if anyone attempts to tell you otherwise you must advise me at once."

Louise Peters finished off, "Thank you and goodbye for the moment."

She didn't know why but she kept the telephone to her ear rather than putting it down. She could hear a voice in the distance talking. It was not a voice she had heard on the conference call. She wasn't quite sure who it was. Obviously he had failed to disconnect.

The voice sounded as though it was speaking to someone else in the room where the speaker was located. "That woman is out of her mind. She isn't going to control anything. Peters will have the situation locked up so tightly she won't be able to touch it with a ten-foot nuclear hotrod. And I'm going to make sure she doesn't. What a true bitch she is! I hear she's shacking up with some deputy minister in Ottawa. He's the current one in a long list of boy-toys. If she were a man she'd be called a stud, Senator Stud."

15

Senator Peters was in her office reviewing her notes for her presentation to the standing committee in Foreign Affairs and National Defence. She had heard her secretary's words of sympathy on the death of her mother and father and then ordered her to get the chief pilot of the Peters air service in Toronto on the line. "I don't know who he is. They have an office at Avitat. Just track him down. I want to talk with him to make arrangements for him to pick me up here tonight."

It took Betty about five minutes. She rang through to the Senator, saying, "He's on the line, his name is Dag Phillips. He's the chief pilot. I've told him who you are and why you're calling."

The Senator picked up the phone and quickly got through the preliminaries. She had to tell Phillips about the accident because nothing was public yet. "I know this is all quite a shock to you because you would have had a close personal relationship with my father, both of you being pilots."

"Absolutely. When he was on board, he used to do most of the flying from the left seat. He was an excellent pilot. Jesus, I can't believe it! And your mother too. This must be a very tough time for you, Senator."

"Yes, the loss of my mother is really hard to take. She was a real sweetheart and very close to me . . . Now, you will appreciate that my father's death puts me in a difficult position. I have to take over control of the Peters family. My brother is badly injured and he is out of it just for the moment, unconscious. I'd like you or someone from your staff to pick me up at the Ottawa Airport at six tonight. That will give me enough time to get things straightened away here. I have an appearance before the Defence Committee and a whole bunch of other things to do. If you pick me up at six that will give me a good chance to get to my Toronto apartment tonight and my office in the morning. And then I want you to stand by because I will want to go to New York, probably tomorrow afternoon, to meet with our executives there."

"Sure, Senator. We'll be happy to do whatever we can for you, but I take my orders directly from Mr. Foster and he's already booked for us to pick him up at the Muskoka Airport this evening at six. He's on his honeymoon you know."

"Sorry, Mr. Phillips, I'm in charge here now and I want that goddamn airplane here at six. Tell Mr. Foster you'll pick him up at eight after you drop me off."

"I'm sorry, Senator, I don't think I made myself clear. I know who you are but I work for Brad Foster and your father. I take orders only from Mr. Foster. I have no authority to take any instructions from you. I hope you understand what I'm saying. I'm in a very difficult position."

"I hear what you're saying, Mr. Phillips, but if you want to keep your job, that airplane better be at Ottawa International Airport at Hudson General at six o'clock. You can reach me through my secretary. She'll give you the number."

She banged the telephone down into its cradle. The Senator was furious. Brad Foster. She had never met him but she knew a great deal about him. Her father's alter ego. A clever chartered accountant who handled the Peters corporate affairs and financing arrangements with skill and dedication.

Her next instructions to Betty were to find Foster wherever he was. "Get on to his secretary. Tell her it's absolutely urgent, that my father's been killed and I have to speak with Foster immediately."

In short order Betty reported, "His secretary won't give me his telephone number. She simply says he's on his honeymoon and he's given instructions that he's not to be disturbed under any circumstances whatsoever."

"But, my God, my father's dead, surely she can give you the number. Nothing could be more important than to let Foster know."

"She says he already knows."

"What! How would he know? There hasn't been any word about it yet. Somebody from that telephone conference this morning must have gotten through to him. Tell her I want to leave a message on his voicemail and I don't want to hear a negative on that one."

Foster's secretary had no alternative but to go along with that demand. As soon as the voicemail signal came through to Louise she began. "Brad Foster, you and I haven't met but I know all about you. Evidently you know that my father has been killed. In the circumstances I have no alternative but to move to take over control of the family corporation and I expect to have your full support. I had a teleconference with all of the CEOs and senior executives of the main operating companies in the Peters group, but unfortunately I couldn't reach you because you're on your honeymoon. And your secretary, loyal as she is, just won't give me the telephone number. You should know that I plan to take over control of my father's interests, starting with the Peters holding company of which you are the president and the CEO. As I say, I expect your full cooperation, starting with directing Mr. Phillips, the chief pilot, to pick me up at six o'clock at Ottawa International. He tells me that he was to pick you up at that time at Muskoka but we'll move your pickup back to eight o'clock. I simply must be in my Toronto office this evening and then I'll meet with you at your office tomorrow morning at nine. When you get this message, would you please contact me here. I have a committee meeting that I have to go to now and you can leave word with my secretary or on my voicemail, whatever you wish. I expect to hear from you, and I say again I expect to have your full cooperation."

She was satisfied with her position statement. There would be no doubt in Foster's mind that she was going to take over and be the boss. None at all.

She gathered up her notes for the committee meeting and stuffed them in her briefcase. As she went by her secretary's desk she said, "I'm about ten minutes late already for the committee meeting but I shouldn't be any longer than a couple of hours. I expect to hear from Foster. If he calls before I get back, get his telephone number and ask for a best time to talk with him. He may want to leave a message on the voicemail. That's all right. But I really want to have a word with him directly. Okay?"

It was twenty minutes to twelve when she finally made it into the committee room. By that time the news of her father's death had been released by the people at Trenton and word had quickly spread throughout the Parliament Buildings. When she walked in, an unusual thing happened. All the committee members of all parties including the chairman of the Minister of Defence, the Chief of the Defence Staff, everyone stood as a mark of respect for her and for her deceased parents. As she made her way to her designated seat, the chairman spoke to her on behalf of those assembled saying how profoundly concerned they all were to hear of the death of her father and mother and spoke of the great contribution that they had made to Canada and for that matter to the world and expressed their profound sympathy.

She responded by thanking all very briefly, saying, "In the best Peters tradition I have chosen, in the presence of this dreadful news, to complete my obligation as a Senator by being here to express my opinion about what Canada's position should be in relation to the ready-to-go American Nuclear Missile Defence System. When that is done, Mr. Chairman, I will spend most of the day making arrangements for funerals and tonight I will go to Toronto and begin the task of taking over the direction of my father's group of companies."

The members of the press, particularly from the *National Post* and *Globe and Mail*, recorded the event and her words very carefully. She knew there would be a scrum when she left the committee room. She could handle that with no problem.

When everyone was again seated, the chairman invited her to make her statement saying, "You were scheduled for a little later, Senator, but in the circumstances I will be obliged if you could give us your views now."

Fifteen minutes later, Louise Peters had almost completed her presentation. She looked at her watch. There was so much to do, so much to think about. She just had to shorten this.

"Mr. Chairman, my time is running short. I ask your indulgence so I can summarize my recommendations to this committee and to the government and, for that matter, to the Prime Minister."

"Please do so, Major Peters."

"Thank you. It is my urgent recommendation that the Government of Canada pledge its full and unconditional support to the United States in the development and operation of its National Missile Defence system.

"And it is my urgent recommendation that the Prime Minister and the Government of Canada communicate to the White House and the Congress, Canada's support for the National Missile Defence program."

As promised, Senator Louise Peters had delivered her

opinions, even though they might cut across the bow of government policy.

She had finished.

There was complete silence. The distinguished citizens and soldiers in the room could scarcely believe what they had been hearing even though they knew that the Senator had it exactly right. The scribes were scribbling furiously. The chairman was so nonplused it took him a full minute to realize that he had to make some response. It was simple. He sort of gasped, "Thank you, Senator."

"Mr. Chairman, if there are any questions that anyone in the room wishes to put to me I'd be happy to respond, then if the press wish to talk with me we can do so out in the corridor."

The chairman pulled nervously at his tie, "Yes, well, all right, are there any questions any of you want to put to Senator Peters?"

It was as if the chairman had asked anyone in the room if he or she would like to put his head inside the mouth of the biggest, hungriest crocodile they had ever seen. There were no takers.

"If I may be excused, Mr. Chairman, I have a thousand things to do before I leave Ottawa tonight."

He was only too pleased to be able to graciously consent to her departure with appropriate thanks for her—"how shall I put it? Straightforward and from-the-heart opinions."

For the scrum with the press including radio and television, she gave her freewheeling answers to questions about her support for the National Missile Defence program and gave responses to queries about the future of the massive Peters corporate organization, underscoring and making it clear that she intended to take over control until such time as a court said that she was disqualified, a decision she would take to the Supreme Court of Canada if necessary. "I've been in touch with all of the chief executives of my father's companies and I will be in the head office of the group at the BCE Place in Toronto tomorrow morning."

"Have you had any problems with the CEOs you've talked with?"

"Not at all. The Peters Group is a family company just like the Thomson Group is the Thomson family's fiefdom. It's family and the family controls. That's all there is to it."

"What about Foster, your father's right-hand man. He's president of the Peters Group and chief executive officer isn't he? What about him?"

"He's on his honeymoon somewhere in Muskoka. I haven't been able to get my hands on him yet."

Some wag at the back chirped up, "That's the bride's job anyhow," which bought a few guffaws.

"So what about Foster? Do you think he'll give you any trouble?"

"Absolutely not. I haven't met the man but he's obviously a very intelligent person who knows a great deal about me and I know a great deal about him. The first thing he knows is that this is a family owned organization and the family will be in control. No, I don't expect to have any problem with him." As she said that she knew full well she was lying. There was something about that open-line voice that she didn't recognize declaring war on her after the teleconference. She still didn't know who it was, but she was beginning to narrow down the possibilities. It could well have been Foster listening in on a secondary telephone hookup. Just a possibility but the possibilities were turning into probabilities in her mind.

Louise terminated the scrum politely but firmly.

Her first question as she went into her suite of offices was, "Have you heard from Foster yet?"

"No and there's nothing on your voicemail, I just checked."

"And what about the chief pilot?"

"Nothing."

"I can tell you he better be here at six o'clock or else. What time is it now?"

"Five to one."

The Senator went into her own office, saying, "Get him on the phone right now. He's got Foster's phone number and he should have been in touch with him by this time."

When Dag Phillips was on the line she came right to the point. "So what's happening, Mr. Phillips? I'm sure you've talked to Mr. Foster."

A reluctant Dag Phillips admitted he had. "I have some bad news for you, Senator. I have strict orders from Mr. Foster not to pick you up. I got the same threat from him as the one you gave me: if I did, I would lose my job. He says he's running Peters Group, not you, and he says you're probably not even mentioned in the will. And he says the animosity between you and your father was very bad, and the last thing Mr. Peters would want would be for you to take over the Peters Group or even set foot in its offices."

Louise Peters was aghast.

He went on. "He says you have a Senate pass on Air Canada or Air Ontario, and if you want to get to Toronto tonight he's sure they'll accommodate you. So, Senator, just leave me out of it. I'm the meat in the sandwich between you two people. I have to do what my boss tells me, and as much as I'd like to accommodate you at this very bad time for you, I'm really not in a position to do so. You understand."

He could hear her hissing through clenched teeth as she muttered, "That son-of-a-bitch. I'll get him if it's the last thing I do. And as for you, Mr. Phillips, I'll get you as well!"

Once again the phone was slammed down in anger.

"Betty!" she screamed at the top of her lungs. "Get me a booking on Air Canada between five and six. I don't care what class it is, just get me a goddamn seat and get my limo service, Yuri, to pick me up in Toronto. Tell him I'll need him tomorrow as well. And food, get me some food. A sandwich, anything. And open that bottle of white wine in the fridge. I've got about fifty phone calls to make and people are going to be after me . . ."

Betty came from her desk to the door where she stood saying, "You already have people after you. The coroner's office in the Sault has been on the phone. They need somebody to identify the bodies."

"Well, I sure as hell am not going to do it. Telephone that Phillips person. He knows them both well. He's got the company airplane. He can go up to the Sioux, identify the bodies and get back to Muskoka in time to pick up his favourite boss. You've got his number, we were just talking with him. Never mind the food, it can wait."

Louise was still seething from her conversation with Phillips, but she forced herself to turn her mind to the funeral arrangements. What a job that was going to be. She put a call to the head man at Humphrey Funeral Home to give him instructions to have the bodies picked up as soon as they were released by the coroner. Airlift them down by charter. The best of caskets. She wanted the service at St. Paul's on Bloor Street. Would they please make those arrangements and if they had any difficulty to let her know and she would speak with the Archbishop. And she wanted the Archbishop to handle the service. After all, her father had been a substantial supporter of the Anglican Church in Canada. She was looking for something in return. There would be no visitation. Subject to what was in their wills, Louise directed that there be cremation. The Humphrey people would draft the obituary for both of them and arrange for placement in both the *National Post* and the *Globe and Mail*. As to a Québec French-language newspaper, why bother? The caskets would of course be closed. The funeral director had been in touch with the coroner's office and the damage to the face and head of her father was severe. He regretted having to tell her but it was something he felt she should know. It would be the next day at the earliest before the Coroner would release the bodies. With all the arrangements that had to be made the funeral director recommended that the funeral be held four or five days from the date that he received the bodies.

Her next telephone call was to the senior partner of the Fasken firm. She knew that they would have the last will and testament of her father and very likely of her mother, as well if there was one at all.

George Mitchell, the senior partner, was courteous to the point of being deferential. Yes, they had her father's but not her mother's. She might never had made one. The Garth Peters' original was in their safekeeping and, yes, he was one of the designated trustees under the will and would be pleased to let her have a copy. Mitchell would fax it to her Ottawa office immediately and also to her office at the Lang, Michener firm. To his recollection there were no directions in the will as to funeral arrangements so the matter would be left in her discretion, subject, of course, as to what her brother had to say. Louise informed him that her brother was still unconscious so the arrangements would have to be made by her. There was no one else to do it.

Betty reported that she had spoken to Phillips, who had reluctantly agreed to make the identification. He was departing for Sault Ste. Marie immediately.

Louise put in another call to George Mitchell to say that she had overlooked one thing: under no circumstances was he to provide a copy of the wills to anyone other than herself and certainly not to Brad Foster or any of the corporate people. Mitchell told her that, as a matter of fact, he had just received a call from Foster asking for a copy. The senior partner had been planning to speak to Louise about it, but with her clear instructions nothing would go to Foster or anyone else. Then he put the delicate question.

"As you are aware, Senator, we have acted for your father since 1945, and we have a whole corporate division of twenty lawyers and staff dedicated to the legal work for him and his companies including those incorporated in Bermuda. Is it possible to assume that you would like us to continue to act for the companies?" Mitchell asked.

"For the companies, yes, I have no problem with that at least for the time being. When I see the will, I will determine who will handle the estates."

"Your father gave explicit directions in that regard. We are to act as solicitors for both your father and mother. As I said, she may never have made one."

"Those instructions may change, Mr. Mitchell, after I see what the will has to say."

"Senator, I don't think that you're going to like what your father's will provides so far as you are concerned. But I respectfully suggest that we leave these discussions until such time as you have viewed the will. In the meantime, please be assured that, as a named trustee under your father's will and as designated solicitors for his estate, we will do our utmost to accommodate your wishes, all of your reasonable wishes, that is. This is undoubtedly an extremely stressful time for you and we are here to assist. If there are to be any disputes, I again respectfully suggest that we put them over until after the funerals have been completed."

"That sounds reasonable to me," Louise replied. "However, there is one area of major concern to me when you talk about disputes. Since your firm acts for the companies and in particular for my father's main corporation, you should know that Mr. Foster has already adopted a confrontational attitude toward me, saying that I have no power whatever in relation to the companies. I am giving you fair warning as solicitors for the corporations—and I do this as a practicing lawyer—that unless I get cooperation from Foster and the rest of the corporate group, I will have no choice but to turn to the courts to interpret and give effect to my rights. I want to make that clear."

"That is perfectly clear, Senator. In all fairness I must tell you that Foster has already spoken to me about his concerns about your attempting to take control when, as he puts it, you have no right to do so."

It was time to finish the conversation. "I hear what you're saying, Mr. Mitchell. I think your suggestion was good. Let's leave these matters until after the funerals if we can. We may not be able to but if it's possible that's the best route. If you'll send the Will along right now I would appreciate it very much."

Betty reported that a doctor at the Sault Ste. Marie hospital had called. Her brother was still unconscious. His face had been badly banged up, with a broken nose, cuts, but strangely no teeth lost. He should not be moved, so they were not going to take him to Toronto.

"Obviously there's no sense trying to get up to see him. He's right out of it and, I hope, being well looked after."

"They said they'd let you know as soon as he regains consciousness."

"If he does."

"Yes, if he does. You're booked on the five o'clock in business class. Yuri will meet you at Pearson International in the usual place."

"I'm expecting a fax from the Fasken firm. It will be my father's will, so make sure there's a lot of paper in the machine.

"There's something coming through right now. That's probably it. I'll check the paper."

When Betty put the copy of the will in front of her on the desk, Louise Peters looked at the cover sheet. She immediately knew that her life would be changed by that document no matter what it said. If her father had cut her out of the will completely, she would litigate. If he included her but not an equal portion with her brother, she would litigate. Her mother had confided in her more than once that in the month that Louise was conceived, she had had intercourse with both Mark Tyler and with Garth Peters. Either of them could have been her father. Physically she had facial attributes of each of the men. The same colour hair as Mark, eyes similar to Garth, a nose that could have come from either one of them, just like her full lips and flawless teeth. In her heart and mind she frequently had felt that she was the daughter of Mark Tyler, that she couldn't be the daughter of that son-on-a-bitch Garth Peters. At other times, particularly when she had been much younger, there were moments when she was certain that Garth Peters was indeed her father. In later years she had often considered going the DNA test route but had never gone that far. However, with that last will and testament lying in front of her, she decided that the time might well have come, because if Mark Tyler was her father—and it could be proved genetically through the DNA test—she believed that she could trace the case right back to the death of Mark Tyler. She would ask the court to declare that all of the shares and assets of the Peters Group had been in fact held by Garth Peters in trust for her mother, and therefore under her mother's will—if there was one—for herself and her brother. She was sure that her mother's will would provide for all her assets to go to her two children in equal shares, regardless of whether Garth Peters survived her. Louise's mind raced over all of these factors as she looked at the cover sheet.

A speed reader trained in the law and its peculiar verbiage, she was quickly through the operative parts of the will.

There it was, almost as she had expected it except for a shocking surprise—$5 million dollars to a relative, Robert Ross. "Robert Ross! Who the hell is that? Five million?! Ridiculous. Garth Peters must have been out of his mind when he made that bequest. And look at what he gave me—

a measly one million!" Louise was beside herself, yet she hadn't finished reading. Ten million dollars to his wife, Julie, and the house and cottage with it. Fifteen million dollars to the University of Toronto for the setting up of a Chair of Entrepreneurial Studies in the name of Garth Peters. And the remainder of his estate including all of the shares in the Peters Group corporation to his son, Garth Peters Jr.. Louise knew the value of those shares would be in the range of one and a half to two billion dollars. The son-on-a-bitch had thrown that million dollar sop in there so that, if she tried to break the Will, the court could say that in the circumstances of their hate relationship, Garth Peters had indeed taken care of his obligation to his daughter. And this Robert Ross—was he a lover? Got to cut him out, whoever he is. Break the Will? From that moment Louise Peters had one purpose in life and it was to do exactly that.

She picked up the telephone and dialed the direct line of John Thornton, the head litigator in the Lang, Michener firm. She expected voicemail but to her surprise he answered directly. She quickly outlined the situation including the Ross bequest. "John, I'm faxing you a copy of the will. I have to have a meeting with you and our estate specialists first thing tomorrow morning. And I have to know everything about Robert Ross. I don't have any idea who he is, but we have to find him! You'll see when you get the will. Eight o'clock, your office. Are you available?"

He was available indeed and would make sure the other people were there too.

"And, John, I want no discussion by any member of the firm who gets involved, I want no discussion outside the office whatsoever. I don't want to see any leaks in the press about the will situation. And I want to move to take control of the Peters Group immediately."

At that point Betty put a letter from Mitchell on her desk. It confirmed that Fasken's did not have a will executed by Julie. "There's no will of my mother's. We'll have to do a search. I'll fax down . . ." She was going to say 'my father's will' but at that moment she decided she would never describe him as her father again. "Garth Peters' Will."

"Who are the trustees?" Thornton asked.

"My brother, George Mitchell and that asshole Foster—Garth Peters' right-hand man and president of the Peters Group. Unbelievable but true. If you have any problems putting the meeting together give me a call, you know where to reach me."

It was time to get on to the DNA thing. Her good friend, the Commissioner of the RCMP, would give her some idea as to how to go about making that arrangement. A sample would be needed from Garth Peters' body and from hers. A quick call to the Commissioner gave her the name of the firm in Toronto that would do the work. She made arrangements that the Humphrey funeral firm would provide the DNA company with whatever sample was required once the body was in Humphrey's hands. In turn she would give the DNA people the specimen that they required. The Humphrey's director expected the bodies to be in his hands the next day or the following day at the latest. As arranged, he would be in touch with her to let her know when they were with him.

Betty appeared with a tuna fish sandwich and a glass of white wine. "As you could probably hear, the telephone's been ringing off the hook. The press, the TV people, the Prime Minister, the Governor General. She's been on the line herself. The list is endless. I'm keeping a list by the way. What will I tell the media?"

"Tell them that I'm distraught, that I'm in mourning and I'm in no condition to speak with them. I talked to the media after the committee meeting and that's enough for the moment. Speaking of lists, I'm going to have to think about pallbearers. Ever heard of a woman pallbearer? No? I think I'm going to break that rule just for the hell of it."

"Whom do you have in mind?"

"Garth Peters' current mistress."

16

Lang, Michener's top litigator, John Thornton, sat across from Louise at her conference table. He was flanked on his right by the firm's estate department head, Gretchen Swift, and on his left by the senior corporate lawyer, Graham Orr. It was 8:10 a.m. They had disposed of the condolences, coffee had been poured, documents were piled on the table in front of Thornton and he was ready to go.

He said, "The three of us worked late into the night, Louise, looking at all the material and at the case law and the facts as we know them."

Louise broke in. "Right off the top, how are we going to find out who this Rob Ross is, a so-called relative? I've never heard of such a person. Five million to him and only a million to me!"

Swift answered. "I spoke to Mr. Mitchell. He told me that he has a sealed envelope. It was given to him by Mr. Peters when he executed his Will with instructions that its contents would identify Robert Ross and his relationship to Mr. Peters. But the envelope should not be opened before the thirtieth day after Mr. Peters' demise."

"So we have to wait?"

"We have no choice. There isn't a single clue as to his identity, nothing that we could start a trace on." Swift moved on to the main topic. "Right off the top we think it's going to be extremely difficult to break your father's will."

Louise reacted. "Don't call him my father. He was no father to me. Furthermore, I have serious doubts that he really was my father. I didn't tell you this yesterday but I think you should know about it now."

She repeated the story her mother had told her about her paternity, and explained that she had made arrangements for a DNA test. Louise went on to explain her mother's inheritance of the Tyler fortune and the granting to Peters of the irrevocable power of attorney. It was, of course, revocable but her mother had never challenged it and let the whole thing go because she had not been competent to do anything else. The three lawyers all scribbled notes as she spoke.

"Those are the facts of the situation," she said. "The only question is the DNA test. What if the test shows that Garth Peters was not my father? That doesn't that prove that Mark Tyler was, does it?"

"No," Thornton answered immediately. "To get a Mark Tyler test you'll have to have access to the remains of E.P. Tyler. We should be able to get a court to order an exhumation."

The wills and estates lawyer, Gretchen Swift, reacted, her face filled with astonishment. "If the DNA tests show that Mark Tyler was your father, I think we've got a great opportunity to argue that the entire Garth Peters estate and fortune in whatever form, corporate or otherwise, was in fact the property of the person granting the power of attorney, that Peters was only in a position of trust for and on her behalf. At the time of their deaths—which were simultaneous—the power of attorney was terminated and all assets were vested in the true beneficiary, your mother, and accordingly the provisions of her will would apply if she had a Will."

Louise asked, "But can't we make that same argument regardless of whether Peters or Mark Tyler was my father—if Peters was the trustee for my mother? In other words, don't you think that the same argument would apply whether Garth Peters or Mark Tyler is my father?"

"Yes, I think the same argument would apply but it

would be much stronger if the DNA tests show that Garth Peters is not your father. I agree, there would have to be some followup DNA testing to establish that Tyler was indeed your father, and to do that we'd have to exhume old E.P. You see, if Peters is your father then the inheritance chain is from Mark Tyler to your mother and through her to you. On the other hand, if Tyler is your father, again the chain is through your mother but, even if she didn't have a Will, her estate, which is really Mark Tyler's estate, would go to you directly because he is your father. In that instance there's a very nice question as to whether or not your brother —who would be of no relationship whatever, bloodline or otherwise, to Mark Tyler—there's a real question in my mind as to whether he would be entitled to anything unless she so provided in her will."

Louise was focused on every word. "Can you firm up an opinion on that last point?" she asked. "If my mother did not have a will, what then? What you're saying is that if Tyler is my father and if a court declares that the entire Garth Peters estate was in fact held in trust by Peters for my mother because of the operation of the power of attorney and if she had no will, then I could wind up as the sole beneficiary and my brother, who would then be my half-brother, would be excluded?"

All three lawyers nodded in agreement.

Gretchen Swift spoke again. "You'll have to give me some time to get an opinion together but I'm confident that it will be as I have given it to you now."

Thornton added, "We have to get our hands on that power of attorney. Would the Fasken firm have it?"

Louise thought about that. "I expect so. Either that or they'll know where it is — possibly in my father's safety deposit box, assuming he has one. It will be somewhere in his papers because it is the document that gave him all his power and wealth. If he had been challenged by me or anyone else in his lifetime, he would have had to be able to produce it."

"Had you ever thought of challenging him?" Thornton asked. "I think you would have had one hell of a case—if your father was in fact Tyler."

"Of course I did. Even though he has hated my guts and I his, I've never brought myself to the point where I thought I could really take him on. I would have had to bring my mother into the litigation. It would have been really tough on her. So I just never did it. But everything's changed now, of course. And now that he's dead, I still have to fight him. I have to fight that goddamn Will and I'm ready to do so. So, Gretchen, please prepare that opinion as quickly as possible. And, John, please take charge of the litigation. How do we go about this? Will it be by way of an originating notice of motion asking the court for a declaration?"

"Probably," John replied. "It's central that I get my hands on that power of attorney. I'll get to work on that right away. I'll talk to old Mitchell at Faskens. He'll probably know where the original is and he very likely has a certified copy stuck somewhere. I can't see him refusing to let us have it."

Louise said, "If he says he has the original or a certified copy or if he thinks it's in Garth Peters' safety deposit box and he gives you a hard time and indicates in any way, shape or form that he is not prepared to give it to you—tell him you have explicit instructions to bring an action immediately and to bring a motion for production. And you can also tell him that I have instructed you to move for an order declaring that any money, any shares of the Peters Corporation or any of its subsidiaries, any and all of his assets are in fact the assets of the estate of Julie Peters and that any of the provisions of his Will that purport to deal with those assets will be declared null and void and of no effect—or whatever it is you think should be in a claim in the originating notice of motion."

The next matter on her agenda was how to deal with Foster. Louise described her teleconference meeting with the heads of the subsidiary companies. She told the group that they hadn't been able to track down the honeymooning Foster and that he had refused to allow the chief pilot to pick her up in Ottawa. She told them about the unknown voice who at the conclusion of the teleconference vowed to do everything in his power to make sure that she didn't take over the Peters Group of companies. Louise wasn't sure but in the balance of probabilities it was likely Foster whom she had heard.

"The question is whether I should attempt to establish a working relationship with this man, whether I should attempt to take control of the board at this stage, or whether I should back off and wait until the funeral is out of the way?" She looked at Graham Orr, the corporate expert, asking, "What do you think?"

Without hesitating he replied, "I'd back off. This guy's extremely intelligent. He's tough with a reputation for being ruthless. If he was listening to your conversation with the company heads, he knows exactly where you're coming from and he's undoubtedly got his battle plan in place already. In fact, he may well know what's in Mr. Peters' will. Let's assume that he does. That means he thinks he's got a position of strength and he's not going to give you an inch. So I think that you should just cool it for the moment until we're ready to fire all our guns, and all the documentation is prepared for the litigation. Then as soon as the litigators have launched the motion and served the papers, a letter from us should go to Foster setting out the facts and giving him a clear ultimatum, requiring that on an interim basis until the litigation is decided the corporate status quo must be maintained. No deals, no purchases, no sales of corporations, no financings, nothing except with your consent."

"Or else?"

"Absolutely. Or else, meaning either he complies or he's out at the earliest opportunity." He turned to his colleagues, asking, "What do you think?"

It sounded fine to them. Made good sense. And Louise thought so as well.

She said, "I'll be in the office most of the day. I have arrangements for the funeral to make and I have a couple of closings for clients."

"Can't someone look after those for you?" Orr asked.

"No. These are people who have been with me for years. I know their stuff intimately and I really don't want to take the time to brief someone else. So that's on my agenda. And I have go to the DNA lab. They want blood. So does everyone else so far as I can tell. Can we meet tomorrow morning at the same time, same location? And don't hesitate to talk with me about the facts or the law. You all know my secretary. I have my cell phone. She'll get through to me wherever I am."

By noon Senator Louise Peters and the lawyer had closed the two deals she was working on, one a sale and one a purchase of businesses. Both were share acquisitions and so the complications were few.

The Humphrey representative telephoned to say that the bodies had been released by the coroner and were being flown into Toronto-Buttonville Airport by charter in temporary caskets. The DNA people would take the required sample from the remains of Garth Peters as soon as the bodies were in the Humphrey establishment.

The day was Thursday. It was settled with the Archbishop that the funeral would be on Monday at St. Paul's at eleven in the morning. She had amended in various ways the full obituary but finally approved of it. The

Humphrey people had a specialist who wrote first-class obituaries for well-known persons. Both the *National Post* and the *Globe and Mail* carried their respective versions of the life story of Garth and Julie Peters complete with suitable photographs. Louise picked out two coffins. The entire procedure would be finished off by a cremation. For the funeral proceedings at St. Paul's the caskets had to be seen to be of reasonable quality as befitted the status and wealth of the occupants thereof—the way she saw it.

The DNA results were promised to be available on Monday afternoon after the funerals. The legal opinion on her status as the natural daughter of Tyler had been firmed up solidly by the Lang Michener people as had the alternative if the results showed that she was the natural daughter of Garth Peters. The DNA people confirmed that if it was proved that she was not the natural daughter of Garth Peters then the only way to prove that Mark Tyler was her genetic father would be to get permission to exhume the body of E.P. Tyler to obtain a specimen. If necessary those arrangements could be made with the appropriate provincial government authority and the city health department, and of course the operators of the cemetery. It would take some doing but with the advent of DNA techniques they assured her that bodies were being exhumed on a fairly frequent basis to seek out the genetic truth that lay in those telltale human fibers.

John Thornton, the litigator, had had no trouble in obtaining a certified copy of the power of attorney that had been given by Julie to Garth Peters drafted by the English solicitor, Colin James, back in the summer of 1944.

The Fasken lawyer, George Mitchell, had been so willing to cooperate that there was no need for John Thornton to unload any threats of litigation on him. And so Louise's intent to sue had not been disclosed. As she saw it, better that it would come as a surprise for the general public and more particularly for Foster. She was well pleased with the nature and tone of the letter that had been drafted to be presented to Foster immediately after the court proceedings had been initiated—or, as she had put it to her Lang, Michener colleagues, when the shit hit the fan.

Through her secretary, Louise monitored the condition of her brother in Sault Ste. Marie. He was still unconscious and there was no indication as to when he might regain consciousness, if at all. All the life signs were still there and strong.

When he had advised Louise that the bodies were being released, the funeral director confirmed that the chief pilot had identified both the bodies. It had been a traumatic experience for Phillips because, as he put it, both were "badly beaten up," particularly Garth Peter's head and face. It was Thursday afternoon when the same Humphrey man reported to Louise at her Lang, Michener office that the bodies had arrived at the Funeral Home and were being looked after. There would be no viewing, no reception; the caskets would be sealed. Those were her instructions. There was absolutely no way that she wanted to see the battered remains.

On Thursday and Friday, Louise and her legal team focused intensely on the preparation of the originating notice of motion and the affidavit which she had to execute in order to support the facts that she was alleging. Ultimately that document ran to over a hundred pages, a small book, because the basis of the litigation began with the saga of the intertwining of the lives of Mark Tyler, Garth Peters and Julie, the woman who had been wife to both of them. A certified copy of the original power of attorney drawn in 1945 by Colin James in England was the pivotal piece of evidence attached to the affidavit as one of the exhibits. The affidavit traced the corporate growth of the Peters Corporation from its inception when the E.P. Tyler assets were acquired in 1945. Louise had all of the appropriate information in her computer having kept and maintained clippings from the *National Post*, the *Globe and Mail's* "Report on Business," the *Financial Times*, and every other source that carried any kind of report on the activities of the Peters Corporation or any of its subsidiaries. All that information painstakingly accumulated over the years by Louise proved to be a treasure trove for the drafters of the affidavit.

Of critical importance was the DNA test. The required specimen had been obtained from the body of Garth Peters as soon as it had arrived at the Humphrey Funeral Home. For her part Louise had provided a blood sample at the DNA laboratory.

The application to the court had to be drafted in two ways. In the event that DNA test showed that Garth Peters was indeed her father, then the court would be asked to declare that all of the assets in his name were in fact assets that he held in trust for Julie through the operation of the power of attorney and accordingly those assets were to be distributed and allocated in accordance with the will of Julie Peters if discovered or, if not, then in accordance with intestate law. In the alternative, the court would be asked to set aside the will of Garth Peters on the basis of several grounds including incompetence.

On the other hand, if the DNA test showed that Garth Peters was not her natural father, then the court would be asked to order that the trustees of Garth Peters be prohibited from dealing with the assets in the name of Garth Peters and in particular enjoined from making any distribution of the assets until such further order of the court might be obtained after the DNA tests had been effected that would establish that Mark Tyler was her natural father.

In order to establish that link, the court would have to order that the body of E.P. Tyler be exhumed so that the required sample of tissue could be taken from it for the

DNA comparison of it with that of Louise. She was confident that if the matter had to be taken that far, the DNA test would confirm that she was in fact the daughter of Mark Tyler.

In that event the court would be asked to make the declaration that Garth Peters had held the assets in trust for Julie Peters under the operation of the power of attorney and that the assets of Julie Peters be distributed to the exclusion of her half-brother, Garth Peters Jr., in that she, Louise Peters, was the only child of Mark Tyler whereas Garth Peters Jr. was the child of Garth Peters and his wife Julie.

As Thornton had advised, "Julie, you might as well go for the whole bundle if the DNA test proves that E.P. Tyler was your grandfather and Mark Tyler was your father—and why not? You've got nothing to lose—except the court costs, of course, and the Lang, Michener firm is very generous when it comes to matters of this kind."

Her response was prompt. "Bullshit. But you're right."

He went on, "Here's a draft of my letter to Mitchell over at the Fasken firm outlining what we're going to do, putting him on notice that the corporate status quo is to prevail until the litigation is finished, and requiring that the board of directors and the officers of Peters Corporation and their subsidiaries will similarly hold to the status quo. And I want their undertaking to that effect."

"And what happens if he won't agree, or Foster or any of the executives won't agree?"

"We'll bring a motion for an interim injunction."

"If you have to do that, make sure you join that bastard Foster personally as a defendant!"

17

Toronto's grandly massive St. Paul's Church was packed. The Prime Minister of Canada was there together with some ten members of his Cabinet. The Premier of Ontario was present as was the Lieutenant-Governor of the province. Garth Peters had been a strong financial supporter of both the Prime Minister's federal party and that of the Premier of Ontario's provincial party, even though he kicked with a different political foot.

On the advice of her counsel, Senator Louise Peters had gritted her teeth and prepared and delivered a remarkably eloquent and emotional eulogy which embraced both Julie and Garth Peters and gave no hint whatever of the lifetime of bitterness and animosity that she had endured with the man she chose in her remarks to call her father. Archbishop Taylor Pryce had words of effusive praise for his long-time friends and great supporters of the church, and made much of the fact that God had taken both of them at the same time after a full and long life of achievement on both their parts.

All in all the service was a grand affair, well staged, beautifully orchestrated and with a first-class, high-profile audience. Louise was sure that Garth Peters would have been content and pleasantly satisfied with the turnout.

Following the church service the cremation occurred a few blocks away at the Toronto Crematorium, where the Archbishop again said the appropriate payers and words in the presence of Louise and her close supportive friends as she grieved finally and with tears for her beloved, no-longer-wretched mother.

So it was done, over with. Julie Peters and her husband Garth were no more, just memories and ashes to be disposed of some time later.

After lunch she went directly back to the Lang, Michener firm, her mind filled with the possible consequences of the DNA report she expected to be there waiting for her. It was on her desk, a large sealed envelope from the DNA testing firm marked "Private and Confidential."

Anxious though she was to know what the contents stated, she was nevertheless apprehensive, almost reluctant to know what was inside. She moved slowly around the desk and sat in her chair. Senator Louise Peters picked up her silver letter opener then took the envelope and slit it and pulled out the report. As she read its conclusion, she told herself that in her heart of hearts she had always known what the written words were now telling her coldly, precisely and with unquestionable certainty.

Senator Peters picked up the DNA report and walked down the office corridor to the corner suite of John Thornton, the chief litigator. He was at his desk poring over the final documents that would be served and filed with the court as soon as the DNA results were known. Thornton stood up as she walked in, his eyes fixed on the paper in her hand.

She put it on the desk in front of him, saying, "This will tell you which way to go, John. I'd like everything served this afternoon please and filed with the court in the morning. In the meantime would you tell George Mitchell, the trustee, that I want to meet Mr. Foster tomorrow morning in his office. I think it's time that he and I had some words face to face. Would you tell him I'll be there at nine."

* * * * * * * *

Senator Louise Peters prided herself on being prompt. If she had an appointment outside the office she liked to arrive at the stroke of the designated hour, which is what she did on Tuesday at nine o'clock. She was at the desk of the receptionist of the vast, sumptuous offices of the Peters Group in the BCE Tower strategically located as it was on the south side of Wellington at Bay Street in the business heart of Toronto.

It was the first time she had been into the main office lair of Garth Peters. She was immediately awestruck at the opulence, and the caliber of Canadian paintings—the Group of Seven's and Kreighoffs—that were on the walls of the reception area with its deep plush carpets and leather furniture. The ornate chandelier in the center of the room carried the trademarks of the main operating companies that made up the core of the Peters Group.

The prim-looking receptionist stood up behind her desk, smiling as Louise entered. "You must be Senator Peters. I've been so looking forward to meeting you."

Louise returned the smile. "I am indeed and I believe Mr. Foster is expecting me."

The receptionist's eyes dropped momentarily, perhaps a flash of guilt, "Yes, well, he's just a slight bit late. He's been held up in traffic, you know how it is. But he asked me to show you into his office and perhaps get some coffee for you. You'll have to forgive me, I'm new here, but there's a gentleman who's already in Mr. Foster's office. I don't know who is."

"Perhaps I should wait?"

"No, no, Mr. Foster wanted you to talk with this gentleman before he got here."

"But you don't know who he is?"

"No, in fact I haven't seen him. He was here before I

arrived this morning and Mr. Foster told me it was okay that he could be in his office because that's where you would be meeting."

"That's fine. If you'll take me to Mr. Foster's office...."

Louise followed her down a long wide corridor past a huge boardroom with perhaps twenty or more armchairs around it, leather and oak like the furniture in the reception room. When they arrived at the carved double doors of what clearly was a corner office, the receptionist said, "This is Mr. Foster's office." She opened the doors, saying, "Please go in, Senator. Would you like coffee?"

"Black, please."

"Right away."

Louise stepped into Foster's office, her eyes immediately focusing on the broad stretch of floor-to-ceiling windows that overlooked the Toronto Island and its airport to the south and the cluster of enormous bank buildings now towering over the Royal York Hotel, once the tallest building in the British Empire but now a dwarf. Foster's heavy, old-fashioned dark cherrywood desk sat parallel to the run of the south-facing wall windows just as if he had decided that while working he would turn his back on the magnificent view in order to be able to concentrate on papers or people without distraction.

The tall, high-backed swivel chair behind the desk was turned so that its back was facing her.

Louise told herself that there might be someone sitting in that chair because it was so tall.

There *was* someone in the chair. It was not Foster.

The voice from the chair that greeted her was one that she recognized instantly. It had been imprinted in her brain from the time of her first consciousness. The voice cut through her heart and mind like an eviscerating knife. Louise Peters could not believe what she was hearing. But it was true. It was his voice. No one else's. How could it be?

He was dead. Gone. His body burned yesterday in the consuming fire of the crematorium.

It was the unmistakable voice of Garth Peters saying, "It is unfortunate, my dear Louise, that you and I have to come together after all of these years in these most tragic circumstances."

Like an apparition, Garth Peters—the man she now knew was not her father—swiveled in the chair to face her and to look with enormous pleasure on the horrendous shock and surprise that filled her soul and spirit and showed clearly in her wide, staring eyes and slack-jawed face.

"This can't be!" She gasped as her hand flew to her mouth. "This can't be!"

"It not only can be, it is. I am still very much alive. Badly beaten up around the head, a broken arm. But believe me, Louise, it is I, your loving father, Garth Peters, and you greedy bitch, you have been caught with your power-hungry, money-hungry pants down fully intending to screw everybody in your path."

She was in far too much shock to attempt to respond.

"I've read all the material and the affidavits and documents in your unbelievably stupid court action. Unbelievable. Unforgivable."

Louise wasn't hearing anything he was saying. She shook her head in disbelief, shouting, "I don't believe this! How could this have happened?"

"It was a mistaken identity. When we got back into the airplane, Garth Jr. and I inadvertently switched life jackets. I wore his jacket with his identification and he did the same with mine. We both have grey hair and our faces were banged up. Simple as that. My chief pilot screwed up on the identification, but who can blame him. I regained consciousness shortly after noon yesterday—just after my funeral." He laughed. "As soon as I sorted out what happened, I instructed the doctors and the hospital staff not to say anything, absolutely nothing. With my head bandages and dark glasses nobody was going to identify me. I told them if they kept their mouths shut I'd give the hospital a $5 million donation and of course they went for it. So here I am, dear daughter."

Louise was quickly regaining her composure. Her intense animosity for the man had already returned. "You say you've read my court documents?"

"I sure have. What a lot of garbage! You presumed that I was dead and everything's based on that. The fact is I am not, so you haven't got a case, not a hope in hell. Everything I own is mine. You won't get a red cent from me. Nothing."

"Oh really? Have you read my DNA affidavit?"

"Your what?"

"It's a supplementary affidavit that has the DNA test between myself and my brother, your son—we thought it was you, of course—but the DNA test works the same way, because without question you are his natural father. The DNA test shows that you are not my natural father. Therefore Mark Tyler has to be my father. It was his and his father's estate that you scooped up. I am his direct descendant and you're out of it, Garth Peters, out of it completely. That marvelous power of attorney is clear evidence that all the assets were held by you for and on behalf of my mother. My half-brother is gone so I'm entitled to a hundred percent. And I'm going to get it, I'm going to take control of the entire estate including the Peters Group and all its assets. My lawyers will have a new set of court documents ready to be served on you by tomorrow."

Garth Peters was going to struggle to his feet to argue but didn't have the strength. He slumped back in his chair, a sneer on his face as he asked, "And how you are you going to prove that Mark Tyler was your father? He's been gone since 1944. As far as I know his body's never been found. With the way your mother was behaving back in those days, an easy lay—and I can certify to that—your natural father could have been anybody."

Louise was filled with instant fury. "You dreadful, dreadful man, you son-of-a-bitch. You have the morals and the mind of a snake. To say that about my mother—God, you must be sick. You read the court documents. I'm going to get a court order to exhume the body of E.P. Tyler just long enough to take a DNA sample. That will prove without a doubt that I am Mark Tyler's daughter and E.P. Tyler's granddaughter. And when that's done, Mr. Peters, all of this will be mine, every goddamn bit of it. You won't get anything from me, absolutely nothing. The whole world will cut you off, all your high-falutin' friends in Washington and London and Ottawa, they'll drop you as if you were a red-hot piece of dogshit!"

She realized she was shouting. Lowering her voice Louise put the question, "And who is this Robert Ross you've put in your will for $5 million while you had me in there for only a measly million? Who is he, a sweetheart?"

"God, woman, you are sick! Rob Ross is my son, my secret son, my brilliant secret son who doesn't even know I exist. That's who he is! And y'know what? He's now my only child, thanks to your goddamn DNA test . . ."

"And your murderous flying accident!"

"Yes, my murderous flying accident." Peters hesitated as his mind momentarily was filled with the crash. He shook his head then went on, "And Rob Ross—Rob Ross will be my sole heir, the only beneficiary of my estate. You, you vicious little bitch, will get nothing, absolutely zero." He gathered his strength and stood up. "It hurts my ribs to laugh." Peters snorted. "But I can't help it. You just yourself proved that I'm not your father, which means that I have no connection with you, no obligation to you. I hate your guts and I have for as long as I can remember. And the fact that you carry my name makes me want to throw up. This is my company, these are my offices, you don't belong here so I'm telling you now get out of here! You heard me, get the fuck out of here! I never want to see you again!"

She strode to the door, opened it, and as she walked out she turned and screamed, "I'll see you in court, you asshole!"

From the exhaustive examination for discovery of Louise as part of the lawsuit she launched against me I was able to get the basic details about her reaction to the news of the Otter crash and her subsequent actions in preparation for her take over of control of the Peters corporations. So my account of what steps she took and her delicious shock when she found out that I the asshole was alive—my account is right on the money.

Louise and I eventually settled within a week after her five day discovery. One thing about Louise—when she said she'd see me in court, she really meant it. It took her high powered lawyers about a month to launch her court action against me and my corporations.

And guess what? She claimed ownerships of everything I had—the Peters Group, all of its subsidiaries, the aircraft, my houses, the cottage, all of my personal assets, stocks, bonds and cash. Everything. What a bitch!

My equally high powered legal team put together what I thought was an air-tight defence to her Statement of Claim. That was followed by her Reply—these are all legal terms that I'm now expertly familiar with.

Then it was time for my lawyers to examine Louise under oath—for Discovery to get her personal evidence on the allegations she was making against her favourite asshole. If she's had her way I'd be in the poor-house or one of those homeless street people.

All this legal stuff took about nine months until her Discovery. In that period she had obtained an Interim Injunction from the Court that handcuffed me on what I could and could not do with the shares and assets of the Peters Group. No big deal because by the time I had cooled all acquisition negotiations that were going on.

After Lousie's discovery, I huddled my lawyers to assess the state of the battle ground. The way I saw it, she was Mark Tyler's daughter, not mine. She had an equitable claim and a court would probably award her a sizeable chunk - maybe fifty percent - of the Peters Group and its assets. It would be a horrendous blood-on-the-floor trial, which I didn't want. And the value of the pot was approaching $9 billion U.S.

So I said what the hell, let's settle and we did without ever having to do battle face to face or at all. The lawyers did that.

Louise got sixty percent of the assets and shares and I kept the remainder including one of the company jets.

Simple as that. Made the lawyers rich—again.

I was in my new Toronto office in the Royal Bank tower getting ready to go to England and then getting away on my yacht—it was at Monaco—for a few days with a few friends when my secretary rang through to me. It was the last time she would do so.

Garth Peters
Caged Eagle
11 September 2001

18

Peters' secretary was on the intercom. "Senator, there are two RCMP inspectors here. They'd like to see you. They say it's important."

"RCMP inspectors? What the hell do they want?"

"I don't know. They wouldn't tell me."

"God. Couldn't they have called to make an appointment? All right, I'll see them. But tell them I have a meeting at eleven. And while I have you, call my pilots—they'll be at Hudson General. Tell them to be ready, have my Challenger ready to depart anytime after four. We'll go to Gatwick. I have an appointment with the Prince late tomorrow."

"Yes, grouse hunting."

"Try grouse shooting. Send the RCMP people in."

Peters expected to see the inspectors in civilian clothes. He was surprised they were in uniform—their smart, conservative, dark brown work dress. As they entered his office and walked toward his desk—he remained sitting as a gesture of superiority—Peters sized up the two young men, both in their early forties, old enough to be his sons. As the pair approached, Peters waved his hand, a signal to sit in the two leather chairs opposite.

The taller, with dark hair and long face and carrying a briefcase said, "Sir, I'm Inspector McDonald and this is Inspector Oxon. We're from O Division based in London, Ontario."

There was no offering of hands to shake.

"Yeah. Well, sit down, gentlemen. What can I do for you? I don't have much time."

"Your secretary told us," Oxon, the blond-haired, round-faced officer with glasses, acknowledged.

"You might have arranged an appointment." There was a strong note of disapproval in Peters' voice.

"That's true," McDonald agreed, "but the Commissioner—he's taken personal charge of this case—gave us instructions to find you immediately, catch you before you went flying off to London or wherever in your jet."

Oxon added, "The Commissioner decided we'd better catch you before you flew the coop, so to speak."

"So what's this case about and why are you talking with me?"

McDonald opened up his briefcase and took out a full blue file which he put on Peters' desk. "We have several reports in here, sir. I'll show them to you if you wish, but to save time Inspector Oxon and I will give you a summary of what they say."

Oxon pushed at his glasses with the forefinger of his right hand, an indicator to the Senator that the inspector was nervous although he appeared cool and collected. "A month ago, on the 14th of October to be exact, some farmers in France were draining a swamp near a place called Mantes Gassicourt west of Paris and they found a World War II fighter aircraft in the swamp. It had been badly damaged and shot up. They found the pilot's remains in the cockpit. Experts think the pilot, who was apparently hit by a shell or shells from the aircraft that shot him down, stayed conscious long enough to control his aircraft and land it straight ahead . . ."

"Right into the swamp," McDonald went on, "where it settled in and immediately sank and disappeared. None of the locals saw this happen, according to the stories from the farmers who are in the area now—the children and grandchildren of the farmers who were there when this happened in 1944."

Peters said nothing. He tensed, unconsciously shifting his body toward the edge of his chair, his hooded eyes narrowed to slits as his mind flipped back more than half a century.

"No one knew the plane was there until a month ago," McDonald continued. "The farmers contacted the authorities. The French Air Force identified the aircraft as a Mustang, a Mustang I. From the numbers and letters on the fuselage, British records at their Public Records Office showed that the aircraft belonged to 430 Squadron, a Canadian squadron that was based at that time in Normandy."

Peters spoke. "At B8 airfield between Arromanches and Bayeux, to be exact."

"That's right," Oxon said. "When the Canadian connection was discovered—this took about forty-eight hours—the French left the Mustang where it was including the remains. They didn't want to touch anything until the Canadian Air Force investigation team was sent in from Canada, actually from the CF-18 fighter base at Cold Lake, Alberta. The Canadian airbase in Lahr was closed some years ago, as you probably know, Senator."

"I know. I had a hand in getting it closed."

"Well, the Canadian investigating team had found the wartime log book, the original of 430 Squadron still in the possession of the squadron. It flies helicopters and is based in Valcartier, Québec. So they knew who the pilot was, the mission he was flying on."

"To photograph Rommel's headquarters at La Roche Guyon."

"Right, sir, and you were with him as his wing man. So they knew who was in that cockpit. A man called Mark Tyler."

"What's happened to his body, his remains?"

"They were flown to England and examined by forensic experts in London. They'll be turned over to his daughter, Senator Tyler. She's in London now. She's agreed to receive the body and make the funeral arrangements. She's staying at . . . what's the name of the hotel?" McDonald turned to Oxon for the answer.

"The Dorchester. You may want to talk to her. I have the telephone number."

Peters muttered, "I already have the number."

"So anyway, sir," McDonald continued, "the investigating team found that Tyler's aircraft had been shot down by an aircraft attacking from the rear at close range. The shells from that aircraft, several were found in the fuselage, and one had hit Tyler, gone through the armor plate behind him. The shells were from .5-inch machine guns mixed with .303 shells. Neither the Focke Wulf 190 nor the ME 109 carried machine guns of those calibres. The only aircraft that carried them was the Mustang I."

"We have spoken to two men, both pilots, who were on 430 Squadron at the time. They've told us you hated Tyler." McDonald paused, looking at the unflinching old man straight in the eyes. "You were flying that Mustang I, Senator Peters, and you shot down and killed Mark Tyler, the man you hated."

Both RCMP officers stood up. McDonald spoke slowly, "We are here to place you under arrest, sir, for the murder of Mark Tyler. We caution you that anything you say now may be used in evidence against you at your trial."